Insomnia

It was too late. The Marquis was right. Johnny would never be able to look his wife in the eye again, let alone have sex with her. After this – after *her* – normal sex would have as much effect on him as an aspirin would have on a madman. He knew he would crave more. Darker thrills. Deeper pain to inflict and be inflicted upon him. Life was never going to be the same again. He was addicted.

Insomnia

ZOE LE VERDIER

Black Lace novels are sexual fantasies.
In real life, make sure you practise safe sex.

First published in 1999 by
Black Lace
Thames Wharf Studios,
Rainville Road, London W6 9HT

Typeset by SetSystems Ltd, Saffron Walden, Essex
Printed and bound by Mackays of Chatham PLC

ISBN 0 352 33345 6

Contents

Introduction

I can't sleep.

Insomnia always strikes when I least expect it – and when I absolutely have to get up early the next day. It's pointless fighting it, though. There's nothing I can do now. It's like a disease that's taken hold of my body and won't let go. No matter how pale blue and empty I try to make my mind (like a summer sky; that's the idea), the grey clouds just keep looming over and sending me looking further inward.

It's three o'clock, and I'm wider awake than ever. I was tired when I first turned the light out, but gradually, as I lay here, thoughts crept their way inside my head and now my eyes are open and my mind won't keep still.

Sleep, if I could find it, would be an open door through which my thoughts could escape. Insomnia is the opposite: a door that closes and forces me back inside. Deep inside, into the darkness, into a place where exhaustion twists everything. It's not a comfortable journey, but I lie here and follow my fantasies. I have no choice.

1

He sleeps on beside me, blissfully unaware of the other men and women in the room with us: men and women I've known, or want to know, or wish I'd never met. People from every level of my imagination. The population of my soul.

I lie back. As my eyes grow accustomed to the darkness I can see them, waiting there for me.

Crush

Genevieve had the best job in the world. She told that to everyone who ever asked her what she did for a living, and it was true. How many forty-year-old divorcees got to spend their working lives surrounded by fit young men? How many got paid to touch those fit young men's bodies – to knead their hard, thickening thighs; to smooth the tension out of their backs; to press their fingers into their taut, hairless little buttocks? She did. And every one of those fit young men adored her. Her female friends, and some of the male ones too, were suitably envious.

She'd earnt this job; paid for the privilege with years of training followed by years of dedicated hard work, trying to making a name for herself in the testosterone-soaked world of sport. She'd wanted to be a physiotherapist ever since she was twelve. Her favourite uncle had been one and she'd been fascinated by him, and by the job he did. She'd also loved football since she'd been a little girl and her father had taken her and her brother to every Waltham

Forest home match and a few of the away ones too. So this job, apart from the fit young men and the touching, was a dream come true. She was helping to form the Waltham Forest team of the future. More than that – because she was more than a physio to those boys – she was helping these fledgling footballers into adulthood. And sometimes that was the most satisfying part of the job.

She enjoyed being a woman in a man's world. There were other women at the club, but they were the receptionists and secretaries and administrators and personal assistants; the women who wore skirts and little heels and smiled coyly at the chairman's jokes and put up with being called 'love' and 'sweetheart'. Gen never wore skirts to work; she never got called 'love'. She was the only woman who'd ever made it beyond the offices and down, into the inner sanctum of the boot room; and beyond, out into the light, out on to the pitch, where it all happened. Sometimes, in the middle of a home match at her beloved Forest Road, she'd sit forward on the bench and form her hands into blinkers so no one could see her, and close her eyes. In the dark, she'd be thrown back to her childhood. The smell. The sounds. The excitement clawing in the pit of her stomach. The feeling of belonging, with her father and brother either side of her, a swell and scream of fans surrounding her and in front of her, the Blues. She'd found everything she'd needed on the terraces: passion, family, soul.

Waltham Forest had been her childhood. So, stepping into this job had been like coming home. She'd found happiness; the real happiness that comes with being completely satisfied with what you've got, and knowing that if you died tomorrow it wouldn't matter – you'd done it, and done your best.

4

Of course, there was a downside. (Wasn't there a downside to everything? Who invented downsides, anyway? Was it one of the irrefutable laws of physics, like the law of gravity – for every dream job there must be a downside?) Being appointed physio to Forest's youth team hadn't exactly caused her divorce, but it hadn't helped her relationship with her husband. He'd grown increasingly, maddeningly jealous of the time she spent with 'her boys' – not only every weekday but every Saturday too, and most Wednesday evenings. And of course she had to accompany the youth team on their away matches, some of which were abroad. After a month in the job her husband would physically cringe at any mention of 'the boys', and after six weeks it started: 'Why do you have to spend so much time with those bloody lads? How long does this blasted football season last, anyway? Don't you get sick of watching spotty brats kicking a bag of wind around a field?' He'd never been much of a football fan. He didn't play any sport. He was as flabby and run-down as the lads were lean and fit. But that wasn't why Genevieve spent every spare minute at work – she wasn't that shallow. Those boys had more important attributes sadly lacking in her husband: ambition, determination, drive to succeed. And they gave her something she'd never had at home. Respect.

So now her husband was gone and all she had was the London house, the old Volvo and the admiration of thirty-five young men to keep her busy. Not a bad deal, considering.

She checked her reflection in the hall on her way out. Not bad, considering. She certainly looked better now than she had done a year ago, when the marriage had begun to crack and splinter. There was a confidence in her grey eyes that would have died if she'd stayed with her husband; a confidence that was recharged every morning when she woke up and realised she was alone, and that it felt good. Her hair, kept long for a husband who liked it that way, was now in a short bob that suited her far better. And her tits – she turned side on to the mirror – well, her tits had always been her pride and joy. She'd been embarrassed by them when she was young, but now she'd finally grown into them and walked with her shoulders back and their splendour thrust forward, usually wearing something low-cut and clingy to show them off.

The boys liked her tits. The boys liked to look down her top when she was leaning over the massage table. They liked to watch them jiggle as she rubbed their tight thighs and, she had no doubt, they liked to dream about them at nights when they were lying in bed, wanking.

She would love to know just how many of the youth team had wanked over thoughts of her. Her eyes drifted up to the photo by the side of her mirror, one of many lining her long hallway. It was a team photo, taken at the end of last season. She ran her fingertips along the row of smiling faces. 'How many of you?' she asked out loud. 'How many look at my ripe curves – curves that your young girlfriends just don't have – and wonder what it would be like to surrender your youth to my experience? Which of you put your hands up your girlfriends' skirts and wonder whether it would be different with an older woman?'

She was still thinking these thoughts as she jogged around the pitch at the training ground. The lads were lying on the grass doing their sit-ups in pairs, each one with his legs locked around his partner's.

Each one was trying to concentrate but she knew she was distracting them; could feel their eyes straining to follow her. She was in bloody good shape for a woman of her age and she knew it. If she hadn't known it, the attention she always got when she went jogging would have told her: their greedy, adolescent eyes on her arse; on her long, muscular legs; and on her tits, bouncing only slightly in the constraint of her sports bra. But did they want her? Or did their attention stray simply because they were young men, and leering was what young men did best – and because she wore tight T-shirts?

They finished their exercises and she finished her run and watched, keeping an eye on the couple of lads carrying injuries. There was Paddy, a cocky young lad who was destined for greatness but who was, at the moment, still hobbling slightly with a calf strain. There was Robbie, an arrogant little sod who made up for his lack of height with an attitude that was going to break some hearts; he had a groin strain. And there was Michael.

Michael was different from the other boys. Michael was an only child, and he came from a family of doctors. His mother and father were quietly horrified that he'd chosen to use his physical talents rather than his brain, and it was a major achievement that such a shy, quiet young man had managed to persuade his parents to let him follow this path. He was such a clever defender and a natural athlete, although he was tall for his age and still growing, which was giving him back problems he struggled with. But despite the injuries that tormented him, he was single-mindedly determined to make it. Genevieve knew that he would. If he kept up this level of dedication for the rest of the season – and he would – he was going to be offered a contract with

Waltham Forest for next season. He deserved it, too. She smiled to herself as she watched him.

He glanced at her as he ran past, and caught her smiling. Immediately his cheeks began to turn red. Something flared inside Genevieve – a mixture of motherly pride, and pleasure that such a good-looking boy should choose to have a crush on her. It wasn't so surprising. Such a shy lad, he probably didn't come into contact with many women other than his mother. Gen spoke to him like he was an adult, which of course he was. And she massaged his back almost every day. Those two things alone were enough to make a sensitive young man like Michael adore her.

Still, she was flattered by his embarrassment whenever their eyes met. It was touching, and exciting, to feel a young man's lust, after so many years with a man who barely saw her.

'How's it feeling today?' She pressed her thumbs deep into the twin ridges of muscle either side of his spine. 'Any stiffness?'

She bit her lip as Paddy and Robbie snorted. She had to be so careful – anything could be construed as a double entendre by those two.

'Erm ... no,' Michael stuttered, turning his head away from the other two, as if he was trying to pretend they weren't there. 'It feels fine.'

'Mine always feels fine too, when Gen's giving it a rub.'

Gen gave Robbie a withering glance. 'Are you here to do your exercises, or to muck around?'

Robbie shut up and continued with his strengthening exercises, for now. It wouldn't be long before he piped up again.

Gen leant over the physio bed and put all her

8

weight into her massage. Michael's back was prone to knotting and strains; she had to keep it as supple as possible. He swam and did exercises, but he needed massage too. It was also a good way for her to keep a close eye on him; he never told anyone when he was injured, until it was too late and meant time off. 'Been doing your exercises?'

'Every day.'

She smiled. She knew that he had. She'd heard that he made a habit of arriving early, having a bath to warm himself up and then doing an hour in the gym before training. There wasn't a more dedicated player in the club.

She poured some more oil into her hands and went up to stand by his head. Leaning over him, she worked on his shoulders. He had beautiful, broad shoulders that tapered into a narrow waist. He still had a faint tan from his summer holiday at the family's villa in the South of France. And he had not a hair on his smooth skin. I'm glad I don't have a dick, Gen thought. I'd have a hard-on.

Poor Michael wasn't so lucky. As Gen leant right over him, one breast touched the back of his head, and he flinched. When she finished her massage, and told him he could get up, he scrabbled nervously and held his T-shirt in front of him as he walked out.

'I think he's got the hots for you, Gen,' said Robbie, smirking as he watched Michael's red-faced retreat.

She tried not to look wistful. 'It's Genevieve to you, you little shit. Now get yourself over here.'

It was late. She'd had a meeting. She caught herself rushing back to the changing room, then realised she had nothing to rush for. No husband waiting impatiently at home any more. Nothing but freedom stretching ahead of her.

She smiled to herself as she collected her bag, thinking of the bottle of Chardonnay waiting in the fridge for her. Then she heard something that stopped her in her tracks. She could have sworn she'd heard her name, followed by the faint but unmistakeable sound of laughter. Puzzled as to where the sound was coming from, she wandered around for a moment squinting and listening. It got louder as she drifted into the shower room; louder still as she knelt down and put her ear to the grate in the floor.

'Genevieve? I'd have her. I reckon she's gagging for it.'

'I've heard that's why the first team are so knackered. She has her way with them before every match.'

Genevieve giggled to herself as she recognised Paddy and Robbie's voices. Being crude, as usual.

'What a body, though,' Robbie said, a hint of genuine appreciation in his voice. 'I reckon she fancies me. She wasn't half pleased when I told her I had a groin strain.'

'The only thing that's straining is your cock,' Paddy countered. There was the sound of scuffling – a half-hearted fight breaking out.

'Oh, but have you seen her in those leotards?'

'Seen her?' Paddy huffed triumphantly. 'I've done more than that, mate. I've had her.'

'You what?'

'The other night, in the sauna. Practically begged me, she did. Said she wanted to see a real athlete's body in action.'

There was a chorus of whistles, jeers and 'in your dreams'. Tangled inside that noise, getting louder and louder until it could be heard, was a note of seriousness. 'Shut up. Shut up. Shut up!'

It was Michael. Gen felt a shudder running down her spine, into her knickers.

Beyond the grate, the boys' shower room suddenly went silent.

'I wish you lot would stop talking about her like that. She wouldn't touch any of you. She's far too good for any one of you.'

'What's this?' Genevieve could almost see Robbie's sneer; almost see him swaggering over to Michael and squaring up. 'Has the wonder boy got a crush, then?'

'No. I just don't like to hear you talking about her like that.'

'Think you're good enough for her?'

'No. I just don't know why you have to be so crude about her. You've got such disgusting minds, you lot.'

'Oh. Sorry. I forgot Mister Wonder Boy has never had a dirty thought in his life. You were probably thinking about scoring a hat trick when you rushed out of physio with a hard-on, were you?'

The door slammed. Laughter bubbled up again, followed by a rowdy chorus of the traditional football song 'He's a Wanker'.

Gen got up. She couldn't stop her smile. So it was true, like she'd thought all along – the boys did hunger after her. She took a deep breath. Wow. It was flattering, and dangerous, to think of herself with one of those fit, hard young men; especially one of the arrogant ones. Robbie or Paddy – God, how she'd love to see the look on their faces if she really did give them what they wanted.

Even more dangerous was the thought of Michael – sweet, shy, intelligent boy – having such a serious crush on her. It was dangerous for him because, now the other lads knew, they would never stop teasing him; and for her, because now she wouldn't be able to stop dreaming about him. This was a position she'd never been in before – absolute power. He adored her. He would probably give anything to lose his virginity – and she had no doubt he was a virgin – to the woman of his fantasies.

What goes around comes around, she thought, moving in a dream over to the bench. Slumping down against the wall, she thought back to the time when she'd been in the thrall of a deep and desperate crush. Back then, she'd been the athlete. He'd been her physio: a divorced man in his forties, with blond hair turning to grey and a look of Robert Redford in his blue eyes. Or so she'd thought. He'd probably been nothing to look at, but all those years ago, when she'd been just waking up to womanhood, he'd seemed like a god. When she closed her eyes, she could still feel his firm, warm hands on the backs of her legs. She still felt the mad thrill of the day he'd walked into the changing room and found her admiring her growing breasts in the mirror. It could have been the strange cocktail of hormones whizzing round her body, but in an instant she swung from being mortified to being desperately, nerve-shatteringly excited. He'd seen her. Whatever happened – even if it was nothing – he'd seen her breasts. He knew what he was missing. Now, when she dreamt of him, she could imagine he was dreaming of her, too.

That crush had been so strong, so completely engulfing, so totally, utterly overwhelming, that Genevieve's favourite fantasies still revolved around it. She closed her eyes and rested her head against the wall. Without even knowing she was doing it, she opened her legs and slipped her hand down inside her tracksuit pants. She was wet. It was his

12

finger, delving under the elastic of her knickers, and between her swollen pussy lips. It was his faint gasp that whispered in the air. It was him making her back arch as he tenderly, expertly, rubbed her swollen little clit and showed her what it meant to be a woman.

'Yes,' she breathed, closing her eyes tight and seeing him so clearly. 'Oh. Yes.'

It had been a good season. The youth team had come second in their league, despite the plague of injuries that mysteriously kept the boys lurking round the physio room. A couple of lads had failed in their bid for stardom, and left to seek glory elsewhere, in lesser clubs; a couple had been offered full contracts. Chaperoned by the rest of the coaching staff, those who had something to celebrate, or another year of training to look forward to, descended on Gen's house for her legendary end-of-season barbecue. The sun was shining, as it had done every day since her husband had left.

'Hi, everybody!' Gen turned and waved as the mob appeared from round the side of her house and filed into her huge back garden. 'Help yourself to drinks.'

The adults did. The boys, for once, didn't scramble to get at the alcohol. From her post at the barbecue, Gen stared back at them, wondering why they were standing gawping at her from the patio like a row of badly dressed statues. Realising that the sun was behind her, and that her already flimsy dress was now completely see-through, she smiled to herself and tried to concentrate on the sausages.

Up on the patio, Robbie nudged Paddy in the ribs. 'Christ, man, have you seen that body?'

Paddy grunted in reply.

'Tonight's the night,' Robbie said, loud enough for the other boys to hear.

'What you talking about?'

'I'm going to have her. Tonight's the night.'

'You're joking, aren't you?'

'Never been more serious. I can feel it in my bones.' Robbie grinned, playing to his audience. 'The only sausage she's going to be eating tonight is mine.'

Paddy, and several of the others, snorted derisively. 'Let's hope she's not hungry,' said one of them.

'You may laugh,' Robbie warned, undeterred. 'You won't be laughing when I'm tucked up in bed with gentle Genevieve.' Robbie dribbled an imaginary football across the patio. 'He beats one, he beats two, he's in the box. He shoots. He scores!' He thrust his fist, and his groin, in the air.

Michael gritted his teeth and tried to shut out the tiresome innuendo. He was so sick of it. It was constant; a constant reminder of how desperately he wanted her and how much he completely adored her. Robbie, the foul-mouthed little git, wouldn't have a clue how to treat a woman like Genevieve. The trouble was, neither would Michael.

She was so perfect, it was frightening. He looked at her, standing in a halo of sunlight at the bottom of the garden, and the usual sad confusion gripped him. It wasn't like him at all – he was shy, but that shyness hid a driving determination to get what he wanted in life. He was so sure of what he wanted, and yet so utterly powerless when it came to her. So many times, he'd practised it in his mind: how he'd go up to her, and quietly confess how he felt. She'd look surprised, then, very slowly, she'd smile, take his face in her hands and kiss him softly, then a little

14

harder. She'd ease him into sex so gently, he would forget his nerves and be good at it. He'd even manage to give her pleasure. And then they'd lie there, and he'd just touch her for hours. He'd ingrain the exact shape and softness of her heavenly body in his mind. And for ever he'd hold the memory of his first time, with the woman he'd have done anything for.

He scooped himself a glass of punch and tried to wash away the bitter taste at the back of his throat. Who was he kidding? His first time, if it ever came, would be just like the other lads' first times: a fumbled, clumsy shag in the back of a car, with a girl he couldn't care less about. Trouble was, Michael just couldn't see himself compromising. There was only one woman he wanted to lose it with. He'd rather stay a virgin, and keep his sweet, wet dreams of her, than be like the others, doing anything to get rid of the weight of inexperience around their necks.

He was angry. Furious at himself for falling for her; with the others for talking about her like she was a piece of meat; and with her. Did she have no compassion? Couldn't she see what she was doing to him? Had she worn that flowery, feminine dress that went transparent in the sunshine just to tip him over the edge?

She looked more beautiful than ever this afternoon. He kept his distance, partly to avoid having to speak to her, because that always embarrassed him, but mostly so he could look at her. The other lads swarmed around her, laughing and telling her their dirty jokes and confidently flirting. She sat on the grass and laughed with them, pretending to be offended by their crudeness, but relishing their attention.

He cursed her. How could she even speak to them?

15

They were so childish; so disgustingly laddish. They didn't care about her. He hated her for wasting her time on them.

He adored her. He looked at her neck. She had a beautiful neck. She had a very fine gold chain around it that for some reason he wanted to touch. She had small diamond studs in her ears too, flashing in the sunlight when she threw back her head and laughed, and her hair fell away from her face. She had beautiful ears. Beautiful hair. Imagine that hair brushing against his skin. He could almost feel it. So soft. Everything about her was incredible: her voice, her smile, that dress, her body. His gaze slipped into her deep cleavage. As if everything was conspiring to tease him into a fury, a strap slowly fell from one smooth shoulder, and a little more bare skin was revealed. He watched, hoping that the others would disappear and it would be just him and her, and her dress would fall off and she'd open her arms for him.

He felt her attention and it was a moment before he could pluck up the courage to meet her eyes. When he did, embarrassment immediately poured red, from the roots of his hair to his neck. Very slowly, her laughter faded and her smile turned from wide to slight and gentle. It was the smile of recognition he'd seen in his dreams.

Some idiot kicked a football at him. Hypnotised by Genevieve's beautiful, sensual smile, he didn't see it coming, and it hit him in the face. Livid, Michael lashed out at the bastard who'd kicked it, and ended up spilling his drink and looking like a child, in front of her. 'You stupid sod,' he snapped. 'Look what you've done.'

'Oh dear,' Robbie mocked loudly, from his court jester's position at Gen's side. 'The virgin Michael's having a tantrum, everybody. What's that wet patch on your trousers, Michael? Having a wet dream, were you?'

He escaped into the house, glad to be alone. In the kitchen, he looked out at the party and decided he hated himself. He was so pathetic. He'd always come first in everything. Why was this such a huge, inconquerable problem? Why was he scared to death whenever he was within a mile of her? He always ended up looking like a fool. She must have thought he was such a wimp, always going red and running off like that. He wished he could be like the rest of the lads and laugh it off. To them, flirting with Genevieve was a game. He practically had a breakdown whenever he was near her. They were enjoying themselves, getting drunk and showing off in front of her; he was having the worst day of his life. On top of everything, he knew this was the last time he'd get to be with her. He was joining the first team after the summer break. This should have been the happiest time of his life. One touch, one kiss from her, and it would have been. And yet he couldn't even bring himself to speak to her.

Gen waited until the customary drunken football match had started before she slipped inside. 'Michael! Michael? Oh – there you are.' He blushed, guiltily, as she walked into the kitchen and found him at the sink. 'What on earth are you doing?'

'Oh, I, er, I just thought I'd help. There's so much . . .'

'Michael, you're so sweet.' Knowing she would shock him, she went up and kissed him on the cheek. 'You don't need to wash up though, darling, I can put it all in the dishwasher.' She eased his hands out of the sink.

'Oh. Oh. I'm sorry.'

'No need to be sorry.' She smiled and ruffled his hair. Then she realised how patronising that was, and how it was the sort of thing an auntie might do, and that he was almost dying with embarrassment, and she looked out of the window to give him a chance to pull himself together. 'Look at Robbie,' she laughed, as he put in a flying tackle that would do no good for his groin strain, or her lawn. 'Where does that boy get his energy from?'

Michael didn't answer. Genevieve sneaked a look at him. He was watching Robbie too, with gritted teeth.

'You don't like him much, do you?'

'He's all right.' Tentatively, he glanced at her. 'I don't like the way he talks to you.'

She smiled, more to herself than at Michael. 'I can handle Robbie.'

'I know, I wasn't saying ... I just ... He's so crude.'

'Crude? Oh, most young men your age are fairly crude, Michael. You don't have to worry about me being offended. I've seen and heard it all. I'm old, you know.'

'You're not old,' he said, a little too quickly and a little too eagerly. He waited for her reaction, hoping he hadn't given himself away.

It's too late, she thought to herself. You gave yourself away a long time ago, Michael. The very first time I gave you a massage. 'I'm a lot older than you.'

He blinked several times and turned away. Disappointment was set in his mouth, as if she'd been trying to tell him why it would never happen between them, and that he was silly for even dreaming about it.

She watched Robbie again. Now he was having a

18

mock fight with Paddy. Funny, she thought, how young lads could swing between childhood and adulthood from one minute to the next. 'Robbie's been flirting outrageously with me, all day.' She watched for Michael's reaction. He tensed. 'He's been telling me dirty jokes. Trying to shock me. Paddy as well. What is it with those two?'

He looked at her accusingly. 'You know what.'

'No?' She tried not to smile at his anger. 'What?'

Michael's lips twitched as he tried to form the words. 'They fancy you,' he said quietly.

'Really?'

Nervous, but excited to be sharing a confidence with her, Michael nodded.

'I can't believe it,' Gen laughed. 'What on earth would fit young men like them see in a middle-aged woman like me?'

He bristled. He answered before he thought about it. 'They think you're gorgeous,' he said. 'You are gorgeous. I've told them, you're far too good for . . .' Then his brain caught up with his mouth, and he began to blush again.

'That's very flattering, Michael, but I'm certainly not gorgeous.'

'Well, all the lads fancy you.'

'And what about you?'

He hesitated. He would have hesitated for ever, but she drew his answer out with her eyes. 'I think you know that I think I'm in love with you.' It was only a whisper, barely louder than a thought, but she heard it. And in that instant, she knew what she was going to do. If she'd delved into her mind, she'd have realised that she knew what she was going to do that morning, when she'd got dressed and put on her make-up. This morning it would have seemed ridiculous. Now, it seemed so right that it would have been insane to stop it.

'Oh, Michael,' she sighed. She gave him a gentle smile. Tenderly, she held his face in her fingers. 'You're not in love with me, believe me. You'll meet some beautiful young girl soon, and you'll really fall in love, and then you'll forget all about me.'

'Never.' He shook his head slightly within her hands. 'I can't stop thinking about you. I think about you all the time. I'll never forget you.'

She knew he was telling the truth. She'd never fogotten her first crush. 'Michael.' She caressed his lips with hers. Stunned, he looked at her with wide eyes and open lips. 'Michael, I want to make love to you.'

She could tell he was torn between running away and falling to his knees with relief. 'But I . . . I don't know how. I've never –'

'Don't worry.' She stopped him with another kiss. 'I'll show you how.'

Intense. The noise outside faded to nothing. There was only the sound of breathing; of skin against skin; of fingertips in hair and mouths touching. It was strange and beautiful to have a lover who was so completely in her thrall, mesmerised by every inch of flesh she revealed and grateful for every heartbeat of time they were together.

He watched as she unbuttoned her dress. His eyes were serious, his mouth quivering as he tried to find the balance between the ecstasy and the despair that comes with knowing this moment won't last for ever. She took his hand in hers and brought it to her heavy breast; it hovered there for a moment before gently clasping over her flesh. She watched him, as his fantasy unfolded beneath his fingertips, and the look on his face almost made her cry.

She cradled his head while he suckled on her nipple, then slid down his body, turning him so he had his back to the sink. 'What if someone comes in?' he murmured.

'What if they do?'

He groaned as she opened up his jeans and shorts and sucked his long, smooth cock into her mouth. Rubbing her hands over his long, hard thighs, she moaned in reply, in appreciation of his beautiful body. He tasted beautiful too, or maybe it was just that he was sweeter and more sensitive and more entranced by her than any other man had ever been. I'll show you, she thought, licking all along his prick, sucking his balls and flickering her tongue into his weeping eye until his thighs twitched under her palms. I'll show you how beautiful this can be. Your first time should be beautiful.

With a strangled sigh, half embarrassment, half relief, he came on her tongue. She reached around behind him and held on to his buttocks, stopping him from moving as she drank him down. Slowly, kissing his smooth, flat stomach and his hairless chest, she worked her way back up his body. He flinched as she kissed his mouth, as men always did; then, carried on the tide of her soft passion, he gave in and kissed her back.

She pulled away, to look at him for a moment; to remind herself of what was happening. 'They'll never be able to make fun of you after this,' she whispered, smiling.

His fingers stroked her hair. 'I don't believe this is happening.'

She took his hand and guided it again, down over her soft belly, into her knickers. His mouth opened and closed as he touched her soft, thick hair and the ripe, succulent flesh of her pussy. 'God,' he sighed. 'That feels amazing.' He shook his head in disbelief. 'You're amazing.'

'I'm wet,' she whispered. 'I want you, Michael. I want you inside me.'

Watching her carefully, he gently teased a long finger inside her. 'Oh,' she said, telling him yes, that feels good, give me more. She held on to his wrist as he accidentally rubbed her clit. 'Oh, Michael. Touch me there.' She gripped him tight. 'There. No, there. That's it. Oh . . .'

He watched, open-mouthed, as her body warmed and opened to the pleasure. 'Am I doing it right?' he whispered.

'Michael.' She lightly scratched her nipples, then gently pinched them. He didn't know where to look. 'Michael, oh God, I can't tell you how wonderful that feels. It's like . . . like . . .'

She couldn't describe it. She showed him with her body and told him with her moans. Their conversation was soundless music, flowing in the air between them. Watching her intently, determined to get it right, he held her round the waist and strummed her clit and the heavy, swollen lips of her cunt, getting carried away by her as she became carried away by him.

'I want to make love to you.' She was breathless. 'I've wanted to do this for a long time, Michael. I can't wait any longer.' She eased his hand away and pulled him down to the floor with her. Rigid with fear and anticipation, Michael just sat with his back to the cupboard and waited while Genevieve got into position. Kneeling over him, holding her pussy lips open, she waited for a moment, the head of his prick

22

just nestling inside her. 'Am I dreaming this?' he asked.

She shook her head and lowered herself on to him. She held her breath and held in her groan of release, wanting to hear his. The rush of his breath hit her skin. He closed his eyes tight, wanting to hide his feelings from her. She touched his face, making him look at her. She wanted him to remember every moment. His eyes opened again and fell to where she was touching herself, pushing her breasts together invitingly. He dropped his head and kissed her, stopping when her hands moved downwards, into her thick bush. 'You're amazing,' he gasped, resting his trembling fingers over hers, his eyes on where his cock was disappearing in and out of her.

You make me feel amazing, she thought, rubbing her clit hard – wanting him to see her come. Slowly she stroked his cock, up and down, squeezing him with her pussy. His hands shook as they fluttered all over her: over her breasts, through her hair, down her back and on to her wide hips. Putting one hand against the cupboard door, by his face, she angled her hips so her clit dragged against his cock. He was ready to come again; she was ready too. She began to slide harder and faster on him, making his helpless body jerk beneath her. Her own body stiffened as her clit felt the heat of his cock and her own twitching fingers. Her climax flickered up from her toes as he tensed and flooded her. She rode the feeling, writhing up and down on him still, throwing her head back and rubbing her breasts.

Outside, in the dusk, they sat together for the rest of the evening. Michael asked Genevieve about herself, like he wanted to know everything before the day ended. She told him everything. She could talk to

23

him – it was easy. He wasn't really listening, anyway. Just question after question, so he could listen to her voice and replay what they'd just done in his head.

'Will I see you again?' he asked.

She shook her head, smiling at his disappointment. 'It's for the best, Michael, believe me. It would never be the same again.'

The minibus came and went with most of the party. The few who lived within walking or tube distance of Gen's house were allowed to stay. Michael tore his eyes away from Gen for a moment to look at Robbie and Paddy, lying sprawled on the grass.

'Will you tell them?' she asked.

She'd never seen such an effortless smile on his face. 'They'd never believe me.'

'Maybe they would.'

He turned to her.

She smiled back. 'Kiss me.'

'In front of them? You're joking.'

'Don't you want them to know?'

'Of course I do, but . . .'

'Then kiss me.'

He slid his hand underneath her hair, and kissed her. For once, Paddy and Robbie could think of nothing to say.

Penis Envy

She opens her mouth as I slide my cock between her pussy lips. My huge, black, rigid, silicone-rubber cock. Her sweet eyes widen with the shock of it: the shock of me and her. The shock of what her senses are telling her: that this is wrong. This goes against everything she's ever known. The sight of us together; the smell of sex and desire; the feeling of the dark earth between her fingers and the damp grass clasping at her skin and the hard ground beneath her shoulders. The sound of her own whimpering. The taste of her shame. Two women – I know, even now, it tastes sour to her. Sour but sickly sweet. She can't resist.

I understand how it feels to be a man now. Parting her pussy lips with my false prick for the first time, I'm filled with the violent surge of testosterone. I get no physical sexual pleasure from the sensation, but the look on her face: the way revulsion turns to acceptance in her eyes. The feeling of power; it tastes very sweet to me.

* * *

Do men have cunt envy? Do they long to know how it feels to have soft, yielding flesh between their legs – flesh that opens and beckons and sucks you in; flesh that clasps and relaxes and oozes with longing? Do they ever long to feel that sense of submission we feel, when men thrust their cocks deep inside us and claim a part of us as theirs? Do they yearn to lie down and open their legs and to know how it feels to be taken; to be consumed with a man's hard passion?

I didn't know I had penis envy until I went to work at Andrew and Clare's house. Until then, I was quite happy with myself. I had no cause for penis envy because I didn't have a career where I was constantly banging my head on glass ceilings or being judged by my looks before my ability. I loved my job, and I worked every hour I could to build up my business, but I wasn't branded selfish or career-obsessed because of it, like all my female friends who work in mirror-fronted offices in the City. My friends' lives are full of issues that simply wouldn't be issues if they had pricks and balls. Men have it easy, my friends always say. Men are admired for being ambitious; we're just hard-faced bitches.

But I didn't have those problems and, being a gardener, I never will. My penis envy was different from that of my girlfriends. I envied the organ itself: the power of a hard, thrusting cock. The energy surge of an erection. The pure, selfish desire to dominate; to push rigid flesh into soft flesh and feel it stretch and enclose me; to see a woman giving in to the overwhelming strength of my lust. I wanted to feel what men feel when they fuck us. I wanted to consume rather than be consumed. I didn't want to be a man, don't get me wrong; I just wanted to know what it felt like to take her. To make her mine. To make her admit that she wanted it as much as I did, and to see the guilt and shame on her face when she did.

But I'm getting ahead of myself. When I set out to Andrew and Clare's, I didn't know any of this. I didn't feel anything but a slight, anticipatory twitch in my green fingers at the thought of getting my hands on their neglected garden.

In the beginning, it was just another job to me. A cushy job, in a nice big house with a fantastically overgrown garden that would take five or six weeks to clear and prepare and design and plant out. Six weeks' work meant a tidy profit, and since I had a tendency to undercharge that was good news for my cashflow. When Andrew rang up to say my company had been recommended by his neighbour, and that neither he nor his wife had much idea about gardening, I jumped at the chance. I remembered their house – it had been empty when I'd been working next door. I remembered sneaking round the back of their place to have a look at the garden, and actually feeling my mouth watering. Andrew and Clare's garden was a dream. Three years of neglect by the previous owner, and it had run wild. A job like that wasn't just good money; it satisfied my creative hunger. I loved a challenge.

I went round the day Andrew rang me, to take a look and give them an estimate. Clare answered the door, wearing a delicate, calf-length flowery dress in a pale blue the colour of the sky that day – and of her eyes. She had on pointy little heels that made me think, why on earth do women wear shoes like that? They looked so bloody pinched and uncomfortable. She was tall and had dark blonde hair streaked with lighter blonde and swept back in an immaculate

27

French pleat. She was youngish – about the same age as me, I reckoned. Mid-twenties. But she dressed as if she was in her mid-forties. She looked incredibly clean. I looked dirty. I always look dirty. I always enjoyed playing in dirt when I was a kid. The day I went round to see them was no different from any other day: I had earth beneath my torn and jagged fingernails, grass stains on my ripped jeans and the whiff of sweat and humid summer on my T-shirt. My long, wavy, dark-red hair was tangled and as dull from lack of care as hers was shiny and sleek. There were probably bits of grass and bark entwined in it – there usually were. Clare winced, looking down disapprovingly at my mud-caked DMs as I stepped into her cream-carpeted hallway.

She took me through the living room, through the open French windows and out on to the patio where Andrew was sitting at a wooden table, beneath an umbrella, sipping a Pimm's. He stood up as I arrived and, unlike his wife, he smiled when he saw the state of me. Dirt appeals to men – especially straight types like him. It reminds them of their youth, and of making mud pies and getting into trouble.

He shook my grubby hand and offered me a Pimm's. I asked for a lager instead and Clare was sent into the kitchen for one as if I was one of her husband's mates. When she came back, she held out the bottle of expensive imported stuff and a glass, and frowned as I ignored the glass, took the bottle and swigged straight out of it. I wiped my mouth with the back of my hand and caught the slightest hint of admiration in Andrew's eyes. A woman with balls, he thought. How super.

They showed me around the garden. Or rather, they showed me around the bits we could get to. It was more of a thicket than a lawn. Ivy and brambles had been allowed to creep in whichever direction they chose, and they'd chosen to overtake the grass, the spindly trees, the shrubs and anything else that stood in the way of their total domination. I told Andrew and Clare that I liked the wildness and that, although it had to go, I would want to keep a slightly unruly feel to the garden. The house was old; the garden, too, should look like it had been there for ever. I told them that neat, regimental borders and symmetry were fine in stately homes but wouldn't suit this place. Clare tried to say something but Andrew spoke first. 'Well, I'm sure you know best,' he said. 'You did a wonderful job on next door.'

'Thank you,' I said. 'So, would you like me to do you an estimate?'

'Yes please,' said Clare.

'I don't think there's any need,' Andrew contradicted. Ignoring his wife's black look, he explained that the garden had to be done and I'd come highly recommended and money wasn't really a problem.

I could see that. The house was massive – far too big for two people. I'd seen the asking price in the estate agent's window. There were two cars in the driveway, a Merc and a Discovery, and the furniture was old enough to be very expensive. For a young couple to have that much cash, Andrew must have been something big in the City, like most of the other inhabitants of the big houses round here. A young whiz-kid who'd moved out of town with his lovely young wife and bought a house big enough to breed brats in. The brats would, no doubt, be looked after by a nanny until they were sent away to boarding school.

'When do you want me to get cracking?'

'As soon as you can.'

'I'm really busy at the moment, but I could probably

make a start towards the end of next week. How'd that do you?'

'That would be wonderful,' Andrew gushed.

We went back to the patio and I showed them my book of drawings and photos of other gardens I'd done, suggesting what I might do with their overgrown mess. I was excited – they didn't have a clue what they wanted and didn't dare question my ideas. I'd have fairly free rein here. I would be able to indulge my often suppressed creative streak. Not only that, but I was pretty sure they'd want my company to maintain the garden once it was done. I couldn't imagine either of them wanting to get their hands dirty. It would be another regular contract to add to my growing number of contract customers. A new customer always gave me a thrill.

Andrew gave me a thrill, too. He liked me. He laughed at my jokes and glanced surreptitiously at my T-shirt when he thought I wasn't looking. But I didn't have to look to know he was enjoying the way my T-shirt was stretched tight across my heavy, bare breasts. I never wear bras. Hate feeling constricted. Love the way men can't help but look. Love the tension it creates when young, beautiful and anally retentive wives like Clare notice their husband's leering. Their mouths go tight, their eyes turn cold and their clean, tight little arseholes contract even tighter. You couldn't get a blade of grass in there, I thought, as I shook her soft, clean hand at the door.

I smiled to myself as I drove away. They were the perfect couple, living perfect lives – lives which were anathema to me. Andrew and Clare were symmetry and calm ambition and perfectly planned-out futures; I was chaos. My naughty, rebellious streak reared its ugly head and I longed to throw a handful of chaos in their path; to prick the bubble of their quiet, peaceful existence. Andrew, I suspected, would be a willing accomplice. It wouldn't be difficult to lead him astray.

I started there on a Friday. It was another beautiful day, and Clare spent it sitting on the patio, watching us attacking the wilderness. Most of our clients either leave us to it or offer to muck in. Not Clare. She was there to keep an eye on us. She obviously wasn't there to sunbathe: she sat in the shade of the umbrella all day, with a hat and sunglasses on just in case a rogue ray of sunshine managed to pierce the black shadow and actually warm her ice-cold aura. She had on another long, pretty, flowery dress – the type my mother tells me I'd look nice in, in the vain hope that I'll go out and buy one and therefore, according to her logic, attract husband-worthy material. 'No wonder you can't get anyone to marry you,' she says, quite frequently. 'Look at you. Those tatty T-shirts you wear. Those awful boots. No one can see your lovely figure in those horrid jeans. Men like women to be feminine, darling.' I've given up trying to tell her I don't want to get married. When she starts I just smile to myself, and thank fuck that my boyfriend – 'the traveller', as she refers to him – doesn't define femininity the same way my mother does. He doesn't have any problem with what I wear. But then, I rarely see him, and when I do we spend most of our time naked.

I bet Clare spent as little time as possible naked. I bet she undressed in the bathroom, out of sight of her husband. She brought us a tray of home-made lemonades, tiptoeing over the grass towards us as if it would soil her, and I sat back on my heels and watched her. She almost flinched as my staff – all three of them young, ruddy, sweat-stained and attractively muscular blokes – took their drinks and tried to make conversation. I tried to picture her having sex and I really couldn't. She was so spotlessly clean, I couldn't imagine her allowing her husband to mess up her hair or rub his sweaty hands over her small breasts or – horror of horrors – spill his come on the sheets. I smiled to myself as she approached me, and she mistook it for a smile of sisterly friendship.

'How are you getting on?' she asked.

'It's bloody hard work,' I said, draining my glass and unable to stop a belch from popping out. 'Whoever lived here before you must have been a right lazy cunt, to let it get this bad.'

She looked like she'd never heard the C-word in her life before. I might as well have picked up a handful of mud and rubbed it into her pale, perfect cheek. Shocked, she turned and tiptoed back up to the safety of the patio.

'Keep those drinks coming,' I shouted after her.

We went to the local pub for lunch. We invited Clare but she declined, of course. When we came back, loud with the cold cider we'd drunk a little too enthusiastically, she was just where we'd left her, reading her romantic novel beneath the parasol. The lads' banter was a fair bit louder and coarser after a couple of pints and I could see Clare's mouth tightening as she tried not to listen. It was too much for her when I started to join in, laughing as raucously and being just as crude as the lads, and she went indoors in disgust. I sensed her watching me out of an upstairs window and I felt a strange, perverse pride. I was like the naughty kid in school, relentlessly driving the new teacher towards a breakdown, and relishing my power. I knew that I shocked and fascinated her, and I liked that. I'd always enjoyed shocking people. The day I told my boss that I was leaving the bank and going to be a landscape gardener, the look on his face had physically aroused me.

The lads went off at six, having loaded the back of the truck with the mountain of brambles we'd cleared. I carried on working, cutting away the ivy that was trying to suck the life out of an apple tree. My boyfriend was away travelling, so I had nothing to go home for. I was enjoying myself. And besides, I wanted to stay and see Andrew again. I'd thought about him the previous night when I'd been masturbating with the shower spray. I'd thought about his gaze on my tits and I'd wanted to feel that warmth again.

Andrew came home around seven. I saw him kiss his wife and I felt a sharp prick of jealousy. It was short-lived though, because after only a couple of words to Clare he was striding down the garden towards me.

'This is incredible,' he said. 'I can't believe how much you've done in a day. You're a miracle worker.'

'There were four of us,' I laughed. 'I did have help.'

'Still . . .' He surveyed our work. 'It's amazing. You can actually tell there used to be a garden here, once.'

I looked at him. He was good-looking in a clean-cut, shiny, wealthy sort of way. Everything about him reeked of money – even his after-shave. At that moment, with the evening sun shining on his smooth, childish face and his voice soft and cool as the breeze, I wanted him in me. I had a flash thought of us fucking on the pristine white sheets in his bedroom (I'd had a quick nose around when I'd gone in for a pee), and of Clare discovering us with a look of horror stretching her perfect face.

He turned back to me and smiled. I knew he was thinking the same thing.

My lads don't work weekends. Neither do I, but in the absence of my boyfriend, who'd thoughtfully sent me a postcard telling me he was in Nepal and that the women there were incredibly beautiful, I carried on at Andrew and Clare's. They were out when I arrived. They came back around midday in their tennis gear and invited me to join them for lunch. I refused, saying I had a pint with my name on it waiting for me at the pub, but they insisted in that way rich people do, like they'll never recover if you say no.

We sat on the patio and ate salad, ciabatta, cheese and wafer-thin ham. Clare offered me white wine and failed to disguise her annoyance when I said I'd prefer a beer. I was everything she wasn't and, unlike most of the women she met, I did not aspire to be her. She was beautiful, and well spoken, and wore well-cut clothes and tasteful jewellery. She rode and played badminton and tennis and knew about art and sculpture. She had a gorgeous house, a brand new car and a husband who was worth his weight in diamonds. She smelt of expensively subtle perfume. She was quiet and gentle and refined. Perfect.

And yet it was me Andrew kept looking at. My tits, so full and obvious compared to the delicate breasts hiding in Clare's pink-edged tennis shirt. It was my jokes he laughed at. He was subtle about it, but I could tell he wanted me. When Clare took the plates back into the kitchen, and dropped a knife, and bent to pick it up, I turned at the noise. He didn't. He looked at me, not up his wife's short tennis skirt. Clare had amazing legs: long, slender and with muscles as sleek as a thoroughbred's. I caught a glimpse of her knickers as she swooped down to collect the knife. (They were big, shorts-style knickers. Clare would never risk anyone catching sight of her buttocks.) As she straightened up she glanced round nervously at Andrew, to see if he'd seen. But Andrew was oblivious.

'You've torn your T-shirt,' he said, when he was sure she was out of earshot.

'Have I? Where?'

He reached out and touched my shoulder. 'There,' he said.

I looked down. His fingertip was on the tiny piece of skin exposed by the rip in the material; his palm was hovering over my breast. 'I must have caught it on a thorn,' I said.

Clare came back out with fruit salad and he whipped his hand away. It was only a second; it was nothing. And yet, he was overly attentive to Clare from that moment on, which told me more than if he'd said, 'I can't stop thinking about your tits.'

I worked Sunday, too. It was an overcast day. Andrew and Clare had guests, and they stayed indoors and sent their insincere, harmonious laughter out to me through the open window. I felt myself being watched, and looked up. A small crowd was standing at the French windows, looking out at me. I waved and smiled. Embarrassed, Andrew came out and offered me a beer to make up for his guilt at being rich enough to hire a gardener – and for his gardener to be working on a Sunday while he watched.

'Don't you ever take a day off?' he asked.

'I've nothing else I'd rather be doing,' I explained.

There was one thing I'd rather be doing, but I didn't know him well enough to go into that. 'I love this garden,' I said. 'I'm really enjoying myself. Don't feel guilty because I'm working. You go and enjoy yourself.'

He humphed. 'You obviously haven't met Clare's brother and sister-in-law. I'd much rather be out here, rolling my sleeves up and getting stuck in.'

The thought of him getting 'stuck in' made me laugh. 'Gardening's a dirty job,' I said, showing him my filthy hands. 'Look. I bet you've never had nails this dirty in your life.'

'Not since I was a kid,' he admitted. 'I used to like making mud pies.'

We talked a bit about our childhoods, and the conversation was turning a little racy (as it tended to do with Andrew and me), getting on to playing doctors and nurses, when Clare appeared at the back door and, with poorly disguised annoyance, asked whether Andrew was staying out there all day. He smiled at me and rolled his eyes. 'Excuse my wife,' he said quietly. 'She gets jealous every time I talk to you.'

I'm not surprised, I thought, as he stomped back up to the house. He was making it pretty obvious.

On the following Tuesday, Clare had a coffee morning. A gaggle of identikit Clares arrived, floating up to the front door on swathes of silk and flowery perfume and giving me strange looks as they passed me. I was pushing wheelbarrowloads of weeds and stones and unwanted soil up a ramp on to the back of my flatbed truck. It was hard work, and I could feel the sweat making my T-shirt cling to my back. My nipples were stiff from rubbing inside my top and my hair was stuck to my face. I must have looked like a wild woman. Clare's clones smiled nervously at me as they waited to be let in the front door. Somehow, the sight of a woman doing physical work unnerved and embarrassed them, like I was a freak – like my hormones had been muddled up.

After they'd left, Clare came out with a tray of drinks for us. Sam and I were right at the bottom of the long garden, digging the hole for the pond. We were grunting and talking as we worked, cracking childish jokes and being silly, and for a while we didn't notice Clare standing waiting with the drinks. She coughed politely and we stopped. I poured a glassful of lemonade down my dusty throat and handed the glass back to her, but she didn't move. She was looking at me with a strange expression on her face.

'Everything all right?' I asked.

She shook her head slightly. 'I was watching you,' she said quietly. 'You're as strong as a man.'

'Oh.' I was taken aback. 'Was that a compliment?' I asked.

'Oh, yes,' she said quickly. 'I think it's marvellous how you . . . I wish I could . . .'

She lost track and began to blush. I watched her walking quickly back to the house and wondered what was going on behind that perfect, flawless facade. Just then, out of the blue, my pussy clenched involuntarily, sending a shudder up the back of my spine and putting unanswerable questions in my mind.

Because I worked on after the lads went home, and because I was at their house during the weekends too, I was invited to share more lunches and drinks and even a couple of evening meals with Andrew and Clare. I became more than just a hired help – I

37

was a bit of a curiosity. They shared stories from their tame pasts with me, and I amazed them with tales of the things I'd done. They were shocked by the lack of compromise and convention in my life – and by my repertoire of filthy jokes. Andrew found me refreshingly different to his wife and probably every other woman he knew; Clare, I began to realise, found me intriguing. I helped her clear away the dishes once and turned round to catch her staring at my arms.

'What are you looking at?'

She jumped. 'Oh. I'm sorry. It's just that . . . Your hands. They're so big.'

I held up one of my hands. It *was* big. Big and gnarled, heavily scarred with thorn cuts and dirt. I was busy noticing my hand for the first time when she did something which surprised me. She put her hand beside mine as a comparison. Her fingers were so slender, with their long, pink-painted nails; her skin was white and clean, and cool and soft against mine. I turned and looked at her and realised for the first time that we were the same height – both tall. But her frame was as slender and elegantly proportioned and graceful as mine was heavy. 'Look at your arms,' she said, and she lightly touched the hard muscle in my upper arm.

There was a moment's still, thin silence. It was only a split-second but it felt like for ever, and in that expanse of time I looked at her thin, pale lips and an irrepressible urge gripped me. I wanted to crush my mouth on to hers; to use the thick muscles in my arms to grab her and press her spindly body against mine; to hold her still and silence her pathetic protests with my tongue.

Andrew came in with the rest of the dishes and she span round and took them from him. She began

38

to talk quickly, animatedly, as if she was trying to cover something up. Guilty at the violence of my own thoughts, I rushed back out into the garden and even though it was the most humid afternoon of the summer, dug like an idiot until I was dripping with sweat and almost on the point of collapse. I stopped for a moment and felt coldness stretching across my chest. Looking down, I saw that my T-shirt was soaking and stuck obscenely to my breasts. Glancing up at the house, I wondered whether anyone had seen me like that. Then I refined that thought: I wondered whether Clare had seen me like that. I wondered whether she'd gasped at the sight of my heavy, full tits and had to slip her cool hand beneath her blouse, beneath her lacy bra, to touch her own slight, sweet breast.

That night, I couldn't sleep. I'd had the urge to throw a handful of chaos into their pristine world, but it was me who was in turmoil now. I was confused: my fantasies of Andrew kept turning into terrifying fantasies of Clare. I'd slept with women before, when I was too young to think anything of it. This was different. This wasn't tipsy, giggling experimentation. This was lust. Lust for a woman was surprising enough, since as far as I was concerned I was, and always had been, hungrily heterosexual. Lust for this woman, who I had nothing in common with, was incomprehensible.

But it was there. And it was still there the next morning when, having managed only an hour or so's sleep, I got up at six and went round to Andrew and Clare's to start work early. An hour's hard graft and I would sweat out whatever warped illness had got inside me.

I got there just as Andrew was heading off on the

commuter trail into London. I saw him kiss Clare at the front door. She was standing there in her dressing gown – a flimsy satin robe as creamy and smooth and ethereal as she was – and he was giving her a proper kiss, holding her face in both his hands. I felt an inexplicable, sharp prick of jealousy. But as Andrew picked up his briefcase and turned to see me jumping down from my truck, and I met his eyes, I realised it wasn't Clare I was jealous of. Andrew's flirting with me was flattering but predictable, and it didn't turn me on. It was Clare who turned me on.

Clare waved him off. I went over to say hello to her on my way round to the back of the house, sort of wishing that we wouldn't just say hello, but that we'd drift indoors, upstairs and into their still-warm bed. She'd lie there and let me discover her and then take her, like her husband had just done.

As I got closer to her, I could see there was a veneer of pride on her skin, like a layer of expensive foundation that made her glow. When she smiled at me, it wasn't her usual slightly nervous, slightly uncertain, no-eye-contact smile. It was wide and open and relaxed. It annoyed me.

'You look pleased with yourself,' I said cruelly, wanting to hurt her. 'You've just had a shag, haven't you?'

She dropped her smile.

I don't know what happened to me. I was tired. Something nasty took over. 'I can't imagine you two fucking. Does Andrew have to make an appointment? Do you book it in your diary like one of your coffee mornings? "Andrew, 6.30 am, doggie style."'

Disgusted, she gasped and slammed the door on my sneer.

* * *

40

I could almost hear her seething from the garden. It took her over an hour, but eventually she emerged from the house and stalked her way across the grass towards me.

'You had no right to talk to me like that,' she snapped.

'No I didn't,' I said. 'I'm sorry.'

She didn't hear. She'd obviously spent some time and energy working herself up to do this, and she was determined to have her say. Her voice was higher and more clipped than usual. 'I thought we were becoming friends. I want to be friends with you. I want to understand why Andrew likes you so much. I try my best to be nice and you just turn round and say something like that. Why do you have to be so crude all the time? I've tried to ignore your filthy jokes and your bad language because Andrew seems to find you so amusing, but you've gone too far this time. Our sex life is none of your business. You're paid to work. There are plenty of other gardeners, you know.'

'Andrew likes me?'

'You know he does,' she spat. 'He's a man. He's bound to like a woman who goes round without a bra on. You can see everything, you know.' She glanced disgustedly at my tits. 'No wonder you come highly recommended. Are the cheap thrills free, or do you charge extra for them?'

'I don't know what you mean,' I said, sounding completely serious but teasing her.

Her hand flapped as she tried to explain without resorting to my level of crudeness. 'When you get all sweaty, your top sticks to your ... Watching you work is like watching one of those dreadful wet T-shirt competitions.'

41

'Is it?' My voice was calm but I was screaming inside. 'And do you often watch me work?'

We looked at each other. Her anger was raging as fiercely as my lust. It rushed over me again: that desire I'd felt in the kitchen to hold her; kiss her; have her. I couldn't stop myself. I gave in to it. I grabbed the back of her head in my big hand and forced my mouth on to hers.

I've seen it in films and television dramas and always thought it was ridiculous, but it happened now. For a while she was so stunned by my passion, she just stood there and let me kiss her soft, sweet mouth. Then, slowly, realisation of what she was doing and who she was doing it with took over, and she pushed her hands up against me and struggled to get away. As she struggled I held her, and the tighter I held on, the more desperate her struggling became, until she accidentally pushed at my breast. The feeling of her hand on me was so shockingly wonderful, my mind and body lost their connection and I let go of her.

We stood staring at each other, a little breathless – her with panic and shame, me with lust. I wanted her. I wanted her more than I'd ever wanted any man. I wanted her like a man would want her. Another flash thought, so strong and vivid it made me dizzy: me on top of her, thrusting my cock between the pure cream of her thighs, into her interminably soft, fragrant cunt.

'What did you do that for?' she asked, her voice trembling pitifully.

Whatever had come over me still had control. I didn't hesitate. 'I think you know why,' I said. 'I want to fuck you, Clare.'

Reeling, she took a step backwards and just hovered in the tension between us. Deafened by the rush of my desire, she took a while to register the sound of my lads arriving behind her, but when she did she turned and ran.

My belly felt so tight. My groin felt so hard and full, I had to look down to remind myself I was a woman.

Things changed after that. Clare didn't hire another gardener – that would have meant telling Andrew the reason she wanted me to leave – but she kept out of my way. She went out more than she had done before, and when she was at home, she stayed indoors. She didn't even come round with drinks any more. She told one of my lads that from now on, we could help ourselves. She left a plastic sheet on the kitchen floor to catch the mess from our boots. When I went in for a pee, she'd be hiding out of sight behind one of the many silent, closed doors.

Andrew didn't alter towards me. Every night he'd come for a chat, carrying a beer for me, and we'd stand and survey the garden's progress from uncontrollable into a designer version of 'wild'. He was as pleased with the way it was taking shape as I was. He flirted gently and ineffectually with me and always gave my tits an affectionate ogle, like they were old friends. But the thrill I got from his attention was very faint now, like the warmth from a fire that had died hours ago.

I smiled and laughed along with him and chatted as if nothing was wrong. But something was wrong. I wanted Clare so much that whenever Andrew was talking to me I could barely hear what he was saying because I'd be so aware of Clare's presence in the kitchen window in the distance. My eyes would drift over Andrew's shoulder and I'd send my thoughts racing towards her: I want to fuck you. You're beautiful. I want to enjoy you like a man would enjoy you. Tell me you've thought about it, too.

I said it again and again, chanting silently inside my brain in the hope that she would hear. The way I imagined it, she'd look up from her cooking, catch my eye, smile slightly and tell me, 'Yes. I have thought about it.'

But she never did.

The turning point came when my boyfriend landed back from his travels, hungry for a decent meal and horny for a decent fuck. I didn't work that weekend. I fed him and fucked him and satisfied all the other little cravings that built up when he was away, like wanting clean sheets and Guinness and *Coronation Street*. On the Saturday night, we went into the village and got ratted in the pub. Stumbling out at closing time, we began the long walk home, which was a slow process what with stopping every few yards for a bit of a fumble. I was standing at the roadside, waiting while Jason thoughtfully went out of sight to pee in a bush, when a car I recognised drew up beside me.

'Hello,' Andrew said, as his window slid smoothly downwards. 'Are you all right?'

'Fine,' I said, laughing as I heard Jason swearing and falling over in the distance.

'We haven't seen you this weekend. We were wondering where you'd got to.'

'My boyfriend turned up,' I explained. 'I don't work weekends when he's home.'

'I see,' Andrew chuckled. Clare was driving. He was obviously a bit pissed, otherwise he wouldn't have said, 'Better things to do with your time, hey?' and tapped his nose knowingly.

Jason emerged from the black shrubbery and

arrived by my side. For some strange reason, I felt proud as he curled his arm around my waist, pressed his drunken body against mine and claimed me. I felt ridiculously proud as Andrew and Clare watched him kissing my neck – something he always did after he'd been away from me for a minute or two. Clare's blue eyes darted over his big, scruffy, powerful body and through his wild hair. I could see she was attracted to Jason the same way Andrew was attracted to me. Jason was everything Andrew was not. He was rough and ready and smelt of real life. But, more important, I could see the briefest flicker of jealousy in her nervy smile. Like anyone who thought they owned someone's attention, even if it was unwanted, she was disappointed to see that my attention was divided; and surprised at herself for feeling disappointed.

Back at work on Monday, when I went indoors to make a brew she loomed out of the genteel silence. 'Did you have a nice weekend with your boyfriend?' she asked.

Surprised to find her talking to me again, I hesitated. 'Er, yeah. It was great, thanks.'

'Have you been with him long?'

Where was this leading? 'Three years, off and on.'

She seemed puzzled and her eyes were hard. 'So he doesn't know that you're a . . .?'

My turn to be puzzled. 'A what?'

She summoned all her strength. 'A lesbian,' she spat.

'What makes you think I'm a lesbian?'

Her delicately shaped eyebrows shot up, putting furrows in the perfection of her forehead. 'Have you forgotten about your behaviour with me, that day you said you wanted to . . . to –'

'Fuck you? No, I haven't forgotten.' Neither had

she, by the look on her face and the way her lip was beginning to quiver. 'I do want to sleep with you, but that doesn't make me a lesbian, Clare. Why do you have to put labels on people? Does it make you feel better, up here in your ivory tower? I've got some dope in my house. That doesn't make me a drug dealer.'

'I don't understand,' she whispered, clearly overcome and wilting like the corseted heroine in some costume drama.

'I didn't expect you to,' I said.

'But how could you say those things to me? How could you kiss me if you weren't –'

I put my fingers on her cheek and lightly brushed my thumb across her open mouth. She flinched but didn't move away, answering my question before I'd asked it. 'Haven't you ever wondered what it would be like, Clare – with a woman?'

She tried to shake her head but there was fear in her eyes that said, 'Yes.' She had been wondering, ever since I'd planted the thought inside her mind.

'You're beautiful,' I said. 'When I look at you, I want to fuck you the way Jason fucks me. I want to know how it feels to make such a beautiful woman come. I want to know how it feels to be the man.' I kissed her gently on the lips. 'I think you think about it, too. I think you want to know how it would feel, with me on top of you, instead of Andrew. We've all thought about it, Clare. We've all wondered about doing it with another woman, because a woman would know exactly what to do, wouldn't she?'

She still didn't move. She didn't fight me off, but she didn't respond either when I touched her mouth again.

'Admit it,' I pleaded. 'Just admit you've thought about it.'

46

No reaction but terror in her eyes. There was fear inside me, too, but something made me keep pushing her. I whispered in her ear, 'Can't you feel the tension between us?'

'No,' she said, shakily.

'Admit it. It's not just Andrew who looks at my tits, is it? You look at me, too.'

She let out an 'oh' of distaste.

'I know you think about me,' I said. 'I bet you think about me in bed. Andrew touches you, and you close your eyes and pretend it's me. Don't you?'

'I do not. I've never thought about another woman like that. I certainly wouldn't want to think about *you*. You disgust me.'

'I don't believe you,' I whispered.

'You can believe what you want.'

'I believe you want it as much as I want to.'

'You're mad,' she huffed, backing away from me. 'The only person I want is my husband. I can't wait until you're finished here, then I'll never have to see you again.'

'Andrew's asked me to maintain the garden once it's finished,' I said. 'You'll see me once a week.'

She groaned with frustration and stormed back into the living room.

That was it. From then on, she knew as well as I did that it was going to happen. I wasn't going to go away. She could pump her head full of revulsion or try her best to purify her thoughts, but it was no good. I was in her brain like a poison, slowly taking hold. She couldn't help but think about it; couldn't help but watch me and wonder. And I knew, as well as she did, that she couldn't help but close her eyes when Andrew was touching her and pretend that it was me – another woman.

47

She was lost. My suggestion had infected her, and try as hard as she could to fight it, her disgust was now entwined with strands of curiosity. What would it be like? Could it be as good as with a man? Was there the slightest chance it could even be better? From the sanctuary of her kitchen, she'd look out to where I'd be talking to Andrew and our eyes would momentarily meet. Only a moment, but it was long enough. I could see her admission. It was going to happen. I began to obsess about it, and on the Saturday that Jason went to Wales to do some climbing, I went to London to do some shopping. I bought a big, smooth, black dildo and a harness to hold it in: a soft leather G-string with a hole in the front that my false prick fitted into. That night, lying on my bed, I couldn't believe how horny it felt to have it all: the hard prick and urges of a man, and beneath them, the body and mind of a woman. I couldn't wait to share it all with Clare.

I didn't have to wait long. Good job, or I may have gone insane. But the following Tuesday, I arrived at their house to find Clare's car gone, Andrew's still there but no one at home. A while later, Clare arrived back just as I was setting off to the garden centre.

'Something wrong with Andrew's car?' I asked.

'No,' she said. 'Andrew's gone to Frankfurt. I just took him to the airport.'

'Oh,' I said. 'Is he back tonight?'

'Tomorrow.'

I looked at her. *Then it's tonight.*

The lads went home. I worked late. She ate alone in the dining room with her back to me. Ever since I'd bought it, I'd kept my strap-on under the seat in my van, just in case. Now, it was calling to me. 'Put me on,' it was urging. 'Do it. Fuck her.' I went and crouched in the back of the van and put it on, smelling the leather and silicone rubber as it mingled with the scent of my skin, my sweat and my pussy. It was difficult angling the huge erection so it fitted when I pulled my knickers and combat pants back up. It looked obscene, bulging against the soft khaki cotton. I felt obscene.

Still, I didn't do anything. I carried on working, savouring my ever-ready erection and the feeling of her attention on the back of my head. She was expecting me to come indoors and get her, but I wasn't going to. She was going to have to come outside. I'd made all the moves so far – it was time for her admission.

Sure enough, like a squirming insect brought out by the setting sun, she emerged and silently handed me a beer. We stood side by side, watching the sunset turn the clouds silly colours. The pulse in my pussy echoed along my rigid cock. I let her suffer in silence while I sipped my beer.

'You know what we were talking about, last week?' she said haltingly.

'Yes.' I turned to face her.

She flinched. Looking down, she fiddled with her fingers. 'I have. Thought about it,' she stuttered.

If I hadn't already had a hard-on, her quiet, shy, shameful admission would have given me one. 'I know,' I said.

She looked up. At me. I dropped the beer and grabbed her shoulders. I pulled her tight into me and kissed her so hard, I could feel her gasping for air. At first, she just stood there and let me, but then, when she realised a thunderbolt was not going to strike us down, she began to kiss me back. I could feel her body giving in to mine; and I could hear her mind fighting her body.

'You want this as much as I do,' I said, speaking into her open mouth.

She answered by touching my tongue with the tip of hers. A strange energy flowed between us – two women who had so much and so little in common. 'You want me to fuck you.'

'Yes,' she breathed. 'I don't understand it. I'd never thought about it before I met you.'

Neither had I. Done it, but never really thought about it. Didn't think about it then, either. Thought like a man. Wanted her dress off. Wanted to see her tits; to feel them and suck them and lick them, and pinch her pale pink nipples until I felt her stiffen.

Her breasts were so delicate. Mine were so big and heavy, so achingly full of lust. Hers were like an adolescent girl's, slight and pale and pure, like they'd never been touched. I touched them with reverent fingertips and then greedy lips, feeding on her gentle curves and making her wriggle and whine. I pulled her down with me on to the ground, and before she could complain about grass stains on her dress she was open-mouthed, trying to silently protest about my fingers in her knickers.

Soft, cream satin and lace pulled down over her long legs and thrown aside, like a flower head lying dead on the dark grass. The softest skin on her inner thighs. Soft, blonde pussy hair. Soft, soft lips, and inside, never-ending softness. Everything about her was so soft – even her voice, curling gently upwards into the dusk like the last wisp of smoke from a sweet-smelling bonfire. She made me feel so hard.

I lay flat, face down between her open thighs. Ravenous, I lowered my mouth to her cunt and ate her. Any misgivings she still had were overtaken by pleasure and she bent her legs and lifted her hips up for me. My tongue and lips and hunger were hard. I sucked an orgasm out of her and fed off the shaking of her thighs and the juice pouring from her cunt.

But, like a man, I was impatient to bury my cock inside her. I unzipped my trousers, pulled my knickers down over my thighs and watched the shock distort the pleasure on her face as she saw my big, black cock. 'Oh my God,' she whispered, but before she could say anything else I was holding myself over her body and sliding into her. I bowed my head and watched as she took me in, deep into the core of her. I looked up again at all the emotions in her eyes: the confusion and repulsion and disbelief, and the terrible realisation that her body was taking over, and that, even though I was a woman, she wanted this. Needed it. Needed a cock inside her, whether it was real or fake, white or black, flesh or rubber.

'Oh God,' she whispered again, looking up at me, scared. 'This is so weird. I can't believe this is happening.'

Neither can I, I thought, as her trembling fingers touched my waist and slowly moved upwards, pulling my T-shirt up. As I thrust above her, she revealed my full, dangling breasts. She couldn't stop herself from staring at them, then tentatively touching my wide, brown nipples.

Mesmerised, she gently pulled at my shoulders. I lowered myself on to her, watching as our breasts pressed together. We looked obscene and beautiful, my soft, dark nipples kissing her stiff, pink nipples; my heavy curves slowly engulfing her slight curves. There were sharp thrills inside my stomach as she dragged her eyes away from the sight and up to my face. I kissed her, and, with her shaking fingertips on the sides of my breasts, she kissed me back.

She was gone. She'd lost control. Power surged inside me; it was me who'd made her lose control.

I'd offended her, made her angry and jealous and then curious. Now she was wrapping her legs around my back and pulling me deeper inside her, wanting this to happen – wanting to satiate the strange longing I'd aroused in her guts.

I had control. Of her; of her longing; of this. I had everything. A cock to plunge in and out of her, so big it made her gasp with every thrust. A man's strength to hold her down until I felt her give way. Breasts to press against hers, to remind her that this wasn't natural. And a clitoris, burning inside my harness, being rubbed with every thrust of my cock, which was making me moan in time with her.

Holding on to her, I rolled on to my back. Freed from the safety of my thick limbs, she hesitated for a moment, realising that here she was, straddling another woman who, beneath the leather harness, had a pussy as hungry and wet as hers. Then I reached between her legs and stroked her clit and she stopped thinking and took up the rhythm I'd started earlier. With her knees either side of my hips, she lowered herself up and down on my prick, smearing her juice on the black rubber. My throat felt tight as I realised why my boyfriend likes me on top. A woman on top is like an admission: she sets the rhythm, she makes it quicker or slower or harder because it's what *she* needs. All deep-seated, underlying shame at needing this has gone. He's not fucking her any more – she's fucking him, because she has to. The craving in her cunt makes her do it.

So Clare, the perfect, pristine wife, knelt on top of me and fucked my fake cock. She was naked, and my gaze followed the fading sunlight, caressing her long neck, her small breasts, her slender waist and toned stomach. My fingers worked beneath her soft curls, rubbing her clit until her rhythm faltered and she closed her eyes. 'Oh God,' she groaned, and I bent up my legs behind her and used all my strength to thrust up into her while my fingers drove her insane. 'Oh God,' and she was coming, throwing her head back and touching her own breasts and opening her mouth in a silent prayer.

Still shaking, she lowered her body on to mine and rested her head in my shoulder. I felt her quick breath on my neck, and the way she clutched on to me, and pride swelled in the swollen flesh hiding behind my still-hard cock. Jason had pursued me for weeks before I'd given in, and now I knew how he must have felt that first time we'd fucked, releasing all the tension that had built up between us. Clare had given in, and despite her senses screaming at her not to, she'd exposed her longing to me. It confused and angered and probably upset her even now, as she was lying gratefully in my arms, but like a woman who's always attracted to the wrong sort of men, she'd been powerless to fight it for ever.

She laughed softly. 'I thought it was Andrew you wanted,' she said.

'It was, at first.' She looked up at me as if she wanted to say something. 'You all right?' I asked.

'Yes.' Her voice was weak. 'I'm just a little shocked. Andrew doesn't always ... I've never actually ... Well, I've never come like that before.' The slightest smile quivered over her lips at my look of surprise. 'You were right. Women do know exactly what to do.'

I smiled back. I reached down and felt for her tender clit. Her hips jerked and she pleaded with me. 'Don't. It's too much.' But a moment later, she squirmed and parted her thighs as the pleasure began to wave over her again. A moment later, she was involuntarily reaching for my cock.

'That's another good thing about women,' I said.
'What?'
'We don't have to wait twenty minutes before we do it again.'

A Dangerous Addiction

*H*e met her in a gay bar. His eyes were immediately drawn to her, although that was understandable, since he was the only staunchly straight man in the pub and she was one of only four women there, and she stood apart from them. She wasn't one of the sycophantic fag hags, cackling raucously at the jokes of the vicious queens and gentle queers. She sat alone at the bar, not bothering to turn around when she was jostled and nudged, her eyes glazed with boredom. He watched her drinking – she drank like a man – and something gripped him. It might have been lust, but it felt stronger, more sinister than that. It ran through his veins, quicker and darker and stickier than blood; it pulsed deep inside him, in time with the pounding beat of the music.

He pushed his way to the bar and looked at her while he waited to be served. She was beautiful in her selfish solitude. A beauty that scared him because, like a child wanting to pull the wings off an insect, he wanted to crush her. To stick his cock in her mouth and fuck her. The vision was disturbing but her thoughts precluded him and he wanted to invade her private world. He wanted her to look at him; to acknowledge his existence. To care whether he lived or died.

'Hello,' he said hopefully, then immediately wished he hadn't.

She turned and looked at him. She summed him up with eyes that fell quickly over his body, pausing at his shoes. They were nice shoes. He believed in spending a little extra on good shoes. It was always worth it. But she didn't look overly impressed.

'Can I buy you a drink?'

Her eyes narrowed. 'What do you want?'

'I don't want anything,' he lied. 'I was just offering you a drink.'

'You don't know me. Why on earth would you offer me a drink? Unless . . . Unless, of course, you're going to try and chat me up.'

I see, he thought. It's like that, is it? 'Well, would you mind if I tried to chat you up?'

'Didn't your mother teach you not to talk to strangers?'

'Yes, but . . .'

She smiled slightly. 'But what?'

'You're more attractive than the average stranger.'

'So you're willing to break Mother's rules? Talking to strangers can get you into trouble, you know.'

Her eyes flashed with evil. A stream of pure desire shot from his stomach into his mouth. 'Is that a promise?'

'It's a warning.' Her dark eyebrows flickered suggestively. 'I should also warn you that I'm married.' She gave him a look that didn't exactly say, 'Keep away, I'm married' – it said something else altogether. It said, 'Yes, I know I'm horny. I know you want me. I would have been very surprised and actually quite disappointed if you hadn't tried to chat me up.' At least, that's what he thought it said. But at the same time she lifted her hand and showed him the undeniable, solid-silver proof of her wedding ring.

'Is that why you drink in gay bars? To avoid all the men who would otherwise try and chat you up?'

'How do you know I'm not gay?'

She couldn't possibly be. Lesbians just didn't look like she looked. 'I thought you said you were married?'

'I could be married to a woman. Things aren't always what they seem, you know.'

'Are you married to a woman?'

'No. And I don't come in here to avoid being chatted up. I like being chatted up.' This time she gave him a look that said, 'Don't even think about it/I'll eat you for breakfast/Come and have a go if you think you're hard enough.'

He was confused. There were conflicting signals sparking and clashing in the muggy, nicotine-stained air. Back off. Come on. Try it if you dare. Johnny was out of practice with all these pre-fuck mind games – he'd been married for three years. His relationship with his wife was so comfortable; so easy. He hadn't considered flirting with another woman since his wedding day, let alone picking a woman up in a bar and dragging her into a back alley and pushing her to her knees and dragging his fingers through her long blonde hair and unzipping his flies and –

'So what's your excuse?' she asked, giving him a smile that derailed his train of thought.

He blinked several times. 'Sorry?'

'What are you doing in here if you're straight? If you are straight, that is,' she added, teasing him. 'Of

57

course, you could be bisexual, which would explain why you're in a gay bar trying to chat up a woman.'

'I'm straight,' he said. 'Honestly,' he insisted, at her sneer of doubt. 'You can ask them.' He tilted his head towards the corner, to a quiet group of young men in very tight T-shirts. 'I work with that lot. They dragged me in here. I think they're trying to convert me.'

She didn't even bother to look round at them. 'You're definitely straight?'

'Definitely.'

She looked as if she knew better. 'You sure about that?'

'Very sure.'

Her small, sexy, cock-hungry mouth shrugged. 'Shame. Bisexual men are far more interesting.'

He was silent, and slightly surprised to be kicking himself for not being bisexual. What was it about her? She made him feel conservative with a big C. Since when had plain old 'straight' become so boring?

'So, are you going to try and chat me up, then?

'But you're married.'

'So are you.' She smiled sneakily, obviously pleased with herself and amused at having spotted his wedding ring.

'Just because a man's married, it doesn't mean he has to stop noticing other women.'

'And what about fucking?'

'Sorry?'

'Do you draw the line at noticing other women? Or do you fuck them too?'

Her aggression should have been a turn-off, but it wasn't. It was just frightening. He'd never felt such pressure to impress a woman – and such a need to get inside her knickers.

'Look at my wedding ring,' she invited, holding out her hand.

He took her fingers in his. Jesus. The sensation of holding a part of her body. Feeling her skin on his. The temptation to pull her off her stool, pin her down on the dirty, sticky floor and push up her skirt and fuck her, hard.

'Look at it,' she urged.

Her low, luscious voice wrapped itself around his neck and slowly squeezed. He wanted to close his eyes and roll around naked in the filthy thoughts that were turning his mind into a dirty, muddy swamp; but he obeyed her and looked. Her wedding ring was a flattened band of dark silver with letters engraved all around it.

C K M E F U

'Fuck me,' she said.

He looked up at her. 'Pardon?'

'That's what it says. On my ring.'

He looked down again. The letters rearranged themselves and punched him between the eyes. 'Your husband gave you a wedding ring with "Fuck me" engraved on it? Charming.'

'Don't you want to?'

'Sorry?'

'Don't you want to fuck me?'

He should have thought. Should have realised that this woman, whose husband had married her with a Fuck Me ring, was danger. But he didn't think.

Like a child inching his way towards the edge of the high-diving board, he tried to convince himself he could do it. Would do it. He counted to ten and then flung himself off. 'Yes,' he said, as the air whipped past his face and the force of the fall sent his heart jumping up into his mouth.

She stared at him for a long time, head tilted, eyes

59

narrowed, summing him up. Assessing him. Deciding whether he was going to be allowed to fuck her. 'How will you do it?' she asked at last, as if this was the final question she'd reached in her mind. The final hurdle.

'How will I . . .?'

'Fuck me. How will you fuck me?'

Oh God. This was pressure. This woman had probably seen it all, done it all. What could he possibly offer that was going to shock or arouse her? How was he going to impress her enough to make her stand up and say, 'OK. Let's go'? What could he say?

The barman hovered meaningfully and she looked up, breaking the spell; saving Johnny from coming up with anything witty and/or devastatingly sexy – for the time being.

'What are you drinking?' Johnny asked.

'Southern Comfort.'

He smiled to himself. She could have been the poster girl for Southern Comfort – she'd have fitted in perfectly with its advertising campaign and the image of its drinkers as non-conformists. She certainly didn't conform to his usual idea of what was sexy. Up until now, he'd always gone for shy, small, sweet types – stereotypes of what he thought women should be. Women who wore pretty, flowery dresses and perfume and necklaces and delicate, strappy shoes with little heels and who looked adorably cute wearing his rugby shirt on Sunday mornings. Softly spoken women who flinched at the F-word and got positively upset at the C-word. Sensitive women. Gentle, girly women. She was none of those things. He watched her, her eyes lazily following the barman's movements as he served them, and he longed to see inside her head.

She nodded with casual familiarity as another drink was placed in front of her. She took a big, manly, greedy gulp – the sign of someone who needed a drink rather than enjoyed it – then turned back to him. 'Go on then. Tell me how you'd fuck me. I'm dying to know.' She licked her upper lip. 'Make me wet,' she challenged.

'I . . . I . . .' Oh God. 'Well, I'd . . .'

She grinned. 'Tell me what you thought when you first saw me. The truth.'

The truth? The truth was lurking in a dark place in his brain; hiding behind a door he didn't want to open. He couldn't possibly tell her what he'd thought when he'd first seen her. His mouth flapped. He swallowed air. She raised an eyebrow and waited.

'I, well, I . . .'

She drummed her fingers on the bar.

'I thought . . . I thought you were very attractive.'

'Is that all?'

'Yes,' he lied.

She thought about this for a moment. 'You didn't think about maybe sticking your cock in my mouth?'

She said the words very slowly, deliberately rolling them around on her tongue before letting them out. She left her mouth open in teasing invitation, and he couldn't help staring at her small lips. In his silence, he admitted that she was right.

'I'm right, aren't I? A lot of men want me to suck their cocks. Something about my having a small mouth, apparently.'

His mobile rang. For a while, deafened by the sexual storm raging between him and this woman, he didn't hear its shrill, insistent whining.

'It's my wife,' he said, after pulling the phone out of his jacket pocket and reading the number.

'Ignore it,' she challenged.

His brow dipped. 'It's my wife. I can't ignore it.'

She shrugged disinterestedly, as if this loyalty was a weakness on his part. He watched her talking to the barman as he spoke to his wife, and he wished he could hear what they were saying. They were laughing at some secret joke – laughing at him, he suspected – and he could barely concentrate on the instructions his wife was giving. 'Get home as soon as you can, darling. David and Penny are coming over for dinner then we're going to watch a video. Can you buy some French bread on your way home? Oh, and David will be driving, so you'd better get some mineral water too. Where are you? I can hardly hear you, that music's so loud. Have you been drinking?'

She slid from her stool. On her feet, she was as tall as him. Tall, for a woman. Imposing. Scary. She knocked his shoulder as she brushed past him and weaved her way through the crowd to the cigarette machine. 'Are you listening?' asked his wife. 'Yes,' he said, watching her hips sway; her long strides; her fingers tearing off the cigarette packet's plastic wrapper as if it was his skin. He promised his wife he'd be home in half an hour and put his phone back in his pocket.

'Your wife checking up on you?' she asked, getting back on to her stool. 'Does she know you go to gay bars and talk to strangers?'

'Does your husband know about everything you do?'

'My husband and I have a very trusting relationship. He lets me fuck other men. And I let him.'

Oh Jesus. Oh Jesus. If that wasn't an invitation, what was? He gritted his teeth and cursed his pretty, sweet, clever, loving wife and their happy, comfortable marriage which suddenly seemed too comfy – a bed so soft he couldn't clamber out of it; white, fluffy pillows choking him with mouthfuls of feathers; sheets so clean they'd been bleached of life. A freshly washed nightmare. He cursed dinner parties and friends he knew too well and Friday nights with bottles of wine and videos. He cursed the safety of it all.

She pulled out a cigarette, without offering one to Johnny. He slid closer and offered her a light. She held his wrist and lit her fag. She carried on holding his wrist and studied the inscription on the battered gold of his Zippo. 'To Johnny. Love, Rebecca.' She let go. 'Does Rebecca trust you, Johnny?'

He swallowed hard. 'She trusts me not to sleep with other women.'

'But sometimes you want to.' She sucked on her cigarette and exhaled a thought. 'I know the feeling, Johnny. Sometimes my husband just isn't enough. Sometimes I just want to stay out all night and have dirty sex with someone I've only just met.'

Oh. Jesus.

His phone rang again. Did Rebecca have radar? 'Yes?' he said, a little too forcefully, so that she asked what was wrong and told him not to get uptight, she was the one at home doing the cooking, all she was asking him to do was pick up a few things she'd forgotten, if that wasn't too much trouble. 'Half an hour,' he promised. 'No, I haven't left yet. I'm just about to. No, I won't forget the balsamic vinegar, I promise.'

He sighed and turned off his phone. What the fuck did she need balsamic vinegar for? 'I've got to go,' he said with heavy regret. 'I wish I didn't have to.'

'Don't then.'

'I have to.'

She shrugged. 'You don't have to do anything you don't want to.'

God, how he wished that was true. He spent his life doing things he didn't want to. 'Believe me, I have to get home.'

She blew smoke in his face. 'You just haven't got the balls to fuck me, have you?'

Probably not. 'I just have to get home.'

'OK. Go, then.'

Suddenly, he realised how little he meant to her. He knew that if she never saw him again it wouldn't matter – he would never occupy so much as a second of her thoughts.

She, however, would occupy long hours and days and sleepless nights of his. 'Can I call you?'

'What would be the point if Rebecca doesn't let you out to play?'

'I'd like to see you again.'

She stared at the fingers holding her fag, following the swirling smoke with lazy, drunken eyes.

'Will I see you again?'

'In your dreams.'

She turned away. He did something he shouldn't have done – he reached out and grabbed her wrist. He couldn't help himself, but as she looked down at his hand she withered his bones with her stare and he wished he hadn't done it.

'What do you think you're doing?'

'Sorry,' he said, uncurling his fingers.

'Go home,' she suggested. 'Go and shag your wife senseless.'

'I don't want to.' His voice was bleating. 'I want to shag you.'

'Then ring your wife and tell her you won't be coming home tonight.'

'I can't do that.'

'Then close your eyes and pretend it's me.' She glanced at him; in an instant his innards turned to charcoal: black, flaking, dead. 'It'll be the best fuck your wife's ever had.'

'But . . .'

'But what? I've made it pretty clear I'd have let you fuck me, and still you tell me you have to go home. Go then. I don't give a fuck, either way.'

She looked at him for what seemed like forever. Then she turned her back on him and began a low, private conversation with the barman, who was hovering again.

Johnny fought the urge to pick up her drink and throw Southern Comfort and glass and fury and frustration at the grubby wall, slammed some money on to the bar and slunk back to his friends to deliver their drinks and tell them he was leaving. He could taste anger in his mouth, even more flat and disappointing than his pint. 'Fuck,' he muttered, quickly swallowing his drink because he'd paid for it and didn't want it to go to waste. 'Fuck.'

He watched her. He had never experienced such a violent rush of sexual desire. He wanted to pull her long, blonde hair. He wanted to bite her lips. He wanted to fuck her, hard. Until it hurt. Until she cried. Until those wide blue eyes were forced to show surrender. She had the sexiest eyes he had ever seen.

She had a tattoo on her upper arm that he hadn't noticed before – a small green and blue butterfly. She had a streak of dark blue running through her hair, and her long fingernails were painted dark blue too, to match the short, dark-denim skirt that showed her muscular thighs and shapely calves. She had on heavy black leather boots and a thin leather collar around her neck. Her skimpy T-shirt was a pale blue that matched her eyes. The material was silky and incredibly clingy, and it seemed to Johnny that she wasn't wearing a bra underneath. Her tits looked lovely: pert and just too big to be a handful. He imagined them jiggling as she straddled him. He imagined biting on her nipples until he tasted blood.

She downed her drink in one, stood up and leant over the bar to kiss the barman on both cheeks. Her skirt rode up as she bent forwards and Johnny felt the breath hovering in his throat, burning his insides like a mouthful of dry ice. He imagined those long, tanned, muscular thighs wrapped around his waist. Around his neck. Imagined his thumbs pressing into her flesh. Imagined them shaking – not trembling gently, but full-on shaking – at the force of his fucking. He imagined biting those thighs until they were spattered with dark red teeth-marks.

He blinked and tried not to think of those things. He watched as the barman – a queer so raging that his bald head and pierced tongue and thick moustache made Johnny's skin crawl – whispered something to her and she nodded, and when she turned there was a secret smile on her lips. He felt panicky as he watched her squeeze a path to the door, and suddenly, for the first time since the age of about ten, when he'd developed a fascination for catching butterflies and pinning their beautiful wings down and watching as they slowly gave up the fight for life and died, he discovered that violence lurked inside his mind.

Through the window, he saw her emerge into the sticky summer night. Like a wild animal released into the urban jungle, she blinked hesitantly. She looked up and down the pavement several times, unsure of where to go. Turning her back on the street, she sheltered herself from the world with a long drag of her cigarette while she ran her fingers through her hair. Then she looked directly at him. She smiled.

That was it. Fuck dinner. Fuck balsamic vinegar and videos and David and Penny. Fuck Rebecca. He slammed down his pint, slopping a little on the already sticky table. 'Got to go,' he said to his friends.

But by the time he escaped from The Marquis, she was gone. 'Fuck,' he chanted. 'Fuck, fuck, fuck.'

He would never find her in the dark. His panic inexplicably grew into terror. He hunted for a flash of blue, without success.

He would have to go home, close his eyes, pretend his wife was the other woman and shag her senseless. He started walking to the tube.

Then he spotted her. She was on the opposite side of the road, standing at the bus stop. Laughing at him with her cold eyes. As he waited impatiently for a gap in the traffic he stared at her determinedly. He wouldn't let her get away a second time – not after that smile.

She languidly turned her head as he appeared at her side, breathless. Her self-assurance made him feel inane and childish and utterly stupid, like a spotty, pre-pubescent boy asking a supermodel for a date. 'Hello again.'

'Haven't you gone yet? Your wife'll be getting very anxious.'

'I . . .' What should he say? You smiled at me and I changed my mind? I'd like to fuck you now, if that's OK? 'I don't feel like going home, just yet,' he ventured, hoping he sounded rebellious and a lot braver than he felt. 'I thought maybe we could go somewhere where we can, er, pick up where we left off?'

She tilted her head and weighed him up. 'OK,' she said at last. 'Come on. I owe you a drink.'

* * *

He stood in the corner and she brought the drinks over. The Liberty was much quieter: a back-street pub populated with businessmen. When she spoke, her voice was hushed conspiratorially.

'What did you think of The Marquis, then?'

She pronounced it the French way – Mar-key – rather than the English, Mar-kwiss. He thought nothing of it. 'It's OK,' he said. 'Not really my scene, to be honest. But I'm glad I went. I wasn't expecting to meet anyone like you in there.'

She looked at him over the rim of her glass as she drank. His penis thickened as he realised how beautiful her eyes were. Wide, with thick, dark lashes that didn't match her blonde hair. Pale-blue irises streaked with a darker, dirtier blue. Pupils dilated. Did that mean she wanted him? She looked directly inside his head, baiting him with silence.

'Would you like to see something?' she asked, not waiting for an answer and knowing that he would want to see whatever she chose to show him. A strange expression lit her eyes. She backed herself into the corner and pulled at his sleeve, moving him until he shielded her from the view of the rest of the pub. She put down her glass and turning her back, lifted her T-shirt.

Her skirt was slung low over hips that curved upwards into a slim waist. Her skin was brown and luxuriant, but damaged like a peach that had been repeatedly and cruelly slashed with a blunt knife. Either side of the furrow of her spine, her flesh was scarred with purple streaks of violence. Johnny became aware of the loudness of his heartbeat knocking at his hollow chest. She turned to face him again and, letting her top fall, she eased up a corner of her skirt. First, unavoidable, he saw the black lace edge of her knickers, and dark tufts of pubic hair trapped beneath the elastic; then deep, mottled wounds of green, brown and indigo at the top of her leg. He saw a welt on her inner thigh, recent and long: a raised strip of swollen, pink flesh. Holding his breath, and without realising what he was doing, he ran his fingers over the wound. Either side of the welt her skin was cool, and so soft it made him ache.

His voice, when it eventually arrived in the smothered, smoky atmosphere, was barely audible. 'Who did this to you?' He grabbed her shoulder. 'Who did this? Tell me.'

'My husband.' She seemed slightly, insanely proud of this announcement.

She dropped her skirt. Johnny looked furtively around to see if anyone else had been watching, while she retrieved her drink and bathed in its amber glow.

He looked at her: at her bowed head, her golden hair swishing forward and hiding her shame; at the long fingers clutching her glass as if the alcohol could save her if she hung on tightly enough. And rage forced its way through his gritted teeth. He couldn't get his head round this, at all. Such a strong woman – how could she have let this happen?

'Is he sick?' The hand that held his glass shook slightly. Anger swelled at the back of his neck; worse, his penis thickened further. 'Is he sick?' he said again, not knowing what else to say. 'Why do you let him do this to you? Why do you stay with him?'

She lifted her head, moving in slow motion as if it was a tremendous effort. Her eyes were glazed. She had retreated from the present and moved back into her own, dark world. Her voice was calm. 'You wouldn't understand.'

'No, I don't think I would.' He shook his head.

'Explain it to me. I want to understand. I want to help you.'

'You can't help me. I don't need help. I need him.'

He cupped her elbow in his palm. He wanted to rip her T-shirt at its low V-neck; to suck her breasts. He wrenched his mind away from her breasts and back to what he was supposed to be thinking. 'You've got to get away from him.'

She swallowed the rest of her drink and shuddered as its fire hit her damaged belly. 'I don't want to. I trust him. He's the only man I've ever met who understands me.'

She ran out of the back door, into the darkness. For the second time that evening, Johnny abandoned his pint and ran after her.

He couldn't see her, which meant she mustn't be far away. He felt sweat prickling over his skin with the muggy heat, and swirling confusion in his brain. He stumbled along the empty pavement behind the pub, desperate to find her, although he was no longer sure why.

She was hiding down the first dark alleyway he came to; hiding like a child wanting to be discovered. She stood with her forehead to the black wall, her palms spread against the bricks as if he was about to frisk her. As he approached her, he heard that her breathing was shallow and irregular. He assumed she was having a panic attack.

'Are you all right?' He placed a gentle hand on her shoulder.

She shivered and turned to face him.

He struggled to comprehend the look in her eyes – plea, test or warning? Ashamed by his overwhelming desire to fuck her, he felt responsible. 'Look, you must take my card.' He delved into his pocket. 'If you need any help, or you just want to talk, you can ring me any time. Promise me you will.'

She studied the card for a moment before pushing his hand away. 'Thanks,' she whispered. 'But I don't need any help.'

'I think you do,' he said. 'Jesus, I thought you said you and your husband had a trusting relationship?'

'We do.'

'I'm sorry. I don't understand. He lets you sleep with other men – and you let him hurt you?'

'He lets me sleep with other men but he punishes me for it, afterwards. It's the price I pay for my freedom.'

'I still don't understand.'

'You may never understand.'

'Jesusfuck.' He sighed at the empty hopelessness and the utter madness of the situation. Don't get involved, his common sense told him. But he already was. He was already addicted to this mad, dangerous, frighteningly sensual woman.

For a long time, they stood in silence, looking at each other while her breathing slowed.

Then he kissed her.

Their lips matched. He had kissed women before whose lips had been out of sync with his. Their noses had bumped and they had banged teeth. They had stopped before he had wanted to, or wanted to carry on when he'd been itching to move on to the next stage. They had been forceful against his tenderness, or vice versa. But her kissing was fluent. As their tongues touched and he tasted Southern Comfort, he felt himself floating into insanity. He clasped her face in his hands. Her fingers moved over his back and he felt his cock, straining for release, pressing hard against her hip.

When they parted for air her lips shone with their

71

saliva. She was smiling. 'Would you like me to . . .?' Her fingers moulded tightly to his balls.

'No.' He wanted it desperately. 'No.'

She pressed him against the wall and knelt in front of him. He groaned as she unzipped him. Guilt speared him because he had already envisaged this scenario, long before he'd had the right to. He forced himself to keep still and not to thrust into her, like he wanted to. Knowing what he knew now made the agony of his coming violent and quick. He pulled her up and held her, tasting himself in her mouth. He had never wanted to do that before, but it was different with her. He was surprised by the flavour.

'Your turn,' he promised. 'I want to do something for you.'

She jolted as if he'd hit her. 'No.'

He paused to zip his weeping cock back into his jeans, and she was gone. He'd lost her. He went home, closed his eyes and shagged his wife senseless.

Outside, in his garden, the man and woman who had followed him home lay on the grass with their fingers in each other's pants.

'What do you think?' asked the bald, pierced, moustachioed man.

'I think he's perfect,' said the blonde, blue-eyed, giggling woman.

'Think he'll co-operate?'

'Of course he will.' She closed her cruel fingers around his prick. 'He's dying to fuck me. I know his type.'

He groaned, partly with the sensation of his cock thickening in her grasp; partly at the thought of the man inside that house who was blissfully unaware of the two warped perverts lying on his lawn; and of what they had in store for him. 'Did you show him the whip marks?'

She smiled. 'He didn't know what to think,' she said. 'He had a hard-on and he was ashamed of it.'

'Oooh,' he cooed appreciatively. 'Shame. My favourite.'

'I thought pain was your favourite.'

'Pain and shame. I get the pain with you, but you're no good where the other's concerned. You're utterly shameless.'

She grinned and spread her legs as four of his fingers thrust inside her hungry pussy. 'Shameless,' she repeated in a grateful whisper, as if she'd just been given her mantra.

Johnny went back to The Marquis every night, but she never returned. The barman watched him suspiciously, and Johnny supposed he took him for one of those unhappily married, closet gays. His wife probably thought he was either having an affair or becoming an alcoholic. His boss assumed he had problems at home and told him to take some time off, after he made several mistakes that cost the company minor expense and major embarrassment.

He hid himself in thoughts of her. In his lonely fantasy, he replayed their scene over and over again with the blind obsession of a trainspotter. He catalogued every moment and savoured every word. Sometimes he forgot a minute but essential detail and would have to rewind to the beginning again. Sometimes he would purposely omit a section, so that he could run back to the start and relive that amazing, earth-shattering, mind-altering first moment he'd seen her. Occasionally, he'd skip straight to the end, and his cock would twitch at the thought of her lips around him.

In a way, he didn't want to see her again. It was tempting to hold her in his memory, where he could gain access at any time. His fantasy could have been very satisfying, especially after he began to elaborate on reality, fucking her while he jerked off. It was almost perfect, apart from that look in her eyes: unresolved, incongruous. There was sorrow there, and the look of someone lost. But on top of that, there rested a layer of certainty which intrigued him. He had to understand it; had to find her.

Besides, she needed saving from her husband. Johnny saw every painful blotch in his mind, plotted clearly as if he had a map of her injuries that he'd drawn himself, and each day that passed without seeing her could only mean she was being subjected to some new and unbearable torture. The other man invaded his thoughts – a psychotic ogre who beat her mercilessly. Johnny imagined her being tied up and made to suck her husband's cock, which in his mind was huge and threatening and suffocating. (This thought aroused him intensely, and he hastily buried it like a guilty boy stuffing pornography under his mattress.)

He didn't see her for a month, and he began to fear the worst. He nearly went to the police station to report her missing, but realised just in time how stupid he would sound. He didn't even know her name. He became withdrawn, and his wife suggested they go to marriage guidance counselling.

Then one Friday night, just like every Friday night, he went into his local pub and she was there. She was wearing the same clothes she had worn the night he'd met her, but she looked very different. Her legs were just as he remembered. So were her hips, her waist, her back, her arms – he was immediately intoxicated by the sight of her skin – but her haircut

74

had changed her appearance completely. Her hair had been long and blonde; now it was short and almost black, cropped and slicked down. It showed the length of her neck and emphasised the solemn shine of her eyes. Its severity shocked and excited him: it made her seem delicate and vulnerable and invincible and overtly, rabidly sexy all at once. The pain of his wanting her became unbearable as it honed itself into a white light that pierced his consciousness and made him feel dizzy. He felt jealous of the other people in the pub – other people sharing the space her glory shone in, and dulling her shine; other people touching her as they pushed past her to the bar; other people breathing her air; other men looking at her and wanting her, when she was his. He didn't even register the madness of this thought as he forced his way through the crowd towards her. He touched her shoulder and she turned.

'I've found you. At last.'

'Yes.' She didn't seem at all surprised. As if she'd known, during the torture of this last month, that on this Friday night, in this pub, they would meet again. Her calmness would have been unnerving if he'd thought about it for longer than a millisecond.

He motioned her urgently towards the pub's narrow hallway, watching her hips move as he followed her. They stood close. He felt uncomfortable, not knowing whether to touch her or not. Her lack of emotion when he'd confronted her had disturbed him and for a sickening moment he felt his fantasy drop away like his stomach on the Big One at Blackpool last summer. Perhaps she didn't want to see him. Perhaps she didn't like him. Perhaps she hadn't thought about him at all since that night. And why should she have done? Why would she be as obsessed as he was?

'I thought I'd never see you again,' he said, realising that he had no choice but to let her know she'd filled his every waking thought, and most of his sleeping ones, even if he did make a tit of himself. He didn't care any more. 'I missed you. I couldn't stop thinking about you.'

'Why? What's so special about me?'

He wasn't sure. 'I've never met anyone like you.'

She smiled: not the sort of smile he'd expected. More of a twitching, struggling-not-to-laugh-out-loud smile.

Undeterred, he carried on. 'I looked for you in The Marquis, but you never came back. I went to that other pub too, but –'

'I thought about you too.'

Thank fuck for that. He smiled back: just the sort of smile she would have expected from a poor, obsessed, pitiful, weak, grateful and painfully heterosexual man.

But her attention drifted before his smile grew to full size. She pressed her fingers to her temples as if with sudden pain. 'I was late getting home that night,' she said quietly. 'You know. The night we met. My husband was waiting. He punished me.'

'Oh Christ. Are you OK?' But he knew before the question reached his lips that she wasn't.

Her eyes danced. 'I'm stronger than he is.'

He was confused. 'What do you mean?'

'Control is so hard to define, don't you think?' Her eyes narrowed. 'Do you recognise those moments when you're driving, and you suddenly realise you're not in control of the car, you're just this helpless human trying to control it, but in a second you could lose that control – in a second you could be dead?'

76

'Well . . .' Where was this all coming from? He'd only wanted to know if she was all right.

'If you can accept that realisation without fighting against it, it can be the most thrilling moment of your life. Sometimes it's the powerless who have the real power.'

He didn't listen. He should have done. He only felt his blood congeal as he lifted his hand and touched two fingers to her lips. He kissed her. His tongue slid tentatively on to hers.

Footsteps approached; little noises that became sharp as they emerged from the blurred hum of the pub. He pushed her further down the hall and into the ladies' toilet, locking the door behind them. They stared at each other for a while.

'What happened to your hair?'

'My husband liked it long. I cut it myself. I did it to piss him off.' She laughed slightly. It was the first time he'd seen her laugh. 'It was a very cathartic experience.'

'You used to be blonde.'

'It was dyed. This is my real colour.'

It suited her. Now her eyebrows and lashes matched her hair. Her eyes seemed even bluer. 'I like it,' he said.

'I'm glad.'

He touched her hair, her neck, her shoulder. He felt the tension in her body releasing as his fingers spread over the swell of her breast. The silky material of her T-shirt clung so tightly to her shape that he could see the outline of the tender flesh around her nipple, and he heard her sigh as he touched it. She bowed her head and her gaze followed his hand as it brushed over her, slowly exploring her. She was stunning. Every inch of her. The slope of skin beneath her shoulder, with its gently gathering curve gradually arching into a soft point; the underside of her breast where it met her ribs. The way her nipple hardened instantly beneath his touch into a peak that was obvious through the silk of her top. The way she chose not to wear a bra, so that he could feel the weight and shape of her without the usual impediments. It would have been cruel to keep those beautiful, tender, soft breasts trussed up with straps and wires. Cruelty reminded him of something – one of the thoughts that had haunted him since that night when they'd met.

Her body stiffened again as his hands slowly eased downwards and felt for the hem of her skirt. Watching her face, he lifted it up.

'Don't,' she pleaded, but her eyes encouraged.

He looked down. As he had done countless times in his dreams, he recognised the sweetness of her thighs, but the map he had drawn for himself was obsolete. The old markings were gone, replaced by fresher, harsher wounds. The bruising had faded, the welt he had touched had healed, the scar still there but only faint. But beneath the pale pink stripe was a wound far more shocking. A fresh tattoo, messy like a child's first attempt with felt tips, scrawled across the top of her thigh. It was written large. There was no mistaking what it said. WHORE.

The skin around the word was swollen angrily in protest. He read it again to be certain, as if trying to translate from a language he was unsure of. WHORE. Embarrassed, he searched for the right words of outrage and comfort, but she shook her head.

'My punishment for being late that night,' she explained. 'He said that no man could ever want me after seeing it.'

The cruelty took Johnny's breath away. But also – although he denied it to himself like a murderer suddenly realising with blinding clarity that he was a murderer and he couldn't be stopped – it excited him. His groin throbbed. 'I want you,' he offered, praying the violence of his wanting wasn't in his voice.

She took a slow deep breath and released it. 'You do?'

'Yes.'

She pressed her lips to his ear. She might as well have kissed his prick, the effect her mouth had on him. 'Do you want to fuck me?' she breathed.

The shock gave him an immediate erection. 'You know I do.'

His skin felt cold when she pulled away. She shone with satisfaction. He forced himself to remain calm as he looked again at the obscenity that branded her skin. Then he looked beyond, at the black triangle of her knickers, and his whole body grew hot. Tremulously, he touched her. She felt warm. He traced the edge of her knickers and the backs of his fingers felt the intolerable softness of her inner thigh. He slipped his hand beneath the elastic and eased himself inside. Amazed at the effortlessness with which he entered her, he gasped. She was very wet. As he began to slide in and out, her tender pink flesh clutched at him, and her soft hairs brushed damply against the palm of his hand. He pushed another finger in alongside the first. She held on to his shoulder, steadying her body as every muscle quivered.

He touched her clitoris. She smiled slightly. He smiled back, dizzy with the pleasure glowing like an aura around her. She was captive to the pleasure he was giving her. He would make her come – feel her body give in beneath his fingertips.

She leant against his shoulder and put her mouth to his ear again. 'Do you want me?' she whispered.

He didn't need to answer.

'Do you want to make me come?'

Yes. Yes. Yes. He wanted her. He wanted to fuck her, lick her, suck her, finger her hard until she came; until she cried out for him to stop. He wanted to know everything about her and to do everything to her.

'Do you want to hurt me?'

He froze, unsure why the menace in her voice frightened him and made him feel so guilty.

'Nova?' Someone banged on the door. 'Nova? Are you all right?'

'I'm fine,' she replied, looking at Johnny. It seemed a cloud had lifted from her face. She seemed amused by something. 'I'll be out in a minute.' She flicked her tongue across his lips. 'It's my husband,' she whispered. 'I'll have to go.'

'Don't go,' he begged.

She pushed his hand away from her pussy. 'I have to.'

He grasped at her arms. His desire was a fury inside. It panicked him. 'What did you mean, do I want to hurt you? I couldn't hurt you.'

She ignored him and unlocked the door.

He put his hand on top of hers, delaying her escape. 'When will I see you again?'

She shrugged.

Oh God. Do something now. Think of something. 'It's my wife's thirtieth birthday tomorrow. We're having a party. I want you to come. I have to see you again. Please say you'll come.'

'Tomorrow? I could make it tomorrow. My husband's working tomorrow night.'

'I'll get a friend to collect you here, at eight.'

'Fine.'

Again, that puzzling sureness, as if she had fully

expected the invitation. He locked the door behind her and sat on the toilet with his fingers in his mouth, tasting her, repeating her name to himself over and over again as if it was a cure for this madness that was taking him over.

When he emerged she was sitting at a table in the far corner, with a man Johnny vaguely recognised, perhaps from his imagination – hard to tell where from, since he had his back to Johnny. For several long minutes he watched her, coldness clutching at his spine, his emotions swinging pendulously. At first he was lulled by her, falling into a semi-slumber as he studied her face; then abruptly he fell into panic that he couldn't speak to her, and his pulse raced irregularly. Once, she looked up and he suspended himself in her as they shared a smile; a subtle glance that acknowledged what they knew.

Nova's smile, however, did not acknowledge what they knew. It acknowledged her husband's fingers up her skirt and inside her pussy. Her husband's cruel fingers, discovering how wet she was.

'How much longer?' he asked impatiently.

'Not long,' she promised. 'Tomorrow night, and he's ours.'

The next morning, while his wife was out shopping for the party, Johnny rang his best friend, Phil.

'I need a favour, Phil. A big one. I'll do anything if you'll do this one thing for me.'

'What's going on, Johnny?'

'I'm obsessed with a woman called Nova.'

'What sort of fucking weirdass name is that?'

'Help me. Bring her tonight. Pretend she's your girlfriend.'

There was a long, long pause. 'Tonight is Rebecca's

81

birthday party. Rebecca. Your wife. The woman you promised to love and cherish – remember her?'

'Please, Phil. I'll never ask another favour as long as I live. You have to do this for me.'

'Why on earth should I?'

'I have to see Nova tonight. I'll go mad if I don't.'

Another disapproving pause filled with disgust and disbelief.

'Phil, please. You know what it was like when you saw that woman on the tube. Like a thunderbolt, you said. Well, that's how I felt the first time I saw Nova. I can't stop thinking about her. Please, Phil.'

'Is she good-looking?'

'She's amazing.' His voice got sucked back into his lungs as his head filled with her, again. 'She's . . . I'd do anything for a night with her. Anything.'

'Even cheat on your wife?'

There was terror in his silence, as he realised the idea of cheating on his wife – the woman he'd loved for the last three years – didn't strike any sort of guilty chord inside him.

'You're not planning to fuck this woman at your house. Just promise me that.'

'I just want to see her.'

'I hope you've thought this through.'

'I have to see her.'

It was a mistake. He knew that as soon as they arrived together. Jealousy choked him as Nova was introduced as Phil's woman; he snapped at his wife when she commented on what a good-looking couple they made. He took refuge in brandy, which always made him ill and, mixed with the champagne he'd drunk earlier, gave him a headache that made him aggressive. He gulped down its warmth anyway, hoping it would settle his churning gut and numb his frightening passion. He wanted to be numb. His feelings for Nova were too fierce to control.

His eyes burned into Phil. Phil, the blond, lumbering, rugby-playing sloth. What the fuck did he think he was doing, parading round the room with his huge arm draped around her waist? Laughing at her jokes, eyes flickering over her cleavage. Bastard. You were supposed to bring her to me. Get your fucking hands off her.

She made it worse. She was playing the part of Phil's girlfriend with a little too much conviction. She barely looked at Johnny. She had a knife in his heart and she was twisting it. And enjoying his pain. When their eyes did meet he could tell she was taking a warped delight in this impossible situation. What the fuck was she playing at?

When the lights were turned out for the birthday cake, Johnny gave in to the brutal longing that was hurting his brain. He swiftly manoeuvred himself through his friends until he stood behind her. Singing filled the room, but he was immune to its simple jollity, and trapped by her proximity.

She was wearing a long, straight black dress with thin straps and no bra. Beneath its hem, mock snakeskin peep-toe sandals with four-inch stiletto heels peered provocatively at him and whispered, 'Fuck me hard.' I will fuck you, he promised, his eyes on the smooth, bare cups of her shoulders. Tonight.

Ignoring Phil, ignoring his friends, ignoring his wife, he eased his body closer to hers until he could smell the summer on her skin. He slid his fingers around her waist and pulled her backwards on to him. His cock, hard as it always was when she was near, nestled between the tight curves of her glorious arse. One hand slipped around to her front and he infiltrated the lips of her pussy through her dress, delighted to find her cunt bare and willing beneath the thin material. 'I want to bite your tits,' he mouthed to the back of her head. 'I want to hear you scream.'

The singing stopped and the lights came on. He pulled away from her and reluctantly went to kiss his inconvenient wife.

When Phil and Nova left, Johnny abandoned the party and followed them. Alcohol and envy made it dangerous for him to drive, trailing Phil's dark-green sports car instead of watching the traffic. 'He barely fits into that poncey car,' he muttered resentfully. 'Great big fucking oaf.' He strained his eyes for the back of her head, searching for clues in her movements. It surely wasn't possible that she had connected with Phil as dramatically, as definitely, as she had done with him. And yet they'd left together, with no more than a cursory, 'Goodbye. It was a lovely party. Thank you,' to him and Rebecca. She'd shaken his hand as if he was a stranger. 'But I want to fuck you,' he'd wanted to say. He'd almost wanted to see the shock in his wife's sweet eyes, and for her to know the sordid truth.

He watched them disappear into a doorway next to The Marquis pub, and as he searched frantically for a parking space, he knew that he would do whatever it took. This was where he had first seen her. This was his fantasy, not Phil's, and Phil had no right to be trampling across his tortured soul with his size-thirteen boots.

Johnny found the doorway. The buzzer said NOVA CAINE & THE MARQUIS, but he thought nothing of it since he didn't need to use it. He should have thought. Should have thought. Nova Caine. Why did that remind him of the dentist? And she lived with the Marquis. Not Mr Caine. The buzzer did not say Mr and Mrs Caine. He should have registered these thoughts, but the front door was open and he thought of nothing but having her. He ran up the dank, gloomy staircase. At the top, another door was slightly ajar, and he pushed at it further until he could see.

If he had been more aware, he would have heard the soft, repetitive thud of the music from the pub downstairs, and the jumpy buzz of male voices. He would have realised she lived above The Marquis, and perhaps found this interesting, particularly bearing in mind the name on her doorbell. As it was, he was only aware of the dull red light; of the black strap of her dress, slowly falling from her shoulder. Of Phil's gigantic hand, cradling one bare breast. Of Nova's eyes turning to meet his: a challenge.

'Get out. Now,' he hissed at Phil.

Phil jumped. He looked to Nova for approval. She nodded. 'You'd better go,' she said.

Yes, he thought. You better had, before I kick your stupid head in.

'I didn't mean for this to happen. It just . . .' He looked confused, as if Nova had lured him here without him knowing what he was doing. 'I'm really sorry, mate,' Phil said quietly.

'You will be if you don't fuck off, now.' Johnny slammed the door behind his friend, feeling brutal – feeling scared by the force of his own emotions. 'What the fuck is going on, Nova?'

'Isn't it obvious?' She waited, eyes wide, lips open – mocking him. 'Would you like me to spell it out for you? Phil and I were just about to fuck.'

'But I asked him to bring you to the party tonight because I . . .' His head was spinning. 'I . . . I wanted to fuck you. You know I did. I thought you wanted me but you're laughing at me.'

He wanted to hit her. To make her feel as helpless as he felt. Her smile was so cold it made him feel sick. He sucked in air, trying to fuel his brain to make the words. 'What the fuck are you doing to me, Nova? You make me feel so . . .' He clenched his fists to show her.

She laughed, but her eyes were vicious. 'You don't have a divine right to fuck me just because you want to. You don't own me, Johnny. You're not my husband.'

He could barely breathe. A fist gripped his wind-pipe. 'I didn't invite you to my wife's birthday party so I could watch you flirting with my best friend.'

She shrugged. 'Then you shouldn't have asked your best friend to pretend to be my boyfriend. I was supposed to be with Phil, remember? What did you want me to do? Stand on my own all night and not talk to anyone in case it hurt your feelings? I liked Phil. I wanted to fuck him.'

The life was draining from his body. 'Are you doing this on purpose?'

'Doing what?'

Torturing him. Smiling at him as if it was all a joke. Sliding the other strap from her shoulder and letting her dress fall to the floor. Stepping out of it and standing there in only her fuck-me shoes. Sucking on the tip of her middle finger and rubbing it between her pussy lips. Driving him insane.

Her body was incredible; her perfection somehow heightened by the scars and marks and that tattoo across her upper thigh. She was like a statue, her marble purity made even purer by the dirty graffiti streaked across her. Or a fallen goddess. Or a kami-kaze angel that had taken a dive into the temptations of hell and come up dripping with lust and carrying memories of the horrors she'd seen in her eyes. The light from the red bulb was coating her skin in the colour of desire. The air was full of tension and the smell of sex.

Before he knew what was happening, his thoughts became words. 'I want to fuck you more than anything else in the world,' he said. 'I've never wanted anyone so badly.'

'I know.'

Her finger disappeared all the way inside her cunt. His knees went weak. 'I lied to my wife to come here because I couldn't bear the thought of you with my best friend.'

'I know.'

'I think I'd have killed him if he'd slept with you.'

She nodded and sighed as she fingered herself. 'We're alone now, Johnny. What do you want to do to me?'

So many things. Where to start? He wanted to hit her; to slap her hard across the face and make her gasp and let her know the force of his anger at how weak she made him feel. He wanted to push her down on to the bed and fuck her from behind, taking her body for his own selfish needs and to hell with what she needed. But he wanted to see her face, too: to see her gratitude and watch the coldness in her eyes melt into pleasure. He wanted to hear her whimper. He wanted to make her come. He wanted to look inside her mind.

He drifted towards her. 'I, I . . .'

'Don't say anything.' She took his hand and put it where hers had been, cupped over her pussy. 'Just show me.'

He showed her. He slid his finger deep inside her cunt. She shuddered and sighed and he sighed too, knowing that at last she would be his, even if it was for just a moment.

He fingered her hard, rubbing her clit with the heel of his hand between long thrusts and making her squirm and cling on to him. Her nails dug into his arms and the pain spurred him on. He fingered her harder and quicker. 'Show me what you want,' she whispered.

He showed her. He fed her on her own juice, poking his soaking wet fingers into her mouth and letting her lick them, then rolling his tongue on top of hers and stealing the taste back again. He held on to her head and gripped her neck as hard as she'd gripped him, showing her how much he wanted this; how much he'd thought of it; how nothing else mattered but his hard, violent lust.

He grabbed her arm and pulled her over to the bed that was waiting against the wall. He turned her to face the wall, so she had her back to him, and jerked his knee into the back of her knee so her legs gave way. She knelt on the edge of the bed with her hands on the mattress, her body open and vulnerable and waiting for him. Not bothering to undress, he just unzipped his flies. Standing behind her, he held on to her hips and plunged his cock inside her.

Her groan was full of anguish. He smiled at the sound and grimaced at the sensation of fillng her tight, wet, hot cunt. She deserved this. She deserved to feel as helpless as he'd felt every day since they'd met; especially tonight, when he'd had to watch her with another man. She deserved to be turned into a trembling, whimpering body. Nothing more. Just a body. A pussy. His pussy.

But she wasn't just a body. He didn't just want her pussy. He wanted her. He wanted to know that she was his. He pulled out and pushed her down on to the bed. Flipping her over on to her back, he knelt over her sex-flushed body. He lowered his already oozing penis towards her open pussy. She bent her knees up and spread her legs in readiness. He looked down, saw the WHORE tattoo, saw the dark strip of her pussy hair, and plunged into insanity.

He watched her as he fucked her. She was silent, the only sound her breathing as with every stab of his cock he felt the short bursts of breath on his face. Her thighs were wrapped around his waist and he could feel her heels digging into his back. Her hands were on her breasts, squeezing and rolling her nipples. Her eyes were on him. She was waiting.

She smiled. The sight made his longing burst from his cock and he thrust hard, wanting to flood her; wanting to stain her for ever with him; wanting to mark her like her husband had done. She hadn't come, but he didn't care.

He'd taken what he wanted. He should have felt relieved. But as she smiled he realised he was addicted. He didn't just want her for a moment – he wanted her every day and every night. He wanted to feed from her. He didn't want to ever go home; he wanted to exist in her shadow.

Detached from his own body, he suddenly saw himself for what he was: not a lust-fuelled man selfishly grabbing what he wanted, but a poor, help-less insect, blinded by her irresistible light and now slowly dying in her arms. He felt small and weak, and angry that she made him feel like that. And when she asked him, 'What would you do for me?', he answered truthfully, 'Anything.'

'How touching,' said a man's voice.

Johnny jerked his head around towards the voice. Another man was in the room with them – another man who'd stood there, silently watching, as he'd fucked her.

'Johnny, I'd like you to meet my husband, the Marquis.'

He flinched in fear and tried to pull out of her, but her thighs were incredibly strong and she wrapped her legs tighter around him and wouldn't let him move. He just had to lie there, his cock still throbbing inside another man's wife, while the other man looked on.

Johnny recognised him this time. He was the barman from The Marquis: tall, pierced in places he shouldn't have been, with a bushy moustache and a bald head. He had a broad, muscular chest that was bare apart from the huge, sprawling, bluish-green tattoo that covered his breasts. Gold rings hung from his nipples. He was wearing fingerless leather gloves. His legs were long and huge and heavy, and tightly wrapped in black leather trousers.

Johnny looked down at Nova. He could feel his face twitching as he struggled for comprehension. 'Your husband?' he asked. She smiled up at him. 'But he's . . .'

'Gay?' The Marquis came closer. Standing at the side of the bed, smiling as if nothing out of the ordinary was happening, he put a hand on Johnny's shoulder. 'Things aren't always what they seem, Johnny. You mustn't judge people by their appearances. I like men and women.'

What could he say? 'Oh.'

'If you judge on appearances, Johnny, you can get the wrong impression.' His cruel fingers – the same cruel fingers that had inflicted all that pain on Nova's skin – clasped Johnny's cheek. 'You can look at a man like me and make assumptions. Yes, I fuck men.' He leant forward and whispered into Johnny's ear, brushing his skin with his coarse moustache. 'But there's nothing like pussy, is there Johnny? Blokes like you just can't resist pussy, can you?'

'I'm sorry. I'm sorry. I didn't know you were . . . I'm sorry,' stammered Johnny.

The Marquis wasn't listening. 'If you judged people on their appearances, you could look at a woman like my wife and make assumptions. You could look at all those scars and you could think that this woman is married to a cruel man. Is that what you thought, Johnny? Is that what she told you?'

'I . . .' Please God, let this be a dream.

The Marquis sat down on the bed. Johnny felt dizzy from too many emotions and thoughts that wouldn't mix. Here he was, his cock limp now inside her, while her husband sat inches away and stroked Nova's hair. This was too weird.

'Did she tell you that I punish her? That I hurt her? Did she tell you that whenever I know she's been with another man, I whip her until she begs me to stop?' He grinned, showing a gold tooth. 'Did she tell you that I carved the word "Whore" into her thigh to stop any man from ever wanting her again?'

Johnny was scared. More scared than he had ever been. More scared than before his finals or during his first job interview or just before he'd lost his virginity. More scared than when he'd been playing rugby and someone had stamped on his face and his cheekbone had broken and poked out of his cheek so he could see it out of the corner of his eye when he looked down. 'I don't know what's going on here,' he said, 'and I'm really sorry but I think I'll just go now and leave you to –'

'But did she tell you that she begs me to hurt her?' The Marquis paused for effect. 'You see, that's what I mean about judging by appearances. Such a beautiful woman, isn't she? Such a strong woman. You'd never believe it.' He stroked her cheek, ran his fingers over her neck and on to her tit. He pulled her nipple until her back arched slightly and she gasped. 'She's addicted to pain, poor girl. She likes to be hurt.' The Marquis winked salaciously at Johnny, as if they were sharing a secret. 'She likes to be treated like a whore.'

Johnny swallowed. He was scared shitless. He didn't want to be here, listening to this and sinking further into the nightmare. He didn't have a clue what was going on, and he wasn't sure he wanted to.

'Would you like to hurt her, Johnny?'

He looked from Nova to the Marquis. Both were grinning inanely at him, like a couple of teenagers urging the square kid in school to try a cigarette and knowing that he'd become addicted and smoke himself to an early death. 'What?' he said quietly.

'I bet you'd like to try it. I bet you'd like to pay her back for making you feel so helpless.'

How did he know that was how he felt?

'I bet you've thought about it already, haven't you? I bet you thought about hurting her the first time you saw her.'

He gulped down his guilt and tried to prise Nova's legs away from his waist. 'I think I should go now.'

'I bet you wanted to make her feel as helpless as you do.'

This was too bizarre. For the first time since he'd met Nova, he thought of his wife, at home, and the thought gave him the strength to fight his way out of Nova's grasp. He zipped up his flies and practically ran to the door.

But it wouldn't open. He spun round to find the Marquis standing on the bed and manhandling

Nova. She knelt up obediently and held up her hands. He cuffed them in the leather handcuffs hanging down from chains hooked to the ceiling. Johnny hadn't noticed those before. He hadn't noticed lots of things.

What he noticed now was that his fear was subsiding and being replaced by something far more terrifying. He should have been looking for the door keys, letting himself out, running away – doing anything but edging his way slowly back to the bed. Shuffling inch by inch across the floor, he watched – intrigued, bemused, exhilarated – as the Marquis unzipped his flies and brought out his monstrous cock. He watched as, with her beautiful, scarred back to him, Nova wriggled and moved her head from side to side to try and escape that enormous cock. He watched as submission shivered through her spine and her head was held still. The Marquis's fingers pulled at her hair and kept her where he wanted her while his hips began to thrust.

'See, Johnny?'

He saw things inside himself he didn't want to see. He felt his prick getting hard again and he was ashamed. But his shame didn't stop him from wanting her; it propelled him nearer and nearer to her and to the insanity in her eyes.

He stood by the side of the bed and watched that massive cock sliding in and out of her small lips. There was terror stretched across her face – her husband's cock was far too big, and was slamming far too hard against the back of her throat. The sinews in her neck were taut with fear and the strain of trying to get away from him. Johnny wanted to make her feel like that. He wanted to make her feel like he'd felt. He was ashamed of his desire, but he wanted to hurt her.

She coughed and spluttered obscenities as the Marquis pulled out and shot come over her throat and breasts.

'See, Johnny? She's a whore. That's the only way to treat her. Like the whore that she is. Isn't that right, darling?'

He pulled her head up by the hair. She looked exhausted and excited and edgy, like a junkie. 'Hurt me,' she whispered hoarsely.

'Hear that, Johnny?' The Marquis raised one eyebrow. 'She wants you to hurt her.'

'I can't,' he said. Her skin was so beautiful. There were so many scars – so much pain already embedded in her flesh. 'I couldn't hurt her,' he whispered. But he wanted to.

'Hurt me,' she begged. The Marquis clambered off the bed and strode across the room. He picked up something that was coiled on a chair and brought it over to Johnny. It uncoiled and trailed along the floor behind him. It had a thick, smooth handle that he placed into Johnny's sweating hand.

'Hurt her,' the Marquis said.

Johnny looked from his hand to the bed. Strung up, waiting, Nova whimpered. 'I can't,' he said, incredulity in his voice. 'I can't do this.'

The Marquis stood like the devil at Johnny's shoulder, muttering all the reasons why Johnny could. 'Think,' he urged. 'Think of how she makes you feel. Think of what you wanted to do to her the first time you saw her. Think of how she flirted with your best friend and made you feel like she had your balls in her hand and she was squeezing them and digging her fingernails in. She was flirting with him on purpose, to torture you. She would have fucked him in front of you just to get a reaction. She wants you to hurt her. She's a whore. Hurt her.'

The tension in his guts shot into his hand. He gripped the handle tight, raised it behind his head and brought the leather tail whipping through the air. The crack was loud. Her cry was louder. Her whole body jerked with the shock. Immediately, a fresh red slash marked her skin and shame speared him. What was he doing? What was he thinking?

'Again,' she groaned.

He did it again, flailing the whip across her buttocks this time. Her arse cheeks quivered uncontrollably in reponse to the pain. 'Again,' she said, and he whipped the backs of her thighs, her shoulders, her waist, feeling his own lust curl around her like the whip's rasping leather tongue. At last, he felt release.

'She's a whore,' the Marquis said again and again. It was like a subliminal message that Johnny picked up and repeated. 'Whore,' he murmured.

'Yes,' she sighed, between yelps of pain.

'Whore,' he said, louder this time.

'Oh yes,' she moaned. 'I'm a whore. Punish me. I deserve it.'

He whipped her again and again. Her buttocks were his favourite; expansive curves of soft flesh just crying out for sharp punishment. The way they trembled after the whip's caress; the way he wanted to bury his cock between them.

'Whore.'

'Yes. Hurt me.'

'Bitch.'

'Whore. Hurt her. She's a whore. She wants this. Look at her. She's so far gone, the only thing she can still feel is pain.' The Marquis eased the whip out of Johnny's hand and pushed him towards the bed. 'Fuck her, Johnny. Fuck her hard, until she cries.'

Hovering on his shame, he moved to her side. He climbed on to the bed and knelt up in front of her.

Her eyes were full of the mad mindlessness of the addicted. Tears fell down her cheeks. 'Show me,' she whispered, her voice shivering like her body. 'I'm a whore. I'm your slut. Show me what you want to do to me.'

He unzipped his flies and moved closer. He ran his fingers through her tears, over her come-stained breasts and through her damp bush. Parting her pussy lips, he bent slightly to bring his penis to the mouth of her cunt. Then, holding on to her hips, he sheathed himself inside her.

He fucked her hard. He fucked her the way he'd wanted to that first time he'd seen her. He pumped into her like she was one of those repulsive moulded pussies they sell in sex shops; fucked her with as much respect. 'Whore,' he snarled, revelling in the freedom of this. He bit her neck until she flinched and pinched her nipples until she begged for him to stop it. At last, he had her where he wanted her. He felt the surrender flowing through her trussed-up torso.

But then the Marquis carried on where Johnny had left off. The whip screamed through the sticky air again and landed across her shoulders. Her eyes and mouth jerked wide open; her expression a frozen moment of fear. 'Fuck her, Johnny,' the Marquis said. 'She wants this. She deserves this.' Again, the whip. Again, the jolt of every muscle in her body. Johnny fucked her faster, forcing deeper, but he knew now that what her husband had said was true: the only thing she could feel was pain. She was numb to his prick and the desperation in his fingers as they clutched on to her. She was immune to pleasure. Her only pleasure was hidden deep within the pain.

All right. If that's what she wanted. He withdrew from her cunt and went over to the Marquis. He took the whip and returned to the bed. Standing up behind her, he unbuckled her hands and pushed her down on to all fours. 'Give me that,' he said to her husband, pointing at a tub of face cream on the table by the bed. He unscrewed the lid and threw it away, then scooped out a handful of the white goo. Slapping it between her open cheeks, he worked it into her anus, muttering all the while about how if she wanted it, she'd get it. Then, before her tiny hole had even got used to the width of two fingers, he pushed the whip's moulded handle into her arse.

She went rigid. He heard the breath being pulled into her lungs and could tell by the bunched muscles in her shoulders that her eyes and mouth were wide open again. He had her now: she was gripped by the agony. 'Do you like that, you whore?' He pushed the handle in and out. Her anus was distended unnaturally. His lust was distended so far it wasn't recognisable as lust any more. It had turned into anger. He was disgusted with her, kneeling there and letting him treat her like this, with her arse a mess of white cream and the whip trailing out of her hole. Her pussy lips were swollen and streaming juice and her clit looked painfully hard and red. One hand was busy with the handle but he raised his other hand and just touched her clit with his thumb. Spasms took hold of her.

He lost control. He slid one finger after another into her cunt until all four were inside her and his thumb was on her clit. He fucked her in both holes at once, both hands pushing in a rhythm that synchronised with her screams. He fucked her too hard, wanting to hurt her. He fucked her until her whole body shook, ravaged with the terror of having both orifices filled with friction. Her scream was shrill and loud and time slowed so much he thought the music downstairs had stopped. But it hadn't. Time had stopped up here, in this little room, while he'd made another man's wife give in.

Pulling the whip out of her arsehole, he pushed her down and flipped her over on to her back again. The Marquis got on to the bed and knelt at her head, cradling her in his lap and holding on to her wild arms, keeping her still. 'Take what you want,' he suggested to Johnny.

That was exactly what Johnny was going to do. He pushed her legs apart. Drained by the force of his fingers, her knees flopped open. He was going to fuck her again now. He was going to fuck her again and again, until she couldn't take it any more – then he was going to do it again. He was going to leave bruises on her inner thighs.

'What would you do for me, Johnny?' she asked.

It took a moment for her faint, wisping voice to register. 'What?' he asked.

'What would you do for me?'

He didn't want to answer that. He filled his mouth with her soft breast and bit down hard until he felt that any harder and he'd puncture her skin.

'Tell me what you'd do for me,' she said, her voice a relentless echo in his mind.

He tried not to say the word, even silently inside his head, fearing that once he'd acknowledged it he'd be bound by it.

'You'll never be able to fuck your wife again, after this,' she warned.

'Shut up,' he said, putting the whip's slimy handle in her open mouth to silence her. She was completely helpless: her wrists gripped in her husband's huge fingers, her body pinned down by Johnny's, her gaping cunt waiting to be fucked and her mouth full. But she was the one who was smiling.

He slid his penis inside her. But it was too late. She was right. He'd never be able to look his wife in the eye again, let alone fuck her. After this – after her – normal sex would have as much effect on the yearning inside him as an aspirin would have on a madman. He knew he would crave more. Darker thrills. Deeper pain to inflict and be inflicted upon him. Life was never going to be the same again. He was addicted.

He would do anything to fill his craving. Anything to find the elusive high.

Anything.

And so, later that night, when she asked him to prove it, he lay down on his stomach and bit the pillow as the Marquis buggered him. As the sensation swung between shame and desire, excruciating agony and excruciating ecstasy, and a power surge electrified his body, he knew that life as he knew it was over. He was trapped in the dark side of pleasure. He would never get out.

Five

'*E*conomics students should know better,' my father said, when I broke the news that my student loan was already spent.

I argued that I was only a fresher, and not yet *au fait* with the basics of my subject, but he just chuckled in that patronising way that dads do, and told me that being broke would teach me the basics of economic theory quicker than any degree course could. 'You carry on converting your money into alcohol, and you'll soon learn, my dear. Banks aren't charitable institutions, you know. They're there to make a profit, not to fund your social life.'

'But I'm a student!' I laughed. 'I'm living in London, Dad. What do you expect me to do, stay in every night and study by candlelight in this grubby dive they rather grandly call a hall of residence? We don't have mice here, Dad – they're afraid of the rats.'

'Don't exaggerate, darling. If you're short of money, you'll have to do what everyone else does. What your mother and I did, when we were your age. What your brothers did when they went to university. Get on your bike and get a job.'

I might have known I'd get no sympathy from him.

So that was it. Go teetotal, live off fresh air on toast for the rest of the year and scrap my blossoming social life – or get a job. The great tradition of the student sponger, cut dead by my father and his right-wing politics.

I couldn't work in a burger joint – that would have compromised my ethics – and a bar job was out of the question, since I needed my evenings free to spend in bars. So I took a job retuning video recorders to receive Channel Five. Not exactly my idea of fun, but the pay was OK and the hours fitted in with mine. If I did have to crawl out of bed for a lecture, I worked evenings; if my evenings were booked I could skip the lectures and work days. And I got to indulge my middle-class nosy streak and poke around inside other people's houses. Not the ideal job for a young woman, perhaps, but like I told my dad, I can look after myself, and anyway us retuners were under strict instructions not to venture inside any house we didn't like the look of. And there were a few of those, believe me. I thought the other tuners' stories of dog crap on the floor and flats full of vicious cats – and the smell of their pee – and assorted weirdos and loonies acting out roles from *One Flew Over the Cuckoo's Nest* were exaggerated, but they weren't. The most disturbing sights lurked behind the most respectable front doors.

But I liked the look of this house. I especially liked the look of the guy who answered the door. 'Well, hel-lo!' he greeted me, Leslie Phillips style. 'Come in,' he invited, before I'd even told him what I wanted to come in for.

101

'I've come to retune your VCR so you can receive Channel Five when it begins transmitting. Don't I know you?' I asked, smiling in a way that said, 'If I don't, I'd like to.'

'We were talking in the student union bar, last Friday,' he said, smiling in a way that said he'd wanted to do more than just talk.

'I don't remember that.' I could rarely remember much about Friday nights. 'Was it an interesting conversation?'

'Very.'

We stood smiling at each other for a moment. Then I realised there was no smell of cat's pee, no dog crap – not even the stale smell of sweat and baked beans that usually lingers in student houses and which hung like a smog over the halls of residence. I realised this wasn't your average student house. 'This place is fantastic,' I said, looking round enviously at the space and the light, and wondering what it was like to live in more than one room and not to have damp clawing at my clothes.

'Yeah,' he said, nodding and looking round as if it was the first time he'd really looked. Which it probably was. Rich kids just don't appreciate stuff like space and light and lack of damp. 'It's all right, I suppose. It was all we could find in our price range. Saves paying rent, anyway.'

'You own this?' I was gobsmacked by the thought of students actually owning something.

'Dipped into our trust funds and pooled together,' he said, ushering me into the living room. Another four, equally tasty lads were slumped across furniture that couldn't have been more than a year old. 'We were all at school together. Thought it'd be a laugh to buy a place together down here. We can live in it while we're at uni, then rent it out or sell it or keep it, or whatever.'

Whatever. So fucking nonchalant. I looked with awe and jealousy at the fresh paint, the relatively clean carpet, the wide-screen TV, the stereo with speakers as big as my wardrobe, the full drinks cabinet and the sliding doors leading to the garden. A garden! I wondered whether one of these trustafarians would like to marry me.

'This is Owen,' he said, waving at the tall blond hulk taking up most of one of the sofas. Owen waved back and smiled shyly. 'Pete, Jules, Ben, and since you don't remember last Friday night, I'll introduce myself again. I'm Adam.' Adam held out his hand.

I smiled as I took it. 'I'm Eve.'

'Adam and Eve.' He flickered his dark eyebrows suggestively. 'We've just cracked open some beers, Eve. Can I tempt you?'

'Does the pope wear a silly hat?'

He peeled a can from the six-pack he was cradling and offered me it.

'I shouldn't really. Not while I'm working,' I joked. 'But you will.'

I took the beer, had a swig and went over to the telly. Putting the can and my tool case down, I knelt in worship in front of the screen. My finger hovered over the off button. 'Erm, I'm going to have to turn this off, while I retune it. Sorry about that. I know *Neighbours* is riveting at the moment, but some of us have work to do.'

They groaned as the screen went black. 'We're being retuned for Channel Five,' Adam announced.

'What do we want Channel Five for?' one of them asked. 'What's going to be on it?'

'Is it going to show any porn?' asked another.

'Don't ask me,' I said, starting the job that was

supposed to be simple but which I hadn't quite got the hang of yet. 'I'm paid to twiddle knobs, that's all.'

'Hurry up, then. There are a few knobs that need twiddling over here, when you've finished.'

I smiled to myself and got on with my work. I could drink, belch, fart and be crude as well as any bloke. If they thought they could embarrass me with laddishness, they'd have to try harder than that. I had three older brothers. I wasn't easily shocked.

'I wouldn't mind giving you one. You're a total babe.'

Shocked, I glanced round. Pete and Jules were ogling an unfolded centrefold. Adam was looking at me. 'Nice arse,' he said.

Unsure whether he was talking about the centrefold or me (my arse did look nice in my jeans), I turned back to my work. Hoping no one would notice, I got out my instruction manual, since I'd completely forgotten what I was supposed to be doing.

The banter continued behind me. The other two joined in.

'Nice tits.'

'Your sister's got nice tits.'

'Not as nice as hers.'

'What do you think, Eve?'

I looked round as the magazine was held up for my opinion. 'Mmm. She's not a natural blonde, is she? Nice tits, though.'

Ben smiled at me. 'Yours are nicer.'

I looked down. If I had known where I was going that evening, I'd have worn something more revealing. Still, I did look rather fetching in my tight white T-shirt. I was wearing one of those bras that looks like you're not wearing a bra. You could see the heavy shapes of my breasts through the material. Probably, in the right light, you could even make out my nipples. 'Yeah,' I agreed. 'Mine are much nicer.'

'Perhaps you'll show us them, later.'

'Mmmm.' I tried something technical with a screwdriver. 'Perhaps the Government will declare free beer for all students.'

'There's something very sexy about watching a woman work.'

That was Adam again. I sneakily looked at his reflection in the screen, and saw the magazine lower and all five begin to look at me.

Jules took Adam's idea and expanded it. 'I think when I'm rich, I'll hire myself a horny young maid and I'll just sit around all day and watch her cleaning my shoes and polishing my collection of beer bottles from around the world.' Fired up by his mates' sniggering, Jules continued. 'I'll make her wear a very short uniform and black stockings and stilettos. Bras and knickers will not be allowed. I'll ask her to get down on her hands and knees to dust in the corners, so I can cop a look up her skirt.' He was really getting into this – I could tell by the way his voice was aimed at me. This was supposed to be making me blush, and it was. 'When she does something that isn't quite to my liking, I'll take her over my knee and spank her. And when she does something right, I'll give her a little reward. If she's been a very good girl, I'll let her suck me off.'

My eyes opened wide. Hoping the back of my neck wasn't as red as my cheeks, I tried to work.

'What do you think, Eve?' he asked. 'Fancy the job?'

'Sounds like a wonderful career move,' I said, without looking round. 'My parents would be so proud.'

'You'd better retune our VCR properly, or I'll have to take you over my knee.'

My eyes got even wider.

'If you're a good girl, I'll let you suck me off later.'

'Would that be the "little" reward you were talking about?'

The others laughed but Jules wasn't giving up. 'You're blushing,' he said.

'Leave her alone,' Adam said. 'You're embarrassing her.'

'Embarrassed? Me?' I huffed. 'I don't think so.'

But I was. I was also quite wet – incomprehensibly turned on by the thought of myself in a short little maid's outfit, with no underwear underneath, being spanked over Jules's knee.

Get a grip, I told myself. I was an economics student, not a lad's soft-core dream dredged from the pages of *Loaded*. I was intelligent. A feminist.

But I was wet.

And Jules was still going. 'Have you ever slept with a woman, Eve?'

'Yes,' I lied, hoping to stun him into awed silence. 'Have you?'

The others laughed. I threw them a smile over my shoulder.

But Jules wasn't letting go. 'Have you ever had more than one bloke at once?'

I ignored him. I finished fiddling with the television's programming buttons and snapped the control panel shut. I zipped up my tool bag, retrieved my beer and stood up. 'All done.'

'How about it?' he asked.

'How about what?'

'More than one at once.' He looked from left to right, to his friends flanking him on the sofa, then back at me. 'Fancy it, babe?'

He and the others all watched for my reaction. I did the only thing I could do; the only thing that was guaranteed to impress a bunch of lads. I downed my beer in one. 'I don't sleep with men who talk too much about sex,' I said. 'I usually find that a big mouth is a sign of a very small prick.'

I chucked the empty can at Jules on my way out. Adam got up and came out into the hall with me. 'Sorry about Jules,' he said. 'He gets a bit overexcited when there's a woman in the house. He reads too many mags. He doesn't get out much.'

'You don't have to apologise,' I said. 'I get worse flak from my brothers.'

There was a slightly awkward silence while we both hovered at the door – the sort of silence where each of us was wondering what to say to prolong the conversation. 'What are you taking?' he asked at last.

'Economics. I want to be a stockbroker.' I laughed at his look of surprise. No doubt the women he knew all wanted to be models and three-day eventers and It girls. 'I want to get paid obscene amounts of money,' I explained. 'I don't want to be poor ever again.'

'Are you poor?'

'No. I'm doing this crappy job for the love of it. Of course I'm poor. Most students are, you know.'

He nodded thoughtfully, as if this was the first time he'd come across this concept.

'Well, I'd better get going,' I said. 'I've another five calls to do tonight to make my quota.'

Adam opened the door for me. 'Perhaps I'll see you in the bar on Friday.'

'Perhaps you will.' Perhaps we'll do more than talk this time.

I could tell Adam was trying to think of something else to say, but all he came up with was, 'See you then,' which wasn't much good in terms of keeping the conversation going.

'You're not going anywhere.' Jules motored out of the living room and reaching between me and Adam, he slammed the door shut. 'You've fucked up our telly, darling. We can't get any channel now, let alone Channel Five.'

My blush began to seep back. I stuttered and muttered, going gingerly back into the living room. 'Sorry about this.' I knelt in front of the screen again. 'I haven't been doing this job very long. I've never retuned a set like yours before. Maybe it's your widescreen TV that's the problem.' Maybe I didn't have the foggiest what I'd done, or what to do to put it right. I twisted screws and pressed buttons ineffectually for a bit. I got out my instruction booklet again and squinted at it, searching for clues. But when I'd done everything I could think of, and a few other things besides, the television still wasn't working. *Neighbours* had been replaced by an ominously wavy screen and a low hum. 'Slightly more entertaining,' I said, but the boys weren't impressed.

'I'll ring the office tomorrow morning,' I promised. 'They'll send someone more experienced round first thing. I'm really sorry. I haven't been doing this job for long. I've no idea what I've done, but I'm sure it's nothing major.' Wincing with embarrassment, I went back out into the hall.

Jules followed me. 'We need the television working tonight.'

I looked at my watch. Six o'clock. 'There won't be anyone at the office now. I swear, I'll get on to them first thing. I'm really sorry.'

'You don't understand. We have to have the TV fixed tonight. We've got videos we want to watch.' He was insistent.

I was sorry, and said so again, but there was nothing I could do.

'Great. You've completely ruined our evening,' he said.

The others appeared one by one in the hall. 'What are we going to do now?' asked Ben.

'Report her,' Pete suggested. 'She's ruined our whole fucking evening. She should get into trouble for this.'

Surprised, I looked at him. He wasn't as angry as he sounded. His blue eyes were smiling.

'Yeah,' Owen said – the first time I'd heard him speak. 'She should pay for this.'

'Oh come on, lads,' I said. 'I'll lose my job if you complain about me. Please, just let me sort this out in the morning.'

'The morning'll be too late,' Ben said. 'We need to sort this out now.'

Jules began edging towards me. 'We'll have to report you, babe. Sorry, but you've caused us a major inconvenience. We were going to watch porn films tonight. We were all ready for it, weren't we, lads?' The other muttered agreement. 'We had *Swedish Nymphos* and *Back Door Bandits* and *Convent Girls* all lined up. Three classics. Now we've got blank screens. Just what do you suggest we do with our evening instead?'

'I don't know. You could study?'

He snorted and turned to his friends. 'Any ideas, lads?'

'Perhaps there's a way she could make it up to us,' Owen suggested. 'They were only videos, after all. She's the real thing.'

Adam stood in the living room doorway, looking on in amusement as the other four backed me towards the door. I met his eyes, silently asking him

109

what was going on here. He just shrugged. A little uneasy, a lot excited, I watched as Jules picked up the keys from the hall table and locked every lock in the front door.

'What are you doing?'

'Ask not what we do, but what you can do for us,' he said, which sounded vaguely familiar. Then he took my hand, and the others followed us back into the living room again.

So that was how I came to be their entertainment for the night – their very own live bed show. Of course, I could have got out if I'd wanted to. Beneath the bluster and bravado they were wimps, like all lads their age. They were in awe of me: a real woman with thoughts and emotions and a three-dimensional body. They were used to ogling paper women, and now here I was, with my real breasts and arse and a twinkle in my eye. All I needed to do was laugh at them, turn it into a joke and I'd have been out of that door and on my way to the next call. But I didn't laugh. I played along. I don't know why, but I did.

I hope that doesn't make me sound like a wimp myself. I'm not. I certainly wasn't used to letting men have their way with me. I was used to letting blokes chat me up and then keeping them dangling for at least another four dates before doing the deed. I wanted men to know I wasn't easy; and I wanted them desperate. Desperate men appreciate it so much more. But these guys were different.

I still don't know why I did it. I suppose it had something to do with having three older brothers. They were always trying to treat me like the little girl and trying to protect me, and I was always doing ever more shocking things to show them I was just as bad as they were, and didn't want protecting. I was always trying to impress my brothers. I think I was just trying to impress these guys, too. I wanted to show them that whatever they came up with, they wouldn't shock me. I had a dirtier mind than they could ever imagine.

But I couldn't help being a little nervous as they sat in a line on the sofa, and I sat on a chair in front of them, and they decided what I was going to have to do to make it up to them. It was just gone six, but within a few minutes the whole atmosphere of that autumn evening changed. The door was closed, the heavy curtains were drawn and a couple of lamps were turned on. It could have been midnight. More beers were handed round and quickly gulped down – I think we all needed to be half drunk that first time. And as they talked about me, and we all realised something really, really naughty was going to happen here tonight, you could feel the excitement tightening in the air.

'This evening was going to be a babefest,' Ben said. 'I was really looking forward to *Swedish Nymphos*. She's going to have to do something pretty fucking special to compensate.'

'She's going to have to do whatever we say.' Jules was clearly enjoying his part. 'She's going to have to be a very good girl, or we'll report her to her boss.'

'Oh come on, guys,' I said. 'No need for that. I'm sure we can work something out.'

'I'm sure we can.'

More beer. More talk. The talk turned dirty. I just sat there with my pulse throbbing in my pussy as they discussed what to do. More beer, and I realised that, like most men, they were all mouth and no trousers. They were desperately turned on, and relishing the opportunity to talk about my body like I was just another babe in another magazine, but not one of them had the balls to actually get the ball rolling, as it were. As usual, it was left to the woman to make the first move. I chose a fairly drastic one; one that their soft-core-porn-soaked minds would recognise.

'It's hot in here,' I said, fanning my face. 'Anyone mind if I take my top off?'

That shut them up. They leered in silence as I pulled off my T-shirt. I had never thought of myself as an exhibitionist, but there was an undeniable thrill between my legs as I sat there in my bra and they unashamedly looked at my tits. I looked at each of them in turn, and their lowered eyes and open mouths made me even drunker than I already was. As I glanced at Adam he looked up and smiled slightly. He was impressed, and not just by my breasts. He admired my guts, too.

But it was Ben who was shocked into action; he was the one who'd praised my tits earlier. 'Come here,' he said. I went and stood in front of him. He was tall and lanky, and my breasts were level with his face. He stared for a moment, his lip quivering slightly like a child on Christmas Eve who's just caught sight of Santa disappearing up the chimney. He glanced from left to right, as if he was trying to decide which one was the nicest, then he gave up and buried his face in my cleavage.

He spread his fingers over the sides of my breasts and pushed them together, licking and kissing the deep curves of my cleavage. Sitting forward on the edge of the sofa, he pulled me closer and reached around behind me to fumble with the hook. He couldn't manage, so I did it for him. He pulled off my bra slowly, his jaw dropping as my full loveliness was revealed. Someone whistled softly. Five pairs of eyes caressed me. I'd never held so much undivided attention in my life, and I loved it.

Ben was still for a moment, just staring. Then he remembered he had other options than staring and swirled his fingers all over me. Dipping his head, he sucked on one of my big nipples, squeezing my succulent flesh like he was trying to squeeze the milk from it.

Both nipples were stiff and dark by the time he sat back. He was carried away by now – he knew exactly what he wanted. 'Kneel down,' he said, as he unzipped his jeans, reached into his underpants and brought out his long, thin cock. 'I've always wanted to do this.' He was talking to the lads, I presumed, but addressing my tits. 'Touch yourself.'

That was to me. I obliged, fondling and rolling and caressing my tits; giving him a really good show. I could hear the sounds of him wanking, but for a while I didn't look. I bowed my head and looked down at my own fingers on my own flesh. I wet my fingertips and circled my nipples, then pinched the tips so hard I had to gasp. I cradled one heavy breast in my hand and, lifting it up, I strained my neck and stuck out my tongue and just managed to reach my swollen, pointed nipple. Ben groaned at that and I looked up. He was deep in concentration, focused on my breasts and pumping hard with his hand. He was close to coming, his orgasm no doubt building quickly because of the total weirdness of this whole situation and the lager he'd drunk, and like an old man he reached out for my shoulder to steady himself. Pulling himself forward in his seat, he fixed his eyes on my engorged nipples and gritted his teeth. 'Jeez,' he grunted, as the first drops of white come spattered on to me. I lost it too at that stage. I thought I was in a porn movie. I dipped my fingertips in his come and rubbed it on to my nipple, sighing like porn actresses do. 'Oh fuck,' he said, and shot his load all over my tits. Panting slightly, he slumped back. 'Fuck me. That beats *Swedish Nymphos* any day.'

Well, that was it. The ice was broken. With the come still dribbling down my front, Owen spoke up. 'Come 'ere, darling.' I went and stood in front of him like a wet dream, and waited for my instructions. 'You've got to make it up to me now, babe.'

His cock was out. It was huge. My eyes popped as I knelt down and he put his big hand behind my head and brought it into his lap. He tasted vaguely of beer – or maybe that was just my tongue. He tasted fantastic. I gave it all I'd got, licking and sucking and flickering my tongue as if I was auditioning for *Convent Girls*. I showed him hunger and lust, and took as much of him into my mouth as I could. I even massaged the base of his balls as he was about to come and made him moan appreciatively. 'Swallow, baby,' he said, not shy any more, but he was too late. I was already swallowing.

I lifted my head at the feeling of someone behind me. I quickly worked out it must be Pete who was easing my jeans down and rubbing his hands into my arse. He pulled off my trainers and socks, then pulled me backwards until I was sitting on my heels with my jeans crumpled uncomfortably around my ankles and his body comfortably close behind mine. Sitting right against me, he opened my knees wide and rested his head on my shoulder, enjoying the view as he touched me through my lacy, skimpy knickers.

I could feel my pussy lips opening and swelling and I arched my back against his chest with the pleasure. 'Good girl,' he whispered, putting his hand over mine and lifting it between my legs. 'Now let's see you touch yourself.'

I couldn't help it. When he stopped rubbing me up I had to carry on, despite the fact that five hungry men were watching with their tongues on the floor. I loved that they were watching. I loved the fact that something as simple as my touching my pussy – something I did every day, as often as I could – seemed so deliciously dirty to them. In front of me on the sofa, they all had their hands in their crotches, too; behind me, Pete was rubbing his erection over my arse. 'Oh Jesus,' he sighed, as I slipped my hand inside my knickers.

'Oh. Oh. Ohhhh,' I sighed, as I felt how soft and hot and wet and ready I was. I dipped my middle finger inside me then pulled it out and rubbed the juice over my hard little clit. 'Oh.' This was amazing. Masturbating to an appreciative audience. I was a Swedish Nympho. Or a Convent Girl. Or anything they wanted me to be. I was high. I'd have done anything they asked.

So when a large courgette was held in front of me, and Pete whispered, 'Do it,' I didn't hesitate. I needed something inside me. I pulled my knickers down to my knees and knelt up. Looking down, I held my pussy lips open with one hand and the courgette with the other. And slowly, slowly, drawing out the tension and playing to the dribbling crowd, I pushed the vegetable inside me.

Pete came round from behind me and sat at my side to get a better view. I watched him as he watched the courgette easing in and out of my cunt. I'd done this in the mirror so many times (though not with a courgette; this was a first), I knew exactly how it looked. My delicate, swollen lips would be dragging on it every time I pulled out. The dark green vegetable would be smeared with my juice.

I began to rub my clit with two fingers while my other hand slowly fucked me. As soon as I did, I felt myself starting to come. This was amazing: it usually took me at least ten minutes to bring myself off. The extra tension caused by their attention was making everything faster, deeper and wilder than it had ever been before. The climax hovering just beneath my fingertips was like an electric current. It made me twitch uncontrollably. My inner thighs started to tremble and my hands went into overdrive, pumping and rubbing as though possessed. 'Oh God,' I moaned, 'I'm coming.'

Everyone groaned appreciatively. Everyone except Jules, who was on his feet and pulling at my hands. The courgette bounced as it rolled across the carpet towards Adam. As I stumbled behind Jules to the sofa, I watched as Adam picked it up, sniffed it and then licked it. He smiled at me.

Fuck, I thought. This is incredible. This is mind-blowing. I was dizzy, and it was nothing to do with drinking three lagers on an empty stomach.

'You're a bad girl,' Jules said, sitting back down, unzipping his flies and tugging on my wrist so I knelt on the sofa beside him. 'Your behaviour this evening has been disgraceful. Now, you know what I do with bad girls, don't you?'

I waited while his gaze smeared its way over my glistening tits and down to my pussy. I waited, and hoped.

'I take them over my knee and spank them.'

Oh, yes.

He pulled my shoulders down, manhandling me until I lay across his lap with my face on the seat and my bare bottom sticking up. I don't know why – I'll never know why – but lying there like that was the biggest turn-on yet. I was so wet; so horny; and yet the thing I wanted then, more than anything else, was for him to humiliate me.

He didn't disappoint. He slapped me hard with the flat of his hand, making me cry out pathetically with the force of it. He spanked my bare arse again and again, making my breasts jiggle with every hit. He slapped me a bit too hard. It hurt, and brought tears to my eyes, but I loved it. I felt his cock, hard against my stomach, and felt his fierce, angry lust smarting on my skin. I felt delirious.

He came. His wetness oozed over my belly. Suddenly he seemed self-conscious, like he was embarrassed at coming without having fucked me, and he pushed me off his lap and into a crumpled heap on the floor. 'I hope that teaches you a lesson, young lady.'

I didn't have time to think of an answer. Adam was crouching in front of me. Taking my hands, he eased me down until I lay flat on the floor. 'Poor little Eve,' he said quietly. His voice was so soothing I could have fallen asleep in it. 'What have they done to you?' Gently, he rolled me over on to my front. Beyond the layer of raw pain coating my buttocks, I felt his lips as he tenderly kissed my red cheeks. 'What have they done, you poor girl?'

This was nice. This was calm and quiet. As he kissed and stroked my arse, I was lulled by the sound of his voice caressing my skin. I knew I shouldn't be allowing myself to relax, because I'd seen the way he'd smiled at me before, with that quim-coated courgette between his lips. I knew there was more to come.

Sure enough, my arse was still stinging when he began to move. I heard his flies unzipping and felt his hands around my hips. I was pulled up on to all fours and before I had time to prepare myself, his cock was sliding inside me.

'Ooooohhhh,' I groaned. He was big. He filled me up so there was no room for anything but mindless pleasure. I was barely aware of what was happening as he gave out directions. 'Jules, you suck on her clit. She'll come like an animal. Ben, pinch her nipples. Owen, put your cock in her mouth. Pete, you come round here.'

Five men at once. Five times the pleasure. I'd had good sex before – or so I thought. This was different. This wasn't just good, it was awesome. It was ground-breaking. We were making history. No one had ever come like I was coming now.

Adam's cock was thrusting hard and deep as he shafted me doggy-style. His fingers were tight around my hips, keeping me still. Cruel fingertips were pulling my nipples so hard I cried out; but no sound came out because my mouth was full of cock. Underneath me, lying sideways like a mechanic doing some fine tuning, Jules had managed to find my clit and was sucking and nibbling on it and setting off fireworks in the pit of my stomach. And, just when I thought I was going to burst, Adam said, 'Now!' and a greasy finger was pushed into my arsehole. That was it – I was gone. I wasn't me any more. Wasn't a person. Just a body; a receptacle for their lust; my wet, swollen orifices spewing with their pleasure.

So that's how it happened. Before I'd had a chance to recover, Adam was asking me to move in with them and Jules, with his penchant for the theatrical (he dropped out of uni soon afterwards and became an actor), was informing me I had no choice but to move

118

in with them: they weren't willing to let me go. The next day, I collected my measly belongings from my room in halls and shacked up with five guys I barely knew. But I didn't have to know them to realise that this was perfect. It solved all my problems. The lads don't charge me rent. I rarely buy any food or drink and I don't have to do a crummy job just to survive. I told Channel Five where to stick their job – after I'd got our VCR fixed, of course. Yes, it's our VCR now.

We're inseparable. We do everything together. There's a trust that binds us; the sort of trust that links people who've seen each other at their dirtiest and most vulnerable. Other people don't understand. They think we're weird, always hanging around together. What the fuck would they think if they could see us at home, me dressed in the little maid's outfit Jules bought me, the lads all sitting in a row on the sofa with their hands down their trousers as they watch me, on my hands and knees, dusting in the corners?

We don't care what others think of us. Behind closed doors, we're getting everything we need. We're getting lust in great dripping spoonfuls, and lashings of depravity, and sex so hot, the guys have given up watching videos. I'm being worshipped and wanted and licked and masturbated over and fucked so hard my inner thighs have permanent bruises. I'm constantly wet. I come down to breakfast and one of them greets me with his morning glory and pushes me down on to the table while the others eat their cereal. I go for a bath and one or two or all of them come in to scrub my back. We go to bed and there's a fight over which one I sleep with tonight. I wake up in the middle of the night to find one of them on top of me and another one watching. And if I want even more, I've got Adam who whispers that he loves me when we're alone.

My dad rang yesterday. 'How are the studies going?' he asked.

'I'm learning something new every day,' I said, squirming as Adam put his hand inside my knickers, and thanking God we didn't have a videophone.

Trust

*A*ll eyes were on the blushing bride. She was perfect: tall, slender, her long blonde hair swept up, with a few perfectly formed, delicate curls dangling down either side of her perfectly formed, delicate face. She looked like the brides from the magazines – pure and untouchable, incredibly happy and glowing with the shy sexuality that used to be Princess Diana's speciality. Every green-eyed woman in that room wanted to be her; every drooling man wanted to be with her.

Except two. Tom and Joe didn't want her. They weren't even looking at the bride as she and her tipsy, grinning new husband glided around the dance floor within a circle of oohs and aahs and tilted heads and 'don't they make a lovely couple' smiles. Tom and Joe didn't find tall or blonde or sweetly shy attractive. Their idea of pure sexuality stood in the corner, on her own, sucking her cheeks in as she dragged needily on a cigarette.

Gail was small and dark. Brooding. Her black hair, cut very short and slicked back, was a fuck-off to the clichéd convention of what made a woman sexy. Everything about her was a fuck-off, from her choice of clothes – black, always, even to a wedding – to the slight smile on her thin mouth, to the look of bored superiority in her black, knowing eyes. Even in the soft, pale glow of the wedding reception, she'd managed to find a shred of intense, impenetrable and strangely attractive gloom to wrap herself up in.

Joe had always had a fierce, burning thing for Gail. She was everything he wasn't, and that attracted him in a way it shouldn't have done; a way he wished it didn't. He was an adventurer: an outdoors type, who'd left the conventional world with a flick of his straggly brown hair and a promise to himself never to stay in the same place for too long. Never to settle down. He wanted to feel the wind on his face and to smell the sea and to know he was just a microscopic part of this universe.

Gail was her own universe. She sneered at 'travellers', asking them what it was they were running away from, exactly. 'I've got everything I need right here,' she would say, tapping her pale, slightly creased brow. 'You can find whatever it is you're looking for in your head – if you're brave enough to go inside and find it.'

Gail hadn't felt the wind on her face for years. Her natural paleness had been deepened to a deathly shade by her lifestyle. Cooped up indoors all day, huddled over her desk, the only sunshine she felt was from the slivers that forced their way through the constantly closed venetian blinds; the only colour on her cheeks smudges of navy blue from her leaky fountain pen, leaking her smudged and blurry thoughts on to her tiny hands, and from her hands on to her face.

Her face was clean tonight; her complexion

untainted. But her eyes were stained with the same thing that was blurring Joe's vision. He knew he shouldn't, but he couldn't help staring. The first time he'd ever seen her, he'd felt lust – but it was a different sort of lust from just seeing a pretty girl and imagining her naked. What he felt for Gail, even before he'd ever spoken to her – watching her, from the other side of the party, as he was now – was overpowering and, for a man who'd never been frightened of anything, terrifying. Whenever he was away, he tried to convince himself that she wasn't that special – that there were other women who could make him feel like this. But every night, whether he was alone or with some other woman, Gail would come into his head. And each time he saw her again he knew that was a lie. No one else in the world could make him feel like she did. Gail made him think thoughts he couldn't possibly allow himself to think. Without a word – a look from her was enough – she could put fantasies in his head that must have come from her imagination. He'd never had fantasies like those before her.

Tom looked at his brother staring, and smiled as he read the thoughts so clearly scrawled across his weather-damaged face. It was just like when they were kids, all over again: Joe wanting what was Tom's. 'She's mine,' Tom said to himself, smiling as his brother started across the crowded marquee towards her. 'You're mine,' he whispered, sending his warning across the music and laughter, to his wife.

She was pretending she hadn't noticed Joe approaching. But Tom knew her too well – better than Joe ever would. Almost better than she knew herself. That's why she'd chosen him, and not his

123

better-looking, younger and more adventurous brother. Tom knew what made her tick.

He also knew that, given his blessing, she'd fuck Joe in an instant. She got wet with the knowledge that Joe wanted her so badly. Tom whispered it to her while he was touching her: 'My brother fancies you, you know.' Closer, so he could smell her neck; smell her arousal. 'He stares at you. Don't tell me you haven't noticed the way he looks at you.' Closer, so he could hear her breath catch. 'I swear he got a hard-on when he was talking to you this evening. He couldn't take his eyes off you. He'd give anything to get inside your knickers.' Her moaning would sound different then: higher, fainter, tighter, more desperate. And he knew that she was intensely aware of Joe's attention.

She had angled herself for Joe all night, showing him her best profile and smoking in that incredibly insouciant, sexual way that only Gail and French actresses could pull off. She'd even dressed for Joe, wearing the things that he would want to imagine her in: stockings, suspenders, a short black skirt with little slits up the thighs – far too revealing and attention-seeking for a wedding reception – and heavy-soled leather biker boots that came up to the knee. Not wearing a bra beneath the skimpy, lace-edged camisole top that most women would have reserved for underwear. 'Is this for my brother's benefit?' Tom had said, standing behind her and squeezing her small, perfect tit with one hand as she'd put on her dark brown lipstick.

'Your brother?' she'd said, sounding surprised. 'Is he going to be there tonight?'

'I told you Joe was coming.'

'Did you? I must have forgotten.'

But her faint, crooked smile had given her away.

124

Now, pretending to be entranced by the bride and groom's performance on the dance floor, she studiously ignored Joe's approach. She allowed a slight smile to play on her lips – the sort of smile she knew would make Joe tremble inside. She took a long drag of her cigarette and then let the smoke escape back out of her lips. On anyone else it would have looked silly, but it made her look like the most desirable actress in the coolest black-and-white French film ever made. Then Joe came into her field of vision and she couldn't ignore him any more, and she languidly turned her head and let that smile develop into something that gave Tom a hard-on, despite the fact that it wasn't meant for him.

From across the room, he silently applauded her.

'Bitch,' he whispered, as she gave herself away, touching the soft hair at the nape of her neck, the way she always did when she wanted someone. 'I'm watching you,' he breathed at his brother, as Joe put his hand on her narrow waist and kissed her a little too lingeringly on the cheek. But his prick got hard as their lust crackled in the air. It had always turned him on to see other men looking at his wife. It was all about power; they could look, but he was the one who took her home and undressed her and made her whimper like an animal. He was the only one who knew her. Really knew her. And it was the same with his brother. Power. Joe had been better at everything: sport, school, making money without really trying. He was far better-looking than Tom. But Tom had Gail, and Joe didn't.

They flirted, like they always did. Joe listened intently as she talked, leaning his shoulders down to bring his body closer to hers; tilting his head and nodding and smiling. 'God, you're lovely,' said that smile. 'Tell me what you tell me in my dreams: you're not happy, it's over between you and Tom, you think you married the wrong brother.' And Gail put on her usual performance, looking off into the distance while she was talking, to give him the chance to take her in. She knew it; he knew it; Tom knew it so well it was as if he'd choreographed it. Looking to the right so Joe could look at her beautiful, pale neck. Asking him for a light, even though she'd already got one, to give him the excuse he didn't need to stare at her mouth for a moment. Letting the smoke drift out of her lips and letting him imagine it was his come. Tentatively touching him as he spoke – just on the sleeve, but it was enough to make him lose track. Smiling in the silences between them, in that way that made a man feel like he was the most desirable man in the world. She'd danced the same intricate dance with Tom, the night they'd met. But now that Gail and Tom knew every move, and everything there was to know about each other, this dance was saved for Joe.

I've seen this so many times, Tom thought. Every Christmas. Every time the family gets together. Every party. Whenever Joe rolls in from another remote corner of the world with his exotic stories. That smile from him; that way she laughs. He touches her arm longingly; proprietorially. She lets him, the way she only lets one other man in the whole world. They didn't even bother to hide it any more. Tom could tell, from the other side of that huge marquee, that she was wet. He could almost taste her cunt on his tongue.

Without him knowing it, his hand dropped underneath the white tablecloth and into his lap.

* * *

126

He watched them dancing. They looked odd together; Joe so tall, tanned and unruly and Gail so petite and dramatic. And yet, they looked oddly right as a couple. They moved as one, like they knew each other's bodies inside out – like being this close to each other was totally natural to them. Of course, they did know each other's bodies. They'd fucked each other in their minds so many times. It was obvious to Tom – though no one else in their family ever noticed that these two people were seconds away from tearing each other's clothes off. He should have been jealous. Other men would have been. And, for a fraction of a moment, watching his brother's hand on the agonising curve of the small of her back, and his wife's tiny hand on the expanse of Joe's shoulder, Tom wondered whether she wouldn't rather be with Joe. There were women, all over the world, dreaming that they might be the one to turn Joe from wild into devoted; Gail could snap her fingers and he'd fall. Did Tom know his wife as well as he thought he did?

They turned together. Gail looked round Joe's bulk and searched the room for Tom. 'I love you,' she mouthed when she found him smiling.

He nodded. 'I know.'

Her dark eyes smiled – the smile she kept just for him. Gail and Joe drifted off the dance floor and came over to where Tom was sitting. Joe went to get some drinks, leaving husband and wife both watching his big frame ambling away; both thinking the same thing.

Beneath the tablecloth, Tom put his hand on his wife's thigh. 'Are you wet?' he asked. In reply, she opened her legs slightly and let his hand move up under her dress. 'You want him, don't you?'

She looked across the marquee to where Joe was

slouched over the bar. She looked so beautiful tonight. 'Do you want me to want him?'

As if he had a choice. Beneath the table, between her soft inner thighs, he answered with a touch that made her shiver.

She turned back to him; looked him in the eye the way only she could. Then she asked him a question with an arch of her dark eyebrow.

He nodded again, once, knowing that this was what they both wanted, but terrified that it might change things for ever.

She sensed his doubt, the way she sensed everything about him. 'You do trust me.'

He didn't have to think about it. 'You know I do.'

'Whatever happens?'

'Whatever.'

'Promise me? I won't do this unless you promise.'

He thought about it for a moment – long enough to wonder why he was the one having to say, 'I promise.'

He knew that she would never have done it without his whispered suggestions and that light in his eyes. But, once it was done, would it still be something they shared, deep in their souls and in their silent whispers – or would it belong to her?

Too late to stop it now. Tom could do nothing as Gail asked Joe to walk with her in the garden. Glancing over her shoulder at her husband, Gail took Joe's hand and led him outside. After an unending minute, Tom followed, his heart pounding so fast it made his hands shake.

Tom watched from a distance. It happened very slowly. From the blackness just beyond the marquee's lights, he saw their shadows move together round the garden. He heard Joe's voice, deep and low – low enough to get a woman wet without even seeing him, Gail had once said – and hers answering, soft and faint and laced with laughter. They walked around to the side of the house and Tom followed, staying behind in the dark as they appeared in the light again. There was a wall running all around the house and garden, and they leant their elbows on it and looked up at the stars in silence.

Gail was in love with the stars. Tom felt all the usual feelings when he looked at his wife, her face bathed in an innocence she didn't own, and the light from the moon.

Joe stopped looking at the sky and looked down at Gail. She was oblivious – always was when she was lost in the universe. There was a single tear running down her cheek. Tom had seen that tear so many times. Late at night, he'd wake up and find the bed empty next to him. He'd go downstairs and find her in the garden, staring up at the night sky and crying soundlessly, and he'd hold her and tell her not to be afraid. 'I don't want to die,' she would say. The stars always made her feel morbid – infinity was astonishingly beautiful but terrifying, too. A reminder of one's total inconsequence. 'You're not going to die,' he'd promise, holding her tight until she felt the life rushing back into her frail body.

'Promise me.'

He'd promise her anything.

But Joe didn't know what the tears were for – that she was mourning herself. 'You're crying,' he said, and gently turned her face towards him. He put his hand to her cheek and softly brushed her tear away with his thumb. 'You look so sad. What's the matter, Gail?'

'Nothing,' she whispered. 'Just hold me.'

He didn't hesitate. She looked tiny in his arms. Silence cloaked them for a long, long time.

'Gail,' Joe said. 'Oh God. It feels so good being close to you.'

'I know,' she breathed.

'I wish it didn't.'

'Why?'

'Because it drives me mad not to be able to . . . because I can't . . .'

He stopped as she slid her arms around his waist, pulling him even closer to her. 'Can't' changed into 'can't stop myself', and Joe's hand went to her neck then smoothed downwards, over her upper back, following her spine down, on to one buttock. 'I can't,' he moaned, as he did, 'this isn't right. It's impossible.' Joe closed his eyes and held her tighter, trying to mould her softness into his body. He was wincing slightly – torn between pushing her away and never letting her go. She reached up and put her little hand on his face, and he opened his eyes. 'Oh God,' he said again. 'Gail, don't.' She wasn't doing anything but lightly touching him; but he was having to fight. 'We mustn't. Oh Jesus.' He sighed, beaten. 'You know how much I want you, don't you?'

'Yes,' she whispered, sliding her hand around his neck and pulling his face closer. 'Kiss me.'

He almost did. He bowed his head until their lips were almost touching. But he hesitated. He lifted his head. He looked devastated.

He held her face in his hands and begged her. 'Gail. Jesus Christ. Don't do this to me. If I kiss you now, I won't be able to stop myself.'

'Kiss me, then.'

'Gail, don't. Please. You're driving me insane.'

She glared up at him for a moment, giving him the look she reserved for emotional cowards. Then she stepped away like he'd slapped her. 'I'll stop then. Let's go back inside. Forget this ever happened. Not that anything did.'

Tom's erection flared at the sharpness in her voice; the way her chin jutted defiantly; the way her breasts were rising and falling under that clinging top. 'Are you coming?' she asked.

'No,' Joe said. He stepped closer. He put his hand on her upper arm, stopping her as she turned away. It was bare and, despite the warmth of the evening, Tom could see goosebumps flaring beneath Joe's hand. He could feel the hairs rising on the back of her beautiful neck, just as they were on his neck. Her nipples were stiff, pointing sharply against the soft fabric of her camisole.

'Gail, you know I want to kiss you. I want you so badly.'

'Kiss me then.'

'Tom'd kill me.' The seriousness in his eyes almost made Tom laugh out loud.

'You're scared of your brother?'

Joe nodded.

'How scared?'

She stepped up to him and cupped her hand over his groin. With one squeeze of her evil fingers, Joe had forgotten to be scared; with her hand inside his trousers, massaging his lust, he'd forgotten everything but her.

'Gail. God. Don't. Gail, what are you trying to do to me?'

She rubbed the flat of her hand over his groin. He shuddered and surrendered. He grabbed her and kissed her. Years of voracious desire came out in that kiss.

* * *

131

Tom felt so many emotions all at once. Jealousy; rage, that his brother would do this to him; pride that Gail was doing this for him, even though he knew she was also doing it for herself. Doubt? No, there wasn't any doubt. The physical was Joe's, but only for tonight. Her mind was Tom's, and always had been. Before they'd even met, she'd been his. She'd told him that; she was his from the day she was born – she'd known he was out there, living his life until the day they started their real lives, together.

He trusted her. But it was strange, watching his wife with another man. His brother. A man he knew so well, and not at all. There were lots of reasons why Joe should want Gail. He'd drunkenly confessed to many of them, and Tom had guessed the others. Most of all, he knew, Joe wanted Gail because she was Tom's. But right now, there was nothing ulterior in his passion. Right now, Joe was lost in her lips and her skin and the smell of her and the taste of her on his tongue. Tom knew how good that felt, and that it was enough to wipe a man's brain clean and fill him with a mindless, desperate need that would excuse even the betrayal of his own brother.

Joe was suffocating with his need for her. He paused for a moment, leaving her lips to try and catch his breath. But before he could, she'd slipped the straps over her shoulders and revealed her breasts, and Tom watched as Joe gave up breathing all together. Pride and envy mingled in Tom's head, as they had done when the family had sat round applauding Joe's first steps. Tom had been there before; he could do it any time he liked; but there was nothing like watching someone's first experience. He saw the thoughts streaking through Joe's brain, just like they'd streaked through his, that first night he and Gail had laid themselves bare for each other. Her tits were incredible: small and pert, with sharply pointed, dark nipples and the most exquisite curves that were halfway between adolescence and womanhood. Joe's whole body sighed, just as Tom's had done, and he fell to his knees and touched her with his fingertips and lips and tongue. Gail closed her eyes and pushed his head down, and the next minute he was pushing up her skirt and unfastening her stockings and pulling down her knickers.

Both desperate now, both carried away by the pure, physical rush of it, they shuffled around so that Gail had her back against the wall. Holding on to Joe's wide shoulders, she lifted one leg over his shoulder as he ate her pussy. Her body undulated with the pleasure as he gulped at her, his tongue flailing in and out and his nose pushing into her thick pussy hair. Tom just kept looking at her knickers, discarded on the patio behind them like the past.

Things would never be the same again, he thought, as he watched from another universe; watched his brother, lips glistening with his wife, stand up and unfasten his trousers. Gail and Joe stared inside each other as Joe bent his knees and brought the velvet head of his thick cock between the velvet lips of her cunt. 'Ooohhh,' she groaned, as he pushed all the way inside her. Her fingers clawed into his heavy arms. He groaned, feeling at last what he'd had to imagine for so long. He hooked one arm around her thigh, lifting it up so she was more open for him. Then he fucked her, slowly, wanting to relish every second she was his.

But she wasn't his.

She looked like a slut, Tom thought – her top half off, her black stockings halfway down her pale white thighs, her legs and mouth apart. But she wasn't Joe's slut. She was his. As if she'd just remembered it too, she slowly turned her head and looked into the darkness to where she knew her husband was watching; waiting. The look in her eyes said, 'Thank you.' Thank you for letting me. But there was something else in that look, too – something Tom had never seen in his wife's eyes before. Guilt. Shame. Don't blame me for wanting your brother – I can't help it. Don't hate me for finding pleasure without you.

He didn't blame her. He loved her more than ever; enough to let her find pleasure on another plane. He wanted her to taste everything. And for some reason, seeing her with his brother made her more desirable than she'd ever been before. He had to touch her. Love and lust drove him towards her. He stepped into the light and touched her open lips.

Joe came at the same time, shuddering violently, clutching on to Gail's shoulders and sighing like it was the biggest relief of his life. It was a moment before he opened his eyes again and noticed his brother standing there. His body stopped jerking with the violence of ecstasy and jerked rigid with fear. 'Tom,' he said, his strident voice suddenly pathetic. 'Tom, I –'

'You bitch,' Tom said, pushing his brother away. He was only vaguely aware of the sight of his brother's cock, still hard and shiny with come, before he turned to his wife. Her dark eyes flashed. 'You're so beautiful,' he said, grabbing her and kissing her, hard; intensely aware of Joe's confusion, like a fog, behind him. 'Isn't she beautiful?' he said, looking at his wife but asking his brother. 'You've wanted her for so long, Joe. Was it like you imagined?' He reached under her skirt. Come was dribbling down her inner thighs. 'How did it feel, fucking my wife?'

'Tom, I ... Please, Tom ...' Joe stood at his shoulder, but Tom didn't look at him. He was looking at his wife. He couldn't stop looking at her. She was a different woman. On fire.

'Did you enjoy her?'

'Tom, please don't.'

'I love her, Joe.'

'I know you do. I love her too, Tom.'

Tom watched for a reaction from his wife. There wasn't one; her gaze was fixed to his.

'You don't know her.'

'No. God, Tom, I'm sorry. I'm so sorry.'

'Don't be.' I feel sorry for you. You'll never know her like I do. 'She's a bitch,' he whispered, his fingers following the flush that was seeping over her throat. Dark, ferocious desire overwhelmed him. 'Help me,' he grunted. 'Help me teach her a lesson.' He gripped her slender wrist in his hand and jerked her away from the wall. She struggled to keep on her feet as he dragged her into the darkness again, down to the bottom of the garden. Joe hovered behind them, helpless as he always was against Tom's rage, despite the fact that he was a foot taller and far heavier. 'Tom, what are you doing? Please, don't. If you're going to take it out on anyone –'

He stopped as he realised what was going on – and that Gail's breathlessness was out of excitement, not fear. Unconsciously, he took a step closer, watching as Tom pushed Gail down on to her hands and knees. In the distance, laughter and music dribbled out into the night. It didn't reach them. They were miles away in their strange threesome, stepping together into a place that was as far removed from the jollity of the wedding celebrations as it was possible to be.

On all fours on the grass, Gail waited as her husband pushed her skirt up around her waist to expose her bare arse. He knelt down behind her.

135

'Bitch,' he whispered, rubbing his palm over her pale cheek before drawing his arm back and smacking her. Shock came out of her mouth in a high, thin gasp. She didn't have time to recover before he slapped her again, and again. 'You bitch,' he breathed, arousal tightening in his throat. She was so fucking beautiful, her pussy a dark yearning beneath the moonlight-white purity of her arse. She was so fucking powerful, too. Even on her hands and knees, being spanked like a child, she held the two brothers in the palm of her hand. They both worshipped her, and she knew it. She could have crushed them in an instant.

'So I'm not enough for you any more, you heartless bitch.' Gail whimpered as Tom pushed three fingers into her open cunt. 'Not happy with one brother. Perhaps you want both of us.' Her cries turned to anguish as his thumb found her clit. 'Help me, Joe.'

Slowly, unsure, Joe knelt down at Gail's head. Tom watched from behind as she looked up at him. The distant light from the marquee shone in his brother's eyes. Bewildered and mesmerised, he held Gail's face in his big, gentle hands. He couldn't quite grasp what was going on here, but he couldn't resist it either. Gail's cries were muffled as his fingers pushed into her mouth.

Tom reached over to push his wife's head down into Joe's lap. Joe hesitated, his hands wafting indecisively in the warm air. Looking up at Tom, he searched for approval. Then he looked down at Gail's head, and the sight of her there, where he'd dreamt of having her for so long, made him abandon any sense of what was right or wrong. Unzipping his flies, he gave her his cock, still warm and wet from being inside her. Behind her, Tom held on to her narrow waist and plunged his cock between her lips.

Together, they fucked her. They both held her as her shameful climax ripped through her body. Stunned, Joe prised his gaze away from the quivering creature lying at his feet, to look up at his brother. He shook his head slightly. Unsure.

They left the party without saying goodbye, and went home. But tonight, instead of Tom and Gail going up to bed, leaving Joe alone with the sofa and his lonely fantasy, as they always did when he stayed, they went upstairs together. Because tonight was different. And although doubt was creeping like a tumour inside Tom's mind, and he suspected that this was going too far, he was powerless to do anything but follow her where she led him. He'd started this, after all, because all he'd ever wanted was to make her happy; to fulfil her completely; to watch as she went to a place he could never go to. He looked into her wide, pleading eyes as he undressed her; at her tiny fingers, caressing her own breasts; at her perfect body; and at Joe, standing behind her, kissing her neck. And he knew that he couldn't say no. He didn't even want to. He wanted to give her everything. If she'd told him she was hungry, he'd have ripped out a piece of his heart and fed it to her.

'Is this what you want?' he whispered, touching her mouth.

'Yes.' She kissed the tip of his finger. 'But you have to know that I love you completely.'

She loves me completely. He chanted it to himself as the three of them twisted together on the bed in a mad, destructive tangle of lust and love. None of them could stop it now. Tom and Joe were adrift inside her; hooked on her. They needed her cries wrapped around their necks. She just wanted more.

She would always want more, Tom thought, as he knelt up behind her and eased his way inside her insanely tight arse. 'I love you,' he said into her shoulder, before biting it hard. Lying under her, his fingers loving her so hard he was hurting her, his mouth on her cunt, Joe whispered to her that he loved her too. Caught between them, like some poor, beautiful animal, she arched and threw back her head and let out a silent scream.

Her ecstasy gripped Tom like a seizure; fear coursed through his blood. He wanted to scream – to let out the terror that was hurting him inside. Things would never be the same again. He knew it.

But she didn't sleep in the middle. She lay on the edge of the bed, in his arms, touching his face with her inquisitive fingers, like she was discovering him all over again. 'You're amazing,' she said. 'You're so brave.'

Even in the dark, he could see the infinity in her eyes. And he fell deeply in love, all over again.

'Love me,' he begged.

'I'll always love you,' she said softly, caressing him with her sweet, sex-smelling breath.

'Promise?'

'I'd die for you.'

'I know.' His heart was weeping. 'I'd die for you,' he said.

They fell asleep, wrapped so tightly in each other that they didn't stir when Joe got up, got dressed, and let himself out.

Jump Start

Ask me a year from now, and I'll tell you exactly what you were wearing, the day you arrived in the village. You won't remember, but I will. See, we've been waiting for you to arrive for weeks. Nothing goes unnoticed in our nosy little community, and more fucking Southerners moving in is always a big event. The word has gone round. It leaked out from the estate agent and made its way round the pubs and the auction mart and the doctor's surgery and the gaggle of mothers waiting in the school playground. 'The big house has been sold,' they all said. 'Some rich couple moving up from London. More bloody Southerners asking for organic bloody meat and complaining about the smell of cow muck.'

It was hot. Your husband led the official procession in a Range Rover that had never seen mud. You followed in the sports car. You had the roof down. You drove along the main street towards the edge of the village, where your big house looked down on the rest of us. It was like Princess Diana was driving through. Everyone stopped work and peered out at you. There was a part-reverent, part-resentful hush over the village as a car that cost more than a council house drifted quietly by.

You were wearing a flimsy summer dress. It was dark pink, the same colour as your lipstick. It had straps that tied round the back of your neck. You didn't have a bra on underneath it and I could see the shapes of your beautiful tits. You had sunglasses on and your long hair was tied back. Your skin was pale, despite the fact we were having a cracking summer, for a change. You looked like royalty, or some old-fashioned film star. So bloody perfect. So un-fucking-touchable.

'I wouldn't mind a ride in that,' my apprentice said.

'You don't stand a chance, you little grease monkey,' I said. 'She's class. Way out of your league.'

'I was talking about the car,' he said.

'So was I,' I lied. The car was fucking gorgeous too, but I didn't notice it the day you arrived. I noticed you. That evening, when I rolled in from the pub, I had a wank and imagined coming over that lovely little dress. I imagined my come dribbling out of the corner of your perfect mouth and making your lipstick shine.

It goes round quicker than flu. Your husband is something to do with computers and makes more money than he knows what to do with. He works from home but has to go to Leeds once or twice a week. Your kids are at boarding school, but after this term they're coming back to live with you and go to the posh public school in the next village. Your husband's a snob, but you're 'all right'. I wonder what you've done to get approval like that, so quickly – it's not easy round here, especially for a Southerner. I've lived here all my life, and I still haven't got approval from the narrow-minded wankers who prop up the bars and gossip in the butcher's.

I'm in front of you at the traffic lights – the first lights you come to, twenty miles out of the village. You must be on your way into town, like me. Probably going in search of familiarity on the shelves at Marks & Spencer's.

I look at you in my rear-view mirror. It's a nice morning and you've got the roof down again. You're wearing another skimpy little dress that makes me think the worst. I stare at you until you notice. You're confused at first, not sure whether I'm actually looking at you, or at the car. The car is amazing. A Morgan. Dark silver. There's a waiting list for cars like yours. Really classy. But I'm more interested in looking at you. I keep looking as we travel slowly in convoy towards the next traffic lights.

You're so fucking horny and so fucking classy. Has anyone ever made a move on you without asking your permission first? I don't expect so. I bet the type of men you know are all afraid of you. You're the kind of woman that scares blokes shitless. They'd rather put you on a pedestal and worship you from a distance than actually talk to you. I bet your husband didn't dare fuck you for weeks.

But I'm not afraid of you. I drive so slowly up to the next traffic lights that they turn red, and I stare at you in my mirror until you blink quickly and look away, pretending to find something interesting to look at somewhere in the distance. You're afraid of me, aren't you? Afraid of my intentions. Wondering what gives me the nerve to leer so blatantly.

Afraid of me, and yet it turns you on that I'm staring. Your knickers are getting wet, aren't they?

Your pale, silky inner thighs are rubbing together as you try and squeeze those naughty thoughts out of your cunt. You can't possibly allow yourself to be turned on by me, can you? I mean, just look at me. You've seen me in the village and I'm not your type, at all. Oil stains on my skin; dark, messy stubble; an earring; a tattoo; filthy overalls. If I accidentally brushed past you, I'd leave a greasy black film on your clothes. Not your type. But you can't stop, just can't resist, glancing back to check whether I'm still staring.

I am. This time you don't look away. I raise my eyebrows, giving you a signal. You're shocked. Don't know what to make of this perv ogling you so openly. I smile and raise my eyebrows again, so that you're absolutely sure what I mean. You don't react, but you don't look away either. I turn and look round at you through the back window of my van. I raise my eyebrows again, quickly; a flicker of a suggestion. Your mouth opens ever so slightly. You want to look away, but shock and the shocking desire you suddenly have for me is keeping your frightened eyes fixed to mine. I look at your mouth and long for the day your lipstick will smear on my prick. I know that day will come. You may not know it yet, but you want me, you perfect bitch.

The driver behind you blasts his horn and I turn round. The lights have gone green. I've got a hard-on.

I see you in the village, doing your shopping, showing your support for our pathetic selection of shops and making an effort to get to know people. The fruit and veg shop is opposite the office in my garage and I watch you squeezing the peaches surreptitiously, so you don't offend the grocer with your picky Southern ways. You can't see me behind my grease-blackened window, but I can see you, smiling and laughing and showing everyone how nice you are. It's working. They do all think you're nice, you know. 'That Mrs Greene,' they say. 'Isn't she lovely?'

You are lovely, and you know it. But I suspect that, deep inside, you're probably not at all lovely. Beneath your cool exterior I reckon you're simmering away just below boiling point. I reckon there's a slut in those expensive clothes, just dying to get out. Because I've met women like you before: women with everything. Beautiful woman; beautiful house; beautiful car; husband who'll give you anything, except the one thing you're dying for.

I could give you what you want. I know exactly what it is, you see. I can see what's lurking behind that perfect white smile of yours. I hear the silent scream behind your gentle laughter. I know you're bored out of your head, and dying for a shag. Dying for a dirty bit of rough.

I imagine what I'd do to you, if your husband wasn't around. I'd give it to you the way you'd really like it. I'd pull you into the garage and push you over the bonnet of a car. I'd shove my oily hand up your skirt and into your silky pussy. I'd fuck you so hard, you wouldn't know whether your screams came from ecstasy or fear. They'd come from both: the ecstasy of letting go, and the fear of knowing that you've sunk to a lower depth, and that now you're down there there's no way back up again.

Do you look at me and imagine the same thing? I doubt it. It's too soon for you to consciously accept that you want me. You're still at the stage of trying to ignore me when you see me in the village. Memories of that morning at the traffic lights have unnerved you. You think I'm a perv. My oil-smudged skin and my filthy overalls make you cringe. The dark hair creeping out over the neck of my T-shirt is repulsive to you. You think, because I've stayed in this village all my life, that I'm as uneducated, thick and narrow-minded as the rest. You see me out with the lads, staggering around the village pubs, laughing and singing and being crude, and you think I'm ignorant and unsophisticated. Soon, that will start to excite you. Right now, you think I'm a pig.

You shouldn't judge a book by its cover, Mrs Greene. If I judged you by what I see, rather than what I see underneath, I'd expect you to be an uptight, prissy, anally retentive snob. And we both know you're not.

'Don't think much of Mr Greene,' they say. 'Makes you wonder, doesn't it, what such a nice lady is doing with a man like that?'

I'm asking myself the same question. Was it his money that attracted you? It can't have been his charm. He summons me to your house, early in the morning, to look at his precious car. It won't start. He tells me it's pointless calling the AA: it'll take them an hour to get to him. 'That's the downside of living out here, in the sticks,' he sneers, 'miles from civilisation.'

'Fuck off back to London then,' I mutter, under my breath.

He's the ignorant, unsophisticated pig. He owns a classic car and doesn't even know how to open the bonnet. He stands over me while I work, telling me 'it could be the spark plugs'. I thank him for his invaluable help, and tell him it could be that the battery's flat because he left his lights on all night.

I go back to the garage to get another battery. By

144

the time I get back to your house, the pig has gone off to Leeds in the Range Rover. It's still early, and I realise you're probably still in bed, alone, in that huge house. I almost get a hard-on at the thought. I wonder what you'd do if I forced my way inside and found my way up to your bedroom, dripping oil on your carpet and smearing the muck that's inside my mind all over your sheets.

I feel someone watching me. I look up and see a figure at an upstairs window. It's you. I wave. You wave nervously and move quickly out of sight. You hide behind the curtain and watch as I work on the car. Your eyes are on my filthy hands, my broad back and my messy, greasy hair. It's not surprising. Women like you, if only they'd admit it, love to fantasise about men like me. I'm the opposite of your clean, clipped and manicured husband. There's something about men who work with their hands, and who spend their lives dirty, that really excites rich, clean women like you.

When I've finished, I glance up at the window. I can't see you, but I know you're still there, just out of sight, looking at me. When you've heard me drive off and you know that it's safe, you'll lie down on the fragrant sheets and stick your fingers in your sticky pussy. You'll close your eyes and pretend your dirty, greasy, ignorant mechanic is fucking you senseless.

I go back to the garage, lock myself in the office, pull down the blinds and do the same. My cock is so hard for you, it hurts.

You and your husband grace the pub with your presence. It all goes quiet as you walk in. It's the first time you've been into the village at night. Everyone listens, waiting to see what the pig is going to order.

145

'A pint of your best bitter, landlord.' Pompous twat. I bet he's never drunk bitter in his life. He wouldn't know the difference if I pissed in it.

You drink gin and tonic, as I expected. It has an unexpectedly lovely effect on you. Your porcelain cheeks turn pink and your brown eyes blur attractively. While the pig pontificates loudly at the bar, you do what the locals do and circulate, chatting to the other women who've been allowed out by their husbands. The pig snorts. You smile and laugh and nod politely to conversations you can't possibly find interesting. I admire you for trying so hard to fit in. But you'll never fit in. You're a class above.

I watch you getting drunk, the same time as I'm getting drunk, and I become fixated on your tits rising and falling underneath that tight, soft jumper as you breathe. You're so fucking lovely, and I'm so fucking out of your class. But I'm going to have you.

Closing time. You say goodnight to the gaggle of women who are completely in your thrall – who will go home and dream of having hands as soft and clothes as expensive as yours – and you leave with the pig. You're both pissed, although you'd probably call it being 'tiddly', and I suspect you're planning to walk back to your house. Only outsiders would consider walking home that bloody far with a skinful of booze.

I follow you out and emerge into the middle of an argument. You're cold and too tired to walk; the pig has 'no intention of calling a taxi out to take us one mile up the road'. 'You would have done in London,' you say. 'This isn't London, darling,' he observes. Such wit.

'Can I give you a lift?' I ask.

Pig looks suspicious. 'Aren't you ... over the limit?'

I dismiss him with a sneer. 'No police round here at this time of night,' I assure him. I don't think it's me getting into trouble that worries him, but you're already behind me, walking towards the car park. 'It's the van, I'm afraid,' I say, opening the back door for him to get in. 'Not quite the luxury you're accustomed to.'

'We had planned to walk,' he protested, peering worriedly into the dark void.

'Just get in, Alex,' you say. 'I'm too tired to walk now.'

I see a smile twitching on your lips as he crawls in and his lardarse disappears into the blackness. I open the passenger door for you, not because I'm a gentleman, but because it sticks and a weak woman like you wouldn't get it open. I get in the other side and it's my turn to smile. You're sitting there, in my grubby little van, trying desperately not to touch anything in case it marks.

I start up the engine and rev it unnecessarily. I reverse so fast out of the car park that you have to put your hand out to steady yourself. I drive like a maniac all the way, not because I'm drunk, but because that's the way we drive round here. We don't get much entertainment, you see. And I want pig to have the most uncomfortable ride possible in the back.

We hear him knocking around, swearing under his breath as his head or some other useless part of his body hits the side of the van. I don't need to look at the road – I drive along it every single bloody day of my life – so I look at you. You're right back in your seat, as if the speed is pressing you backwards. You're smiling, and your eyes are shut. You're actually enjoying this: being in my van; going so fast.

Knowing that he's hating this. Putting your life in my hands.

I skid into your driveway. You get out and let him out of the back. 'Thank you,' you say, pausing at my window.

'My pleasure,' I say truthfully, my hand already rubbing the warmth you've left on the seat. I think I see a smile on your lips.

We meet on the road to town again. You're behind me, again. Our eyes meet in my rear-view mirror. This time you don't look away. You smile at me, ever so slightly – I sense it more than see it. We play a game. I drive like a maniac, and you try to keep up. Your car is way more powerful than mine, but you're not used to driving like this, accelerating into bends and overtaking when you're not completely sure it's safe. But you're excited, so you do it. You risk it. The rush you felt in my van, two nights ago, has stirred something inside your guts. You see: you're just like me, beneath it all. You can cover it up with your designer clothes and you can try to mask the smell with your perfume, but scrape it all away and we're just the same. Blood and bone and boredom.

You're getting carried away. You don't notice me slowing down as we approach the lights. Maybe my brake lights aren't working, but when you do finally notice that our cars are rapidly getting closer you have to slam on. Those anti-lock brakes are fucking brilliant, but you still can't avoid shunting into the back of my van. I smile to myself. We were bound to come into contact, sooner or later. We were an accident waiting to happen.

I wave for you to pull over at the next lay-by. You pull in behind me, and we get out to look at the damage. It's sod's law, isn't it? My clapped-out old

148

van is fine. Your beautiful sports car has come off worst. Your hand is over your mouth, and it's shaking.

'Are you all right?'

'Oh my God. Alex'll kill me,' you say.

'It's only a little dent,' I say, crouching down to look at it. 'I can fix it.'

'He'll kill me,' you whisper, in shock. 'This car's his pride and joy.'

'It's cosmetic,' I assure you. 'He'll be more concerned that you're OK.'

You snap out of shock. You look at me – really look – for the first time. 'Believe me,' you sneer, 'he'll be more concerned about the car.'

'He's got his priorities wrong then, hasn't he? It's nothing,' I insist. 'I'll have it good as new in a couple of days. We'll take it straight round to the garage now.'

'But you were heading into town.'

I shrug. 'I can go later. Let's get this mess fixed.'

You touch my overalled arm. 'It's very good of you. Thank you so much.'

'My pleasure.'

We leave your car at the garage and I drive you home in the van. We're silent. You're enjoying the way I drive, and I'm enjoying being so close to you, again. I drive with one hand on the gearstick, intensely aware that your thigh is only inches away. You keep your eyes fixed straight ahead, but I know that you're intensely aware of me beside you, and that you're dying to look at me.

Look at me. How filthy I am. How different from that scrubbed-clean prig you married. It makes me sick to think of that pig grunting between your legs. He can't possibly satisfy you.

Look at me. Touch me. Open your legs for me. I'm real, Mrs Greene. My desire is so real, we can both smell it. I won't fuck you out of a sense of duty or because I'm feeling randy (I bet he uses words like 'randy'). I'll fuck you because I know you're gagging for it. I won't tell you I'm too tired, or I've got a lot of work to do, or I have to get up early in the morning. I'd give my right arm to feel knackered from fucking you. And I won't stop as soon as I've shot my load. I won't stop until you come. Because I want to see you come, Mrs Greene. I want to feel you shaking and hear you screaming and I want to be wet and sticky with you.

For a split second, I have to close my eyes. Doesn't matter that I'm driving. I have to shut my eyes and see the image that's just behind them. It's you and me, Mrs Greene. Your leg is hooked over my shoulder and I'm eating your pussy. You're squirming with the shame of letting me do this, and moaning with the pleasure of my tongue on your cunt. Your words are telling me not to, but your voice is telling me not to stop.

I open my eyes and glance over at you. You glance at me and smile nervously. You're thinking the same thing, aren't you? You're wondering what it would be like with someone like me. Would it be as filthy as your fantasy?

We pull into your driveway. I go to get out, but notice you hesitating. 'You all right?'

'He's going to go mad,' you say.

'He won't,' I insist. 'I'll handle him. Let me do the talking.'

We go inside and down to the end of the hallway, into your husband's office. 'What's happened?' he asks. Then he sees me. 'Phil!' He smiles, trying to be chummy with me – one of the lads. 'What . . .' He

150

looks at you; you're looking at the floor. His voice changes. It goes hard and cold. 'What's happened to the car? Has something happened to the car?'

You look at me. *I told you.*

'There was a slight bump,' I explain. 'It's nothing serious. Cosmetic damage. I've taken it into the garage. I'll have it back to you by the end of the week.'

'The end of the week? What the hell happened?'

'Nothing,' you say. 'I was driving a little too fast, that's all, and I didn't realise Phil was braking until it was too late. I bumped into his van.'

The pig doesn't ask about my van, or whether you're OK. 'You were driving too fast?' His face is very ugly. His expensive after-shave can't hide the smell of his sweat. 'Why?'

'The road was clear. I just didn't notice Phil braking.' You glance at me. We share a knowing look. 'I wasn't concentrating,' you say quietly. We know why, don't we?

Your husband shakes his head slowly. His mouth's in a horrible sneer. 'I can't believe this. You stupid –'

'It wasn't her fault.'

He remembers I'm there. 'What?'

'It wasn't your wife's fault. My brake lights aren't working. It was my fault.'

It takes a couple of days to get hold of the paint to touch it up, but soon the car's like new, and back with your cunt husband. He bans you from driving it. You come in the Range Rover into the village, to pay me and to let me know that you've decided to let it happen.

Work stops as you waft in. It's like that scene in *Cool Hand Luke*, where the woman's washing the car in front of the chain gang. You're completely aware of the effect you're having. You probably chose that dress on purpose, because you know the neckline is low enough to show your cleavage, and the material is soft enough to leave just enough to the imagination, and flimsy enough that as the sun shines through it, behind you, we can see the outlines of your legs. You probably arranged for the sun to be behind you. Even old Joe stops his work and has a look.

I straighten up and wait, making you walk all the way across the workshop floor towards me, through all that sexual tension. You're scared but loving it, too. You women are strange, aren't you?

'I've come to settle the bill,' you say. You pull an envelope out of your handbag. 'And I wanted to say thank you.'

'Come into the office.'

I motion you to go in front of me. I tear my eyes away from your delicate heels and your long legs and your arse, and look round to see jaws hitting the floor. Behind you, I make a gesture no one will have ever made to your face.

I write you out a receipt. 'It looks as good as new,' you say. 'Thanks for doing such a good job. And thanks for covering up for me.'

I stand up and come very close. 'My pleasure,' I say. 'If there's anything else I can do to help, just let me know.'

'Thank you. I will.'

We stare into each other's eyes for a moment. And I know that you will.

Everyone leers as you float out over the filthy, greasy floor. So clean and perfect and pristine. Unsoiled. One of the younger lads can't help whistling. Another one makes a crude comment about what we got up to in the office. You can hear, and you're embarrassed, and that gets me hard. I look at the back of your neck and want you so badly it comes out of my mouth.

'I'm going to have her,' I promise, as you disappear out of sight.

Jim snorts. 'You're fucking joking, aren't you? She's way out of your league.'

'You can laugh,' I say, and they do. 'But she wants me.'

You're walking down the hill into the village as I'm walking up. Our eyes catch while we're still a long way apart, and that makes it difficult. Where do we look as we're approaching each other? You look at your watch, then down at the pavement. I look at you. You're wearing yet another pretty, flimsy summer dress. Your tits are bouncing slightly as you walk. The slight breeze and the force of your movement down the hill is making the material clasp to your legs. The late-evening sun is making your skin shine. You're like a fucking goddess.

We meet halfway. 'Hello, Phil,' you say, smiling shyly.

'Hello, Mrs Greene.'

You let out a delicate little laugh. 'Why do you always call me Mrs Greene? Call me Fiona, please.'

'How's that lovely car of yours? Running all right?'

You shrug. 'I don't know. I haven't been allowed to drive it, since I . . .'

Since you were so busy wondering what it would be like to let me fuck you, you forgot about driving. I smile; you look away, embarrassed by your own thoughts. You shouldn't be thinking this. You mustn't. Mustn't think about me. You don't want me. Say it enough times and you might be able to put me out of your thoughts. I bet if I reached under your dress right now, I'd find your knickers were wet.

Wet for me, Fiona.

I bet you lie in bed at night, while he's snoring beside you, and wonder. You touch yourself and imagine my grubby hands on your pure white breasts; my greasy fingers inching their way up your inner thigh. My hard, hairy, sweaty body rubbing over yours, sliding into you, fucking you. You tell yourself to stop it, but you can't help thinking that there has to be more to fucking than what your insipid little husband gives you – has to be something harder and faster and deeper and fuller, something that can match that yearning in your pussy.

Some kids on skateboards, pretending they live in the middle of a city rather than in the middle of nowhere, whiz past. One of them knocks you and your handbag falls off your shoulder on to the pavement. You crouch down but it's too late – things you don't want anyone to see have been spilt. As you scrabble to collect your tampons before they roll away down the hill, I pick up your dog-eared paperback and your slim, smooth, gold vibrator. Trust you to have a gold fucking vibrator.

We stand up. Mortified, excited, you can't do anything but wait as I study the dirty novel. There's a picture on the front of a man like me: dark, muscular, heavy and hairy. A bit of rough. I look up at you and the shame tainting your perfect face is almost enough to make me come in my pants. I look down at the vibrator in my right hand, and the realisation that this has been inside you, lubricated with thoughts of dirty men with dirty hands and minds – men like me – makes me want to ask if I can keep it. I want to take it home and smell it, and roll it around on my tongue, and touch myself with something that's fucked you.

You hold out your hand. That pure, soft hand tipped with pale-pink nail varnish; the same pure hand that forces that buzzing vibrator deep inside your cunt when you need what your husband can't give. How often do you masturbate? Often, knowing your husband.

'I'd be grateful if you kept this to yourself,' you mumble. I hand the book and vibrator back, and you stuff them deep inside your bag, trying to hide them.

'What you get up to is your business,' I say.

You thank me, again, knowing that this'll go no further. You trust me. You must do. That's why you say, 'I used to have a job, but Alex doesn't like me working. I miss London. I miss my friends.' You take a deep breath and let it out in a long sigh. 'Sometimes I get bored.'

'Don't we all.' I take a risk. It's now or never. I sense that a direct approach would be welcomed by you, you poor, rich, frustrated slut. 'Perhaps I could help to relieve your boredom.'

Your eyes cloud and drift to my mouth, then slowly up again to my dark, dirty eyes. 'Perhaps you could.'

A loud beep makes us both jump. It's your husband. He pulls up to the kerb, waves at me and leans over to open the passenger door for you. 'I'm only going to the Co-op,' you say. 'I'll walk.'

'Let's go for a spin first, up on the moors,' he says. 'It's a beautiful evening.'

'We need milk.'

'We'll get the milk later.'

You get into the car. You look at me as the pig does a U-turn and screeches off back up the hill. You look at me, and I look back, and we both know that it's going to happen.

You hold out for as long as you can. Probably because a part of you doesn't want it to happen. Then, the tension will be gone and we'll have to look for another thrill. I understand your hesitance. A part of me doesn't want this to happen, either. A part of me would be strangely happy to carry on wanting you and knowing you want me, and going home and wanking over secret thoughts of you and me and how wrong we are for each other. We have nothing in common but this.

But a part of me wants to be buried inside you, making you scream; making you cry out and hold your breath; making you confront your sordid little fantasies. That part of me goes hard, every time I think of you with that vibrator.

You turn up at the garage, late on Friday night. I hear the throb of your Range Rover's engine as you park, and I know it's you before I see you. It's so late that it's dark outside, and the lads have long gone to the pub. I carried on working, alone. Couldn't face the pub tonight. Planned to go home and pin up my thoughts of you on the grubby walls of my cottage, and wank, all night, over you.

But here you are. I'm just locking up when I hear your heels tapping up behind me. 'I hoped I might catch you,' you say.

I turn round. It's dark, but I can see your eyes shining. 'What can I do for you, Mrs Greene – Fiona?'

'Well, it's a bit of an emergency. You see, my battery's gone flat,' you say.

We both know you're not talking about your car battery. We're silent for a moment, enjoying this. I can smell gin on your breath. I imagine you sitting at home, getting yourself drunk, working yourself up for this.

'Can I help?' I ask.

'I hope so. What do you suggest?'

I think for a moment. 'I could give you a jump.'

'What would that involve?'

'Come inside, and I'll show you.'

I unlock the door again and slide it open. You step inside behind me and wait while I turn on the light and pull the door shut behind us. Lust that's close to rage bubbles up inside me and I grab your arm and pull you over to the old Ford Capri that's sitting in the middle of the workshop. I turn you round to face me and slam your arse up against the side of the car. You gasp at my roughness: it's even better than you imagined.

I stand very close, at your shoulder. I put one hand on the bonnet, just by your waist, and the other on your thigh. I rub up and down. I'm marking the pale pink of your dress with dark streaks of grease, but you don't care. Your lips are apart, your eyes are moving all over my face and neck and you're just gagging for me. 'How come your battery's gone flat?' I ask.

'I've been very bored,' you say, looking at the dark chest hair at the neck of my once-white T-shirt.

'That's the trouble with living in a village.' I reach down and slip my hand under the hem of your dress. 'There's nothing to do.'

Your thigh is even softer than I imagined. It's just like a woman's thigh should be: long and taut, but soft. So fucking soft. You part your legs enough for me to slip my hand on to your inner thigh. Oh fuck. That's the softest skin I've ever felt.

'You're right,' you whisper. Your words come in short gasps, as my fingers move nearer to your pussy. 'I need something to keep me occupied.'

'Perhaps you should take up flower arranging. Or join the WI.'

'Mmmm.'

Fuck. Fuck. Your knickers are almost as soft as your inner thighs. Your pussy hair's soft too, and damp. You take a sharp breath and put your hands behind you, reaching for the bonnet as I slide a thick finger into you. You are so wet. 'Fuck. You little slut,' I grunt appreciatively. 'What would your husband say?' I lick your neck. 'What would he say, Fiona?'

You don't answer. There's fear in your eyes. With your hands pushing behind you like that, your tits are pushed out towards me. The buttons on your dress are straining. I look down the front of your dress as I finger you. Your pussy's so wet, you soon need another finger. Then another. Three of my fat fingers inside you. You slut.

'I've wanted to do this since the day you arrived,' I say.

You blink slowly, thinking for a moment. 'I didn't meet you the day we arrived.'

'No, but I saw you. You drove past. You were wearing a skimpy little dress. You had no bra on, you fucking slut. You wanted everyone to look at you, didn't you? Why else would you wear a dress with no bra? I could see the shapes of your tits. Everyone could. I wanted to come all over them.'

'Oh,' you whimper, as my free hand squeezes your tit. I move closer to you, and speak with my foul mouth almost touching yours.

'I wanted to stick my hand under that little dress and touch that sweet, wet pussy of yours.'

'Oh.'

'You didn't fool me. You looked expensive, but I knew you were a dirty slut.' I poke my tongue into your mouth. At first, you're taken aback by the way

I thrash it around violently, rolling it over your tongue and then pulling it out to lick your lips. I can taste your lipstick. It's sweet and soft, like your cunt. 'I told them I was going to fuck you. D'you know what they did?'

You don't answer. You can't: my tongue's filling your mouth again.

'They laughed at me. Said a woman like you would never go for a bloke like me. They thought you were posh and genteel and clean.' I stick my tongue in your ear, then bite the agonisingly sweet flesh of your earlobe. 'I could tell you were a dirty bitch.'

You don't know what to say or do. You do nothing. You jump with the shock as my fingers pull out of your pussy and I grab your dress at the cleavage and rip it to the navel. Buttons fly off and land in the pools of grease on the floor. Your lacy cream bra undoes at the front and I tear it open. Your tits. Oh fuck, you're beautiful. You're more beautiful than I imagined, and I thought I'd painted a picture of perfection. Your tits are pale and full enough to fill my hand, but small enough to look so delicate I have to bite them. Your nipples are pale pink, like your dress. They're big and tender and you jerk as I bite them.

Your hands are in my tangled, messy hair. They stay in my hair as my head moves down. My tongue drags behind, leaving a trail of lust over your flat stomach. I kneel down and push up the skirt of your dress. 'Hold it up,' I say, and you do, showing me your little knickers. I pull them down to your ankles and lift one foot out of them. You don't have to be told – you hook your leg over my shoulder. I bury my face in your cunt and breathe you in. Oh fuck. You smell of soap and expensive body lotion, but most of all you smell of pussy. I lap you up, you slut, and you make my lips and chin wet with your filthy desire.

I could eat you for hours, but my prick is hard and my balls are so heavy they're hurting, and you're pulling on my hair and trying to bring me further into you. You need my prick inside you, now. You beautiful, horny bitch.

I stand up. I push you back over the bonnet of the car. I slide my hands behind your knees and lift them up so your legs are bent; open; ready for me. You hold on to your knees and look up at me. Fuck. I want to make you scream.

I unbutton my overalls and bring my prick out of my shorts. I'm so hard, and I know that I'm big. Your eyes are wide. Your mouth opens wide as I plunge between your thighs. 'Slut,' I hiss, pounding into you. 'Bitch.'

You hold on tight. You look up at me with fear and revulsion and gratitude and shame and complete, utter abandon. You're mine now, you bitch, and you know it.

I'm going to give you the fuck of your life. I bet the pig never gave you one like this. I lean over you and bite your neck. Squeeze your jiggling tit. I slide my hand between us and rub my thumb over your clit. Not so ignorant and unsophisticated, see? I know where your clit is. I know what to do with it to make you cry. I bet the pig doesn't.

You start to moan and shake. I rub harder. Thrust deeper. Bite until I leave imprints in your skin. I'm coming inside you but you're not there yet. I push harder. Rub faster. You're soaking wet. Your cunt's streaming with juice and come and I'm trying to keep my thumb moving over your hard little clit, despite the fact that my whole body's in spasm. All of a sudden you jolt and your body jerks rigid underneath me. You hold your breath and I carry on, watching you. You close your eyes so tight that tears squeeze out from underneath your eyelashes. Your mouth's so fucking beautiful I have to pull you down off the car. You land in a crumpled mess at my feet, and take my hot, sticky prick between your lips without a whimper. You suck me clean. You beautiful, beautiful slut.

'Well,' you say, holding your dress together, looking round to see if we've been noticed as I lock up again. 'I . . .'

I turn round to face you. I don't care if anyone's looking. I put my hand between your legs.

For a moment, you can't speak. Just my touching you there is making you dizzy. 'I'd better get home,' you say at last, very quietly.

'See you.'

'See you.' You try to go but can't. Your knickers are hanging out of the pocket of my overalls. My finger's pressing your dress up into your naked, wet pussy and anyone could walk by, but you can't leave as long as my dirty hand is on you. We hear footsteps coming up the street and I wait until they're close, lapping up the fear in your face, before I take my hand away.

'Thank you for your help,' you say, raising your voice so whoever's about to walk past hears its innocent tone. 'It was very kind of you to do it at such short notice.'

'Don't mention it, Mrs Greene. Glad I could help. You will let me know if there's anything else I can do?'

'I will. Thanks.'

'My pleasure.' I watch you walk unsteadily back to your car. 'Any time.'

Read Me

November 15th
 My first thought when I meet a man is this: Does he want to fuck me?

Most of them do. (I think this is a reflection on men rather than on my physical attributes, although in the last week I have been variously described as having nice legs by the builders across the street from the office, lovely eyes by a man in a wine bar late last Friday night, and a beautiful body by my boyfriend when he rolled in drunk and horny very early yesterday morning.) Where was I? Oh yeah. Most men would fuck me, given the chance.

I can tell in that first instant when we meet. It's in his eyes and his handshake and his smile, buried just beneath the surface like DNA – invisible to the naked eye but shaping everything we are and everything we do. If he does want to fuck me – and, like I said, most of them do – then it's just as obvious to me as if he'd said it out loud. He might as well get it tattooed across his forehead. I can tell.

I want men to want me. I want to feel their lust,

immediate and strong. I want to ask the question, 'Do you want to fuck me?' and get the answer, 'Yes. I want to bite your nipples. I want to lick your pussy until I feel your legs shaking and your body coming. I want to slide my cock inside you.'

It's funny, but even if I don't want to fuck a man, I need him to want to fuck me. It's an ego thing, quite obviously. My mother was always telling me I was too fat, too clumsy, too shy, too stupid to ever get on. I'm not fat, or clumsy, or shy or stupid, and although I know it now, I need confirmation all the time. I need men to want me; I feed off the hunger in their smiles. My batteries need constant recharging, and I get that charge from the spark of attraction in a man's eyes. Even if I don't want him, I'm glad that he wants me. It means my mother was wrong.

I want every man to look at me and think, 'I'd like to fuck her.' I want married men to consider cheating on their wives with me; I want one-night-stand addicts to offer to give up their ways and devote themselves to me. I want ugly men to worship my beauty and beautiful men to appreciate my ugliness. I want young boys to lust after my experience and older men to crave my youth. I want big men to smother me with the weight of their bodies and skinny men to shelter in my rolling curves. I want filthy men to cleanse themselves in my body and pristine men to get themselves dirty with me. I want my boyfriend's friends to look at me and get hard-ons.

I want to be all things to all men. I want to spread my legs and let them all into the heaven of my cunt. I want to be Gulliver and have leagues of Lilliputians tie me down and live on my body. Ten could suck on each nipple. Two of them could fill my belly button with water and use it as a bath. Whole families could get lost in my pubic hair and live for days eating only the juice oozing from my cunt, of which they would ensure a constant supply by stroking the inner edges of my lips with their tiny, eager hands.

I want to be wanted, not only by my boyfriend but by a constant stream of men.

I realised all this today when I was sitting in the conference room in the middle of an intensely boring marketing strategy meeting. I'd just done a presentation on my department's plans for the next eighteen months. I sat down, and while some other boring fucker was doing his presentation I looked all around the table. There were fifteen men in that room, ranging in rank and age from graduate to chairman. I wondered what each of them had thought of me as I'd made my speech. I didn't give a toss what the other women had thought. I realised something insane – something which would have had me drummed out of the feminist movement and paraded in the streets as a traitor. I actually hoped that each of those men had been too busy looking at my cleavage to listen to what I was saying. I knew at that moment that I'd worn my tight shirt that hugs my tits and my short grey skirt with that thought in mind. I hoped that at least a couple of them had had to drop a hand under the table, into their laps, as I'd reached up to pull the screen down and my skirt had risen another inch or two up the backs of my thighs. I closed my eyes for a split second, not caring whether anyone noticed, and I fantasised about leaving the room and hovering outside the open door and hearing the men talking about me: 'Fuck, she's horny. Didn't listen to a word she said – couldn't take my eyes off her tits. I get a hard-on just listening to her reading out those sales figures.'

Most of those men are repulsive. Sweaty; pompous; overweight; middle-aged, or if not physically middle-aged, at least mentally in their fifties; stuffed with mediocrity. And yet I wanted for every one of those men to come out of that meeting wanting to fuck me. I have to feel wanted.

November 19th

I am intensely aware of men. I try not to be – after all, I'm fairly successful in what I do. People think I'm a confident career woman, and confident career women don't spend their time thinking about men, do they? But I can't help myself. If there's a man in the room I become very self-conscious: planning my movements, giving him my best profile, willing him to notice and to want me – even if I have no interest in him sexually. I take on different characters – because he certainly wouldn't be attracted by the real me. The real me is dark. He'd be scared witless by her. I'll show him other women, but not me. I'll be laughing girl, the fun type; I'll be the serious, nodding, quiet intellectual; I'll be one of the lads. I'll be whatever you want me to be. I'm a piece of clay. Mould me into whatever shape you want then wrap me round your prick and fuck me. I'm whoever you want.

There are signs I look for; signs that I take home with me and rub between my fingertips to make them warm before wanking with them. The second glance – that heart-stopping, gut-twisting moment when he gives me another look. The second glance is wonderful. It means he's admitting he wants me. He's actually showing that he wants me. Fuck politeness and political correctness – this is sharper, harder, faster. This is lust. Yes, I want you.

The slow smile is another favourite. Talking to a

man; listening intently; nodding at the right moment; pretending to be interested in whatever self-obsessed drivel is spewing from his mouth. Then, when he finally lets you have a word in, he nods and then slowly, slowly smiles. That smile has nothing to do with what you're saying. He's not even listening to what you're saying. He's telling you what you wanted to hear: this conversation is a sham. We both know it. We both want to rip each other's clothes off and suck each other's bits right here, right now. But we won't, because we're adults. And now we're all grown up we don't behave like that, even though we all want to.

Last night there was a man who didn't care about politeness or political correctness or behaving like he should. I had to go to a party, a work thing, some poncey Soho design agency we'd used and which, propelled by the huge sums of money our company and other suckers had ploughed into it, had now moved to bigger, brighter, even poncier premises. This was a party for its clients: a way of thanking us all for our business and welcoming us to the new offices and, therefore, keeping the company name in the forefront of all our minds. I munched through the usual unimpressively delicious selection of canapés and drank the expensive wine and studiously ignored the stream of self-consciously trendy designers trying to talk non-business with me in an overly relaxed way that was worse than screaming, 'Please use us again next year! Please! Please!' I stood on my own in a dark corner and watched the self-consciously trendy, overly arty promotional film being played on a loop on the television screen, and I wondered why I was there. Then I was reminded.

'You look bored.'

Danny. The guy who owns the company. (I've told you about him before.)

'I'm bored shitless,' I said.

'So am I,' he said.

I looked at him with a directness that would make some men nervous. But not Danny. I knew what Danny wanted. Knew how to play this game. He smiled slowly in acknowledgement. Slowly, disinterestedly, I turned back to the film.

Aware of every movement, I ran my fingers through my hair, took a sip of my wine and pretended to concentrate on the telly. I felt the vivid colours flickering on my face. I felt his eyes sneak down the front of my jacket. I felt him wondering whether I had anything on underneath. I didn't. Just a bra that barely held my tits.

'Why don't we go up to my office?' It wasn't really a question. We both knew it was going to happen. Just a case of drawing out this moment for a few seconds longer.

I kept my eyes on the screen. 'What would I want to go up to your office for?'

'We need to talk,' he said.

'What about?' I said.

He moved closer to me so he could speak quietly. 'About what I'm going to say to my wife when she asks why I've come home smelling of another woman.'

My turn to smile. Couldn't help it. He took it as a sign. He took my hand. I let him. We went up to his office. I suggested he tell his wife I was an important client, and he'd had to sleep with me to get my company's contract next year. It was almost true, I told him. I had been asked to check out some other design agencies. He asked if he should be worried. I shrugged and told him I was pleased with his work,

167

but that it wasn't just up to me, who gets our contract.

He unbuttoned my jacket and licked his lips. I wasn't sure whether it was an unconscious reaction to my black satin Wonderbra or a conscious, corny one – either way, I liked it. He asked if I would put in a good word for him. I said I could only tell the truth. I felt my pussy clutching in anticipation of his fingers; fingers that were touching my cleavage but which would soon be inside me, searching for the inner me – the crying, writhing, screaming me. I promised to tell my boss that Danny goes to great lengths to satisfy his clients.

He did, he promised, speaking into my neck. He'd do anything to satisfy his clients. And I was his favourite client.

I know, I thought. I've seen the way you look at me in meetings. I've watched your eyes fall down my top; I've felt your attention slide between my thighs as I cross my legs. I've warmed myself in the slowness of your smile and brought myself off in your toilets after I've turned on my way out of your office, to find you staring at my arse. I know.

We fucked on his desk. It was good, although I didn't come. He'd had a lot of wine and he came too quickly. All of a sudden guilt pangs took hold and he started mumbling about his wife, wringing his hands and generally behaving pathetically. I didn't feel guilty. It's sex, that's all. I don't consider it to be cheating. Perhaps that's a selfish point of view; perhaps it's a liberated one. It's the point of view men have been peddling for centuries, anyway. 'It didn't mean anything. I still love you.' Well, it's true. I love John. But sex is sex; it's immediate and physical and chemical. You don't have to love someone to fuck them. You do have to love someone to clear up their sick.

Danny quickly came to the same opinion. His guilt dissolved when he saw me touching myself as I lay on his desk, my pussy lips swallowing up my fingers, and he lost it. He fucked me again, grunting and sweating and moaning into my neck, really going for it this time. He came too quickly again. Again, I didn't. But I didn't care.

Men would never understand, but sometimes it doesn't matter that I don't have an orgasm. Sometimes I get a more intense high from the sense of abandon, or the fact that we shouldn't be doing it but we are, or simply from the violence of his hips banging on to mine and his bollocks slamming between my legs. Sometimes I just need to feel a man's lust burning me up. I can make myself come, later. I don't need a man for that.

In fact, and I've only just realised this as I'm writing it down, not many men I've slept with have made me come. Some of them didn't know how to. Some of them couldn't be bothered to. Some of them managed it through sheer diligence or just by accident. But not one of them – not one – knows the secrets hidden inside these pages. Only you. You're the only one who knows that there is a way to make me scream. A way I long to come; a way I dream about and write about and think about every day. But no one will ever know, and so I'll never know how good it feels. Because to tell a man that that was how I wanted it would ruin it. He has to know instinctively, but at the same time to have that fear that he's got it wrong. The fear is what would make it so good; and it's what will stop it from ever happening.

I'll never tell anyone. Sometimes I feel sad and

guilty, knowing that my boyfriend, the man I share my life with – the man who's seen me vomit into the toilet and shave my legs and pluck my eyebrows and have a shit and who's observed all the other mundanities of my life – doesn't know what really gets me; what gives me goosebumps of terror and longing; what wakes me up in the middle of the night. But I swear, he'll never know. Because unless he works it out for himself – and he never will – it just wouldn't be any good. That's why you must always be a secret. You're the only one who knows.

November 22nd
John went out with his mates last night. I purposely left work early, knowing I would have the flat to myself for a few hours. Knowing exactly what to do.

It's a ritual; one I rarely get to perform. The rarity of it, of being guaranteed solitude for a whole evening, makes it even better when it does happen. It has me shaking as I walk from the station up the hill to my flat. It has my knickers soaking wet before I've laid a finger on myself. You know all about it already, but I'll tell you again. It's part of the ritual – telling you.

First, I pretend that there's nothing going on. I say to myself, I'm going to have a quiet night in, read my book while I lie in the bath, shave my legs without him moaning about my using his razor, then fall asleep with a bottle of wine and a video. I tell myself this, out loud, but my subconscious already knows what I've really got planned. My subconscious is doing cartwheels and showing its knickers to the boys and lighting fireworks without standing back and mixing its drinks in a generally irresponsible way. My subconscious is ready; my conscious mind is not. It has to be coaxed and teased and tricked into this, so it can be taken by surprise.

I make myself some pasta. Take my time. Chop fresh herbs and make a home-made sauce instead of just heating up an M & S one as usual. I make a salad, mix some dressing. Warm some ciabatta. Open some wine.

I sit at the table on my own, watching the news and pretending that nothing unusual is going on. I wipe up the sauce with the bread then I put the pots in the dishwasher and curl up on the sofa and pour myself another glass of wine. I pretend I'm relaxing but I'm not. My heart is pounding.

I run myself a bath. I pour in lots of bubble bath and take my book in with me – as if I could concentrate on reading! I soap my body slowly; as slowly as my fingers will allow. My fingers, by now, are itching to get on with it.

I shave my legs. I run my fingers over them and, feeling how smooth they are, I suddenly have a wicked, wanton thought. But this thought isn't sudden. This thought's been running through my mind for days, keeping me awake at nights and making my legs twitch. That thought's enough to make me soaking wet.

I stand up in the bath. I lean over to get the scissors off the shelf. With trembling hands, I snip at my black curls, trimming my pussy hair until the curls have all gone and there's nothing left to cut. Then, and by this time the trembling has spread to my legs, I kneel up in the bath and rub shaving foam on to the stubble and shave the rest of it off. God, the feeling. I can't explain it. But then, I don't have to explain it to you. You know how it feels to wash away the soap and hair and see myself naked. I stand up again and look in the mirror opposite the bath.

My fingers slide over smooth, secret flesh; flesh that's no longer a secret. I lift one foot up on to the edge of the bath and study my cunt as if it's the first time I've looked. I watch a finger disappear between my pouting lips and I wish I was a man; wish I could fuck my beautiful pussy. Wish he could see me like this.

Of course, there's a man in my head the whole time. I'm doing this for a man. A stranger. The man who knows my darkest secrets without my having to tell him; the man who will fuck me the right way, without having to be told. I've done this for him. I look in the mirror, inspecting the shocking nudity of my hairless body, and I wonder what he'll think when he sees me like this. I wonder whether his fingers will quiver like mine are quivering now.

I step out of the bath and rub myself dry with a towel, taking extra special care over my newly smooth skin and patting gently over my already swollen lips. Wanting to smell sweet for him, I rub oil into my body, pressing my hands all over my skin and deep into the muscles and hoping he will do the same when I finally meet him and he finally undresses me. I rub oil into the bare triangle of my groin. My fingers slip between my legs and I rub oil into my cunt. It is already slippery with juice and before I know what's happening two of my fingers are inside me and my legs are apart, one foot up on the toilet, and I'm clutching at the towel rail with my free hand to steady myself.

My clit's burning now. (And it is burning now – I'm having to touch myself as I write this down, even though I've told you all of this so many times before. In fact, I'm going to have to stop and bring myself off.) I'm back. Where was I? My clit. It's hard beneath my thumb. The need is painful. My muscles jerk as I flicker over it again and again. My thigh twitches.

I can't stand it any more. I need to come. But I'll have to wait.

I go into the bedroom and tear open the top drawer by my side of the bed. I reach for the far corner and there, beneath the silk and cotton of my knickers, is what I've been waiting for all day. But I can't have it yet. I have to build up; have to torture myself first.

I lie down on the bed and spread my legs, ready. I place the vibrator beside me. It lies there waiting menacingly while I wrap myself in my fantasy. It taunts me. Come on, turn me on. You know you want to. Don't think, just do it. You know you want to come.

I do want to come. I want to come with him. But first I have to find him. He hides in the darkness of my mind. I put on the eye mask I wear sometimes when John wants to read and I want to sleep, and I wait for him.

Immediately, he looms out of the darkness. He knows just what to do. He recognises the longing in my eyes and does what I've been praying for. He's afraid to do it and I'm afraid to let him. Our fear gives our fucking an edge of terror. Like fucking on the edge of a cliff.

I'm never aware of reaching for the vibrator or turning it on. But I do it. The buzzing fills my mind. There are no thoughts any more, just the buzzing echoing inside my body and the sense of him enveloping me. I slip the ridged vibrator into my open cunt. It's him. It's me. In and out, in and out. I'm ready. I could bring myself off in a minute but I stop myself, remembering my shaved pussy and wanting to watch as I fuck myself; as he fucks me. I kneel up on the bed and watch in the mirror. The thick black plastic disappears into my pale flesh and comes out coated with my juice. So wet, so hot and sticky. I lie down again and bend my knees up and look between my legs at my reflection. I see my tiny arsehole and my swollen lips and my slit, clasping around the thick dildo. The buzzing enters my subconscious and sparks something in me. I start to fuck myself hard, groaning and rolling my head around like an animal. I feel ready. Ready to come.

I think of him. Think of what he'll do to me. Think of how he'll do it without a word; without me having to say anything. I feel his hands. Feel his teeth and eyes. Feel helpless when I look at him.

I pull the vibrator out of my pussy and press it down hard against my clit. The throbbing reverberates deep inside me, sending aftershocks all around my captive body. Captive – I'm prisoner to this, helpless in my need to come.

I lie there for a long time, stroking myself, smelling my fingers, rolling my tongue around the vibrator's head and tasting my come. And I think of him, and wish he was there with me, and sometimes I cry quietly because I know he doesn't exist.

Then John comes home, slightly drunk and high on the laddishness he's been snorting all night. He discovers my naked pussy and he fucks me clumsily, mumbling about how fucking horny I am and how much he loves me. I don't come. My contempt for him at the moment he shudders into my body is only equalled by my pity: he'll never know. He'd never understand. If he read this diary, he wouldn't be turned on. He'd be confused and upset, and quite possibly disgusted. He knows everything about me, but not that. He'd be devastated that I'd kept it from him, and he'd lash out with disbelief and disgust.

* * *

November 27th

We went to John's mum's for the weekend. His sister and ignorant halfwit brother-in-law were there with their ignorant, halfwit kids. Spent the weekend doing family things and secretly harbouring deeply dirty and totally inappropriate thoughts. There's something satisfying about smiling sweetly at John's mother, who doesn't quite know what to make of me despite the fact we've been together four years, while I imagine my stranger kneeling under the table, his face between my thighs, licking up the apple sauce I've smuggled off my plate and smeared on to my lips. There's something wonderfully depraved about wanking in the bedroom next door to the one his mother's sleeping in.

If only she knew. She'd be disgusted to the middle-class core to know that I wank; imagine what she'd think if she could read my thoughts, and see what I wank about! She'd be mortified. She'd atrophy with shock. Or maybe I underestimate her. Perhaps she dreams of the same things. Perhaps she has her own stranger who lives inside her mind and comes out at night when everyone else is sleeping. Perhaps she longs for the same things I long for. Perhaps she closes her eyes and feels him; smells him; needs him.

I doubt it. I expect she'd find doing it doggie style deeply perverted. I think she's only ever screwed twice in her life, once for John and once for his sister. If there'd been a way to avoid it completely, I'm sure she would have done.

Another example of my non-discriminatory obsession with men. I've decided I want to fuck my brother-in-law. He's rude, ignorant, stupid and smells slightly of BO; I still want to fuck him. I'd like to do to him what I long to have done to me. I'd tie him up and then torture him, wanking in front of him. I'd love to see his face. Love to hear him begging. For years afterwards, whenever John and I went to family get-togethers, he'd stare at me with a slightly frightened look on his thick face. John would ask him what's wrong and he'd bluster and stammer and try to look away but he wouldn't be able to. He'd think I was weird; some wild, perverted woman – well, she is from London, after all, and all sorts go on in London – but still he'd crave another night with me.

I look at his two sons, one sixteen, one almost eighteen, and I long for them to want me. I imagine them stroking their virgin cocks and thinking of my tits. I imagine bumping into them one day in London. They've come down for a day trip. Their eyes light up when they see me. I take them out for lunch and catch them nudging each other. They've been talking about me: about how they'd love to see Uncle John's girlfriend without her clothes on. I take them to a cheap hotel room and show them my body. Teach them how to please a woman. Send them back home with enough knowledge to make their giggling girl-friends' eyeballs burst. From then on, whenever Uncle John is coming to visit they'll ask innocently, hopefully, whether I'm coming too and they'll slink upstairs and toss themselves off, hoping that I'll find a way to sneak into their rooms tonight and teach them some more.

Oh God. I'm sick.

December 4th

We're moving at the weekend. What a time to move, just before Christmas.

What a time for him to decide to take over my mind. I can't stop thinking about him. I always think of him more when I haven't got work to distract me, but this is ridiculous. I've got other things I need to concentrate on, like packing up all the junk we've accrued and informing the electricity and the phone people and the gas and sending out change of address cards. And organising the house-warming party John insists we have the weekend after we've moved in. But he won't go. He's in my head all the time. I wrap crockery in sheets of newspaper and his fingers are around my neck, cold and clasping and cruel. I reach up to take down a picture, and while my hands are full he slips his hand over my breast. I kneel down to pack a box and find myself sitting on his face.

I think it's because John and I haven't fucked for a while. He's stressed out, so I'm not pushing it, but I feel the need. I'm going to have to lock myself in the bathroom with my vibrator and release some of the pressure. I'll have to tell him it's my electric tooth-brush, if he asks what the noise is. He doesn't know I own a vibrator.

It's strange, isn't it. Four years with John and we're moving out of my flat and buying a house together. A house. A mortgage. A big commitment. And yet he doesn't know about my greatest, most longed-for fantasy. He has no idea that I lie in bed at night and long for a stranger to do those things to me – things I could never ask John to do.

Perhaps it's good to keep something hidden; to keep this secret to myself. It excites me deeply to know this craving is mine alone, but it scares me too. What if he ever found this diary? What if I ever found his, and discovered that he was keeping his own filthy secrets?

It's better this way. I'd be disappointed if he had told me everything about himself. I like to imagine him lying awake while I'm asleep, shooting up a sticky black fantasy of his own. I want to look at him and wonder what I don't know.

I hope there's a good hiding place for you in our new house.

December 7th
Our last morning in this flat. We've still got loads of packing to do, and I'm knackered. Couldn't sleep last night. Overtired and disturbed by thoughts of him.

Very vivid dreams. Almost nightmares. I brought them on myself, because I went to sleep running through my favourite fantasy in detail. Whenever I do that, sleep, when it finally arrives, is more a stream of consciousness than a rest in the subconscious side of my mind.

He was more violent than ever last night. Crueller than ever before. And I loved it, because that meant he was more desperate for me than ever. Last night he blindfolded me and left me in the dark in a room full of dismembered hands that were crawling all over my body and inside my body and filling me with fear. I tried to fight them off but there were too many of them. I was helpless.

Eventually he came back in, and at the sound of his footsteps the hands scuttled away like cockroaches into the corners where they scrabbled around, scratching at the walls. I couldn't speak; terror had got hold of my tongue. My head twitched, blind, as I tried to follow his footsteps as they echoed around the room. He came closer. He whispered things to me that turned me cold.

He tied me to the chair, my hands behind my back, my legs apart, one ankle cuffed to each chair leg. He teased me with a vibrator, making me press down on the floor and lift my hips off the seat of the chair to try and reach pleasure. But it was just out of reach.

178

He told me his friends were watching. I should be ashamed. I wasn't sure whether his friends were watching or not. I never know whether he's telling the truth. I was ashamed. But my need was fuelled by my shame and I struggled to find that vibrator. I pleaded for my cunt to be filled.

He stuffed something in my mouth. I gagged and wrestled but the chair was so heavy I was trapped. There's no escape, he warned. His words filled me fuller than any vibrator could. Full to the limit. I cried. He rubbed my clit with his voice. I came violently, without his laying a finger on me.

He scratched and bit and sucked on my skin. He replaced the gag with his cock. He slapped me and pushed me to the floor and made me crawl around like an animal. He tied me to his bed and left the vibrator buzzing inside me. I felt empty. I wanted him inside me.

The buzzing of the alarm clock woke me up. I was sweating and shaking slightly. My pulse was irregular. I reached under the covers and I couldn't believe how wet I was.

John's calling me. I have to go – I've loads to do.

Oh fuck. Oh fuck.

Oh.

Fuck.

I've lost it. Lost it. Lost my fucking diary. Think. Think. Think, you stupid cow.

No. I can't remember packing it. I'm thinking back, retracing my movements during the last few hours in the flat. Thinking of the boxes I packed. Can't see myself packing it. Can't remember doing it. And all the boxes have been unpacked again now. It wasn't in any of them. Not in my handbag either. I go cold as I realise: I've left my diary behind.

Fuck. Shit. How the fuck did I manage to forget it? Too much to do. Hassle of moving. Stressed out. Having an argument with John didn't help. Brain wasn't functioning.

Just check. Look amongst the piles of discarded newspaper and bubble wrap and rubbish. But I already know. It isn't there. The one thing I had to remember and I forgot it. The one thing I really wouldn't want to leave behind, and I left it.

Still, it will be safe in its hiding place. No one will look under the rotten floorboard. Whoever has moved in will be oblivious to the fact that my life's secrets are currently stored beneath a corner of their bedroom floor. Safe.

Have to go back and get it though. Leaving it behind is like leaving a piece of my brain. A piece I can't really function without.

Silly, really. My confidant, my best friend, is a half-full, hardback notebook with a plain dark blue cover. My most treasured possessions are my thoughts.

Stress relief. That's how it started. Someone told me to take ten minutes at the end of each day to write down my thoughts. I was supposed to write down something good that had happened that day, something that had made me glad to be alive, and something I had achieved, no matter how small. All that sounded a little too American for me. I decided to write whatever came into my head. And what came into my head was sex. And I found writing about it as satisfying as doing it, if not more so. A blank page doesn't judge you. A blank page is just waiting to be smeared with your stained thoughts.

Got to get it back. That diary is almost a year old. That diary knows things about me that no one else will ever know.

I tell John I have to go to the shops. Now? I

thought we were going to put the pictures up. I lie. Tell him I'm getting my period and I need some Tampax.

Practically run back to my old flat. Luckily we've only moved five minutes away. Imagine if we'd moved to another borough. Another county. Leaving my diary behind in another world.

Someone's coming out as I go in. Don't bother to buzz. I run up the stairs and nearly trip. Realising I'm panting, and realising that whoever is now renting my flat may think it odd to find a panting, sweating and clearly distraught woman on their doorstep, I calm myself down. Take a few deep breaths.

Ring my old doorbell. No answer. Shit. Fuck. Wonder what to do.

The door opens. 'Hello.'

I smile nervously. I'm taken aback to find he's quite good-looking. Why didn't anyone good-looking move into this block when I lived here?

'I used to live here before you,' I explain. 'We moved out on Saturday. I left something behind. Mind if I come in and ... ?' I step past him without waiting for an answer. 'It's in the bedroom – the thing I left. Do you mind?' He waves me on. 'Your girlfriend isn't in there, or anything?'

'There's no one in there,' he says. He has a very deep, very cynical voice that makes me want to suck his cock. 'Would you like a coffee? I'm just making some.'

I'd like to fuck you.

Mention of coffee makes me think of how rude I must seem. He's only just moved in himself. There are unpacked boxes and suitcases in the hall and living room. 'Sorry to barge in on you like this. It's just that this thing I left behind – a book – I really need it.'

'Don't worry,' he says, smiling. 'How do you take your coffee?'

'Black.'

He goes into the kitchen. Strange to see a strange man disappearing into my kitchen. I go into my bedroom – his bedroom. I hover for a moment, surprised to find it the same but completely different. It's dark in there, like he's just got up. Everything was light and white when we lived here; all his stuff is dark and manly. Not tasteless like a bachelor – no grey-and-red stripes. No chrome or black. Lots of old furniture, a throw on the bed and a wooden blind that filters the light and stains it brown. Murky, hurriedly painted pictures of women on the walls. Women with twisted smiles and distorted bodies and sex slashed across their faces.

Funny. I lived here for three years, two of those with John. It was the first place we lived together in. But I feel more at home here now; now that this place belongs to a stranger.

I go to the bed. I have to kneel on his bed, on the side where I used to sleep, to reach down into the corner where my diary is kept. I don't have to look, I can do it by touch. I feel for the hole in the floorboard, worn smooth by my finger. I ease up the cracked piece of wood. I grab hold of my diary.

Air where it should be. It isn't there. Panic grabs hold of me and I lie down on the bed, flat out, peering over the side. I look. I squint, as if my eyes are failing me. But my diary isn't there.

I feel myself becoming very hot. I'm confused. How can this have happened? My eyes flicker nervously around the bedroom. Had I forgotten to put it back in its hiding place, the last time I wrote in it?

Had I dropped it on the floor or left it on the bedside cabinet by mistake? No. I couldn't possibly have been so careless.

I hear him in the living room and slowly I go out there to join him.

'Find what you were looking for?' he asks.

My smile's been greased; it won't stay on my face. 'No. It . . . doesn't seem to be there.'

'Oh dear.' He pours the coffee from a cafetière. He moves over to me and hands me a cup. 'Are you sure you left it here, this book?'

His eyes are steady and unnerving. I look down into my coffee to avoid them. 'I'm sure,' I say. 'I know I left it here, but it isn't where I thought it would be.' I look at up at him. 'You haven't found anything?'

He shakes his head thoughtfully. 'What's the book? A novel? Who's it by?'

'No . . . It doesn't matter.' It does matter. What am I going to do? I'll never be able to relax, not knowing where it is.

'Did you live here long?'

'Three years.'

He invites me to sit down. We start a conversation. Polite. The area: he doesn't know it well. I do. I tell him where the supermarket is and where the best cafés are. All the while my mind is trying to think. Think. What did I do with that diary?

He asks if there's a good bookshop nearby. He likes a good book, he says. Likes to read in bed – it helps him to sleep. He has trouble sleeping.

For some reason I find it odd, the way he's saying this. I glance up at him, suspicious. 'I often find it hard to sleep,' I say, before I know what I'm doing.

He nods, as if he already knew – as if one insomniac can spot another. Why is he smiling like that?

'Although, sometimes a book is so good it keeps you awake rather than helping you to sleep,' he says.

'It's been a long time since I read a book that good,' I say.

'I'm reading one now. I can't put it down.'

'Who's it by?'

That smile again. It's only slight but it feels like a tongue running up my spine. 'Like a biscuit?'

I take a biscuit. I drink my coffee. We talk some more about our favourite authors. I tell him I love F. Scott Fitzgerald and William Boyd and John Irving and Nicholson Baker and, in a moment of rashness, I tell him one of my all-time favourite books is *Vox*.

'What's that about?'

Oh shit. It's a little too erotic to be talking about with a man I've only just met. An attractive man. 'It's about a conversation between two strangers.'

'Like this one?'

'No.' Nothing like this one.

'Oh, hang on a minute. I've heard about *Vox*. It's about a phone conversation, isn't it? Two people who connect and tell each other their fantasies.'

'Mmmm.'

'Sounds interesting, sharing your fantasies with a complete stranger. Don't you think so?'

'Look, I'd better get back.' Standing, I hand him the cup as he approaches. 'Thanks for the drink. Perhaps ... Could you let me know if you come across anything that isn't yours?'

'Sure. How can I get hold of you?'

I hesitate to give a stranger my number.

He's astute. 'Why don't you give me your work number?'

'OK. Have you got a piece of paper?'

'Erm, hang on.'

Over at the bookcase, he searches for something.

He has his back to me but somehow I know he's smiling that smile again. I watch his fingers skip along the row of paperbacks and stop at one which he pulls out. This one isn't a paperback. It's a hardback, slim and bound in dark blue. He opens it and tears out a blank page from the back.

From the back of my diary.

That smile is all in his eyes as he comes back towards me. He picks up a pen from the table on his way, and holds the biro and the empty page out for me.

The page from my diary.

My heart's in my throat. I'm bright red, I know I am.

I don't need to look back at the shelf, at the plain, dark-blue book lying there on its side, to double-check that it's true. It's in his eyes. This man has found my diary and read it. He knows everything about me.

He knows about my boyfriend; knows about his shortcomings and annoyances and irritations. John doesn't know about them, but this man does. He knows how many blokes I've slept with, and how many times I've been guiltlessly unfaithful. Knows what I think and feel. Knows that I want men to want me. Knows that I enjoy teasing the men at work, baiting them to break out of the politically correct barrier put up by the 'no office romance' rule. This man knows how and when and why I masturbate. He knows how John and I do it.

He knows about my fantasy.

No wonder he's smiling. I have to get away from him. Have to get some air. I blurt something out, something like, 'It doesn't really matter. I have to get back now. My boyfriend's waiting for me,' and I run away.

* * *

I feel sick. Don't know what to do. This man knows everything about me. Everything.

After a sleepless night unsuccessfully trying to convince myself that it doesn't matter that a total stranger has burgled the darkest corner of my mind and stolen all my thoughts, I go to work. But trying to concentrate is impossible. I ring my old flat but put down the phone at the sound of his voice. I hadn't expected him to be at home in the middle of the day. I don't know what I was planning to say to an answerphone, but hearing his voice, so casual, 'Hello?', as if nothing unusual has happened, brings the embarrassment rushing over me like nausea.

I'm not just embarrassed. I'm mortified; rocked to the roots by this. He knows everything!

It wouldn't be so bad if he wasn't so fucking good-looking. It makes it worse, somehow.

And I can't understand what he was doing, lifting the floorboard up in that corner by the bed. It's almost like he knew to check there for a woman's secret journal. Do all women keep their diaries under the floor? Perhaps he lays floorboards for a living. Perhaps he finds diaries all the time and it's the first thing he does when he goes into a room. Perhaps he has a sniffer dog's sensitive nose for secrets.

I go home. John brings home a take-away and I try to eat, try to talk about our new house and what colour we're going to paint the hall and when we're going to go and look at carpets but my mind's elsewhere. I feel guilty – something I don't often feel. I'm guilty that I can't relax with John in our new home, or share his excitement. But I know I won't be able to relax and be myself again until I've got that book of mine back. I tell him I'm going to the supermarket to get some more Tampax – men never

186

question menstrual matters – and go back to my old flat with determination in my jaw.

'It's me,' I say into the crackly intercom, 'I used to live here. We met yesterday. I've come for my diary.' He buzzes me in and I walk slowly up the stairs this time, controlling my breathing and summoning the strength to go in there; to face him without breaking down with the embarrassment of it all. Willing my cheeks not to flush dark pink, I ring his doorbell.

It couldn't be worse. He answers the door with my diary open in his hand, like I've interrupted him reading it, and a look on his face that says it all.

He's been wanking. He's wearing just a T-shirt and boxer shorts and before my eyes flutter down there I already know he's got an erection.

'Come in,' he says, his nonchalance such an annoying contrast to my discomfort that I want to slap his face. 'I'm so glad you called round. I'm stuck on something.' He holds the book up close to his face and studies the page. 'This bit.' He puts his finger to it and then shows it to me. 'I can't read it. Your writing's a bit straggly here. Can you just clarify what this says?'

I look down at the words I'd written; words I'd written for myself, not for anyone else to ever read.

I look at the sentence he's pointing to and read it silently to myself. 'My first thought when I meet a man is this: Does he want to fuck me?'

Oh Jesus. I look up at him. Anger is making me grit my teeth. How dare he tease me like this.

'This is personal stuff,' I say, snatching at my diary.

He's quicker than me. He plays the sort of game my brother used to play with me, jerking the book out of reach every time I grab at it. He's laughing at me. Not out-loud laughter, but silent laughter in his eyes that echoes in my empty skull. I give up and glare at him. 'Give it to me,' I say. 'This isn't funny. This is my private diary. You should have given it back to me yesterday.'

'You didn't ask for it yesterday.'

'I was too embarrassed.'

'Why?'

'Er, hello? I think you can probably work out why,' I snap, 'seeing as how you've read it.'

'What did you expect me to do with it?'

'I didn't expect you to find it, for a start.'

'No. Well, it was one hell of a coincidence.' He shakes his head and ruffles up his hair, chuckling gratefully at the luck that brought him to this. 'I was pushing the bed further into the corner and I heard a crack. I pulled the bed away and had a look at the floorboard. The bit in the corner was rotten. I pulled it up and – well, you know the rest. Do you want a drink?'

'I want my diary back.' I hold out my hand.

He stares at me for a while. He's weighing me up. I try to do the same, but he has a slight advantage. He knows everything there is to know about me.

He probably knows that I want him to want me. He can probably tell that, not quite crushed by the force of my humiliation, a single cell of excitement is beginning to mutate and grow inside me. Because, after all, isn't this what I've been craving all along: for a stranger to know my thoughts without me having to speak them?

Reluctantly he closes my diary and, holding it in both hands as if it's a prize – and I suppose, to a man, it is – he gently places it back in mine. 'Shame,' he murmurs, turning his back on me. He goes down the short hall and into the living room, over to the cabinet, and pours himself a drink. 'I was just getting to a good bit.' He picks up his glass and drains it. He pours himself another and stands staring at me. The mute television flickers light against the wall behind him.

Why don't I go? I've got my diary. I can leave. I never have to see this man again. He doesn't know my name, or where I live or where I work. I can forget about him now.

But I don't go. I just stand here in his hall, looking from my diary to him, my diary to him, again and again. I'm trying to come to terms with this. I'm hoping if I concentrate hard enough, I'll be able to erase his memory and snatch my secrets back.

No I'm not.

Oh Jesus. I must be unhinged. I stand here in silence. I look at the bulge in his boxer shorts and I feel a thrill surge in my stomach. My pussy lips are swelling. His hand wrapped around his glass: I want those fingers wrapped around me. His faint smile: I want to tell him even more.

He knows this. He knows me just as well as I know myself – maybe better. Sometimes an outsider can be more perceptive than those in the thick of things. And he knows just what to say to drive me insane.

'I feel sorry for you,' he says.

'What?'

He strolls back towards me; it's the arrogant, cruel stroll of the torturer in a World War Two film, about to inflict pain. He's practically glowing with power. He's on a high.

I try to deflect his sneer. 'You feel sorry for me? You're the one who gets his kicks alone, tossing off over my diary. Haven't you got a sex life of your own?'

He's standing close to me now. A little too close; but then, he has the right to. He knows me intimately. 'I

189

feel sorry for you,' he says again. He speaks very slowly, looking into each of my eyes in turn. 'You've got this fantasy that keeps you awake at night.' He moves even closer. I can smell him. 'But you can't even tell your boyfriend about it. He wouldn't understand, would he? He'd be disgusted.'

I feel desperately uncomfortable, just as he intended. But with the fear – of being too near to someone I don't know – comes a sexual terror that twists the discomfort into enjoyment. In a strange, warped, masochistic way, I'm relishing these feelings of helplessness.

'Besides, it's no good if you have to tell someone your fantasy, is it?'

I look up at him. He's taller than me. He's looming closer. Unconsciously I inch backwards until I feel the door against my back.

He takes a gulp of his drink. Moving even closer, he puts his free hand on the door just by my face. I didn't realise the door was still open, but as it clicks shut behind me I jump.

That smile again. He's amused by my fear. 'But I could do it.'

I can't look into his eyes. It's too frightening, like looking into a mirror and suddenly seeing someone you don't recognise standing behind you. My eyeline moves down to his throat. There are dark hairs in the V-neck of his grey T-shirt. His neck is thick and strong. Powerful. A thick neck always gets me. My fingers clutch on to my diary. I try and steady myself.

'I could do it now.'

'Do what?' I whisper, speaking to his Adam's apple.

'The things your boyfriend wouldn't understand.'

Oh Jesus. My pussy's throbbing.

'I understand,' he says. Throwing back his head,

190

he empties his glass. He lets go of it, like he's letting go of reality and normality and all the things that should be stopping us from being in this situation and talking about doing impossible things. It falls to the floor and I jump again at the noise. I blink several times. His whisky breath is steaming up my eyes.

'I know what you need,' he says, sliding his hot hand – the same hand that was sliding over his prick as I was on my way over here – on to my cheek. I can smell his prick on his skin.

'Don't touch me,' I say, but I don't mean it.

'You don't mean that.' He eases his body against mine.

Oh Jesus. Jesus fucking Christ. 'Don't,' I warn him.

He doesn't stop. His touch slips down on to my neck. His hand around my throat. He isn't hurting me. He isn't going to hurt me. He's just doing what's written in my diary. But the lightest pressure of his hand just resting on my skin squeezes the air from my windpipe.

'Isn't this what you want?' His head is bowed. His lips against my ear.

Isn't this what I want?

'I understand you,' he whispers. 'You don't have to tell me. I already know exactly what you want.'

My helplessness twists again and becomes fury. 'You don't know anything.' I try to push him away. He doesn't move, so I grab his bollocks.

He winces and backs off. Oh Jesus. His prick is so hard. His balls are like concrete. He's dying to do it. I'm dying to let him.

I can't. This is insane.

He looks down at my hand, still clutching on to him. As I let go he looks up. 'The answer's yes, by the way.'

191

I fold my arms, clutching my diary over my heart to protect me. 'The answer to what?'

'Do I want to fuck you.'

Everything mixes – fear, humiliation, bitter desire – and explodes in a slap across his face that shocks me as much as him.

'Fuck,' he says.

Oh fuck. The way that word sounds on his mouth. The way it hovers in the air.

'Sorry,' I mutter, fumbling with the latch.

I run all the way home.

December 10th

I can't sleep. I promised myself that when I got you back I'd be able to relax. I could enjoy our new house and forget about the embarrassment of leaving you behind for someone else to read. But I can't sleep. Haven't slept for one minute. It's five o'clock now. I've been awake all night, listening to John's slow breathing and worrying whether it's healthy for my heart to be beating this fast. I had to get up, I'm feeling so restless. I'm sitting in our new living room now, shivering – but not from the cold.

I can't sleep, because now my stranger has a face.

It's like fate. For two years I've kept this fantasy, stroked it, fed it and nurtured it. It started not long after John moved in with me. A reaction to the fact that our relationship had passed the thrilling stage and become homely and normal. A rebellion against easy sex. A darkness I could hide in any time I needed to: when I was doing the housework; when I was having a bath; when I was in meetings, at work; and sometimes, when John and I were having sex. It grew big and strong, until it was bigger and stronger than me. Then it was its turn to keep me, to feed and nurture me. I suckled from it. It was a huge, quivering, slavering creature that lived beneath the floor and came out to nourish me with its black milk that ate away at my insides.

I told no one about my fantasy. No one but you would ever know – that's what I swore. And then, on the day I move out of that flat, the stranger moves in and discovers all my secrets. It's what I always longed for – a man who knew without me having to spell it out; a man who would do it without my having to ask.

At last, my stranger exists. He doesn't live in my mind any more. He's stepped out of the shadows and moved into my old flat. He's sleeping in my old bed and making coffee in my old kitchen. He's wanking on my old sofa, with my fantasy.

He has a face and a body. He smells like a man. He has a prick that's hard; hard for me. He has knowing eyes and a smile that eats me up like a disease.

I know that I have to go back to him. I have to do this. Now that my fantasy is five minutes down the road I can't stop shaking, and I don't think I'll ever stop until it's done.

The danger of it all makes me dizzy and very, very wet. I don't know this man, while he knows everything about me. Why am I even considering this? Because the danger is part of it. The danger and panic are linked to it like my pussy's linked to my brain. I feel angry and violated and vulnerable, and that's just how I want to feel. I want him to have the upper hand.

I want to feel his hand on my throat again. At half three this morning, when I'd given up all hope of sleeping, I got up and went into my new hallway. It's much bigger and colder than his, but I closed my eyes and it was his hallway. I put my hand to my cheek and then slid it down on to my neck. It was his hand. I felt his body against mine. I heard him breathing into my ear. I smelt him.

I was so close. Back in his flat, just a few long hours ago, I was so close to letting him do it. If my mind had been able to form my fantasy into the shape of a man, it would have had his face. I want to see that face between my legs. Whatever stopped me then has gone now.

I have to go back. I know exactly what I'm going to do. It's clear now. So clear, it's making my head hurt. I'm going to leave work early this evening. I'm going to come home before John does. I'm going to have a bath, shave my pussy, rub oil into my skin and get dressed again. I'm going to leave a note for John saying I've gone out to a work do, which is exactly where I should be going tonight, and instead I'm going to go back to my old flat. I'm going to post this diary through his letterbox and sit on the stairs outside his flat while he reads this last instalment. This will be the final instalment I write in this diary, because after tonight my fantasy will be reality and I won't need to hide between these pages any more. And if fate chooses to kick me in the guts by making it all a disappointment, then I'll let go of this fantasy and start again with another.

This is to you, the man who knows me. I'm ready. I was ready last night, but something stopped me. Maybe I was afraid that living my fantasy would not be as good as writing it, because once it's your fantasy too, it's no longer in my control. But now I realise that lack of control is what I'm ultimately craving. All my life I've been in control, of my career, my boyfriends – my future. Tonight I won't be in control. Tonight I'm yours. You know what I want.

You say you understand. Let's do it. Let's step inside my mind and see what happens.

I won't pretend I'm not petrified. But what I'm afraid of most is being disappointed. Women always say, in that sanctimonious way, 'Oh, I wouldn't want to actually live out my fantasy. Oh no.' They laugh. 'That's what fantasies are for, isn't it? Trying things you'd never really do, without having to really do them. Fantasies are the safest sex of all. Blah, blah, blah.' Well, I want my fantasy. I want to be able to taste it on my tongue and smell it and feel it. And if it's not as good in reality – if it doesn't match up to the highly defined detail in my head – I will be devastated.

On the other hand, it could be perfect. And we're still strangers. We won't judge each other like lovers and friends do. We're free to do this and then walk away without recrimination, blame or guilt.

I'm ready. There will never be another moment like this. Seize it.

You know all there is to know about me. You know I want things that are dark. I'm tainted inside. Do you still want to fuck me?

Fourteen hours later. Still shaking, worse now than I was this morning. It was dark then; it's going dark again now. Good. I want it dark, to match the mood inside my head.

I can't use the buzzer. I don't want to warn him I'm coming. This has to be immediate. So I stand at the front entrance, fumbling in my bag like I've forgotten my keys, waiting for someone to come home and let me in. I only have to wait a minute. Fate is obviously still on my side.

I walk very slowly up the two flights of stairs to his flat. Everything goes into slow motion and close-up and every sound is deafening. I'm completely focused. It's like tunnel vision. I hear the blood rushing in my ears and watch my fingers drawing my diary out of my bag. I lift the flap of his letterbox. Light shines out and I hear the television talking inside. He's in. I post my fear and longing through his door. I let the silver flap fall and hope he hears it. Then I sit down on the top step and wait.

I'm aware of nothing but how much I'm shaking now. People pass me on the stairs on their way up or down to other floors, but I barely see them. Someone asks if I'm all right and I smile and say something – no idea what. I'm cold.

Did he hear the letterbox flap shut? Has he found my diary waiting on his doormat yet? Is he reading it now?

What is he thinking? Has he got an erection? Is he as scared as I am?

This is taking too long. He must have spotted the diary by now. He's decided to ignore me. He's had second thoughts. Perhaps he has a woman in there with him tonight. Perhaps the moment was last night, and I didn't seize it, and now it's gone.

I don't hear his door open behind me. The first thing I know, his hand is on my shoulder. I emerge from my huddle and get to my feet, gripping the banister like it's the rail on a white-knuckle ride. I look at him, asking so many questions with my eyes.

Is this going to happen? Now that you know, do you still want to fuck me?

'Yes,' he says, grabbing my wrist.

This is it.

Roughly, he pulls me inside his flat. He slams the door then slams me against it. I just have time to notice that he's wearing a suit, and to think that he's just got home from work, and to wonder what he does, before his body is so close. His hand on the door by my face. Blocking any attempt to escape with his presence.

His other hand is on my cheek, then on my neck. His thumb around the front, on my windpipe; his fingers around the back, under my hair. His hand is so big, my neck so slender, he could crush the life from me. This thought is terrifying.

He doesn't crush anything but my lips, banging his mouth on to mine. 'I'm going to fuck you,' he says, talking into my open mouth.

'Touch me and I'll scream.'

'No you won't. Besides, there's no one out there to hear you. There's no escape.'

'You're frightening me. Stop it.'

'I can't. Can't stop myself.'

I don't want you to.

His thumb moves down into the hollow of my throat. Further down, pushing its way inside my jacket. He doesn't kiss me, just rests his lips on mine and breathes into me. His breathing gets slower and deeper as his fingers move over my blouse and on to my breast. He squeezes hard; squeezing a gasp out of my lungs into his.

'Stop it,' I whisper. He ignores me. He's frantic now, fumbling at the buttons of my blouse. His big, hungry fingers are impatient and he tears at the material until it rips and buttons fly off. His hands are all over me, smooth like the black satin of my bra and as urgent as my pulse. He pulls up my skirt and reaches behind me. Squeezing a hand between my arse and the door, he slides it down the back of my thigh and hoists my leg up. I feel my suspender stretching. He hooks his elbow under my knee and wraps my leg around his hip. My skirt is crumpled

197

up, exposing my knickers so that when he leans into me I can feel his prick, beneath his trousers, hard against the softness of my pussy.

'Don't. Don't, please. Stop it,' I whisper, pushing at his thick male neck, trying to push him away, breathing him in and wanting him inside me. 'Please. Stop it,' I beg him, running my hands down over his jacket. Through the material I feel his shoulder blades, the strength of the muscles in his back; then I reach under his jacket for his trousers. Trying to slip my hands between us and get a grip on his hips, I summon all my strength and try to push his pelvis away from mine.

'Get away from me,' I plead, a quiver in my distant voice.

But he doesn't get away. He knows what to do. 'Shut up,' he snaps. Letting go of my leg, he snatches my hands away from their pathetic scrabbling at his hips. He pins both hands up against the door. We both breathe heavily in the silence that follows. I'm waiting; he's controlling this. I dreamt this up. It spewed out of my soul, but it's his now as much as mine. All I can do is wait.

'Don't you dare touch me,' I say, indignant at this violation. 'Let go of me now.'

He smiles. I can feel my breasts rising and falling with every heavy breath. He bows his head and watches for a while, savouring the sight and the fact that I'm helpless to do anything but let him look. My breasts are fantastic and he seems lost in their curves, but when I try to ease my wrists out of his tightly closed fingers he tightens his grip even further, showing me that he isn't lost at all.

'Let me go.' My whisper is barely audible.

'You don't really mean that.'

'Please, I have to go.'

'You can't. I won't let you.' Stepping backwards, he tugs me by both wrists down the hall and into his living room. Walking quickly, he makes me stumble. Ignoring my cries, he drags me to the table and pushes me face down over it. Letting go of one hand, he pulls my jacket off, always keeping a grip on one of my wrists. Then I hear the whip of his belt being pulled from his trousers and a second later I feel the leather being wrapped tightly around my wrists. There is already a chair in the centre of the room – I feel its presence and see it in my mind before I actually see it – and now he pushes me across the room towards it. Pressure on my shoulders and I'm sitting on it, looking down at him as he kneels in front of me.

I shudder at the greed in his touch as he strokes upwards, over my shins and knees and on to my thighs. His skin sounds like a whisper on my stockings. He opens my legs until my skirt is crumpled up around my hips again. Sighing loudly, he eases his hands higher.

'Don't,' I beg him. He repulses me; I want him. 'Stop it, now.'

'Shut the fuck up.'

Everything stops. I hold my breath and watch him watching his fingers as they slide over the black satin triangle of my knickers. I want to close my eyes, the sensation is so soft and slow, but I force myself to keep them open because the look on his face is just like the look on my stranger's face. I've seen that look so many times and now it's real. It's on real features, real skin and bone and there's a real man behind those features, not just a figment of my imagination.

His fingertips move, millimetre by millimetre, over my knickers and down, until he feels my pussy lips.

Does he feel them opening and swelling as he strokes up and down? Does the ache, deep inside my cunt, flow into his bones? Does he feel how wet I am?

'Please stop it.'

He blinks and comes to. His fingers have gone and my pussy's crying for attention. A faint, pathetic whimper comes out of my lips. I wonder how I'm going to survive this – already I could cry, I want his cock so badly.

But I'll have to survive. He's into this; he's doing it just how it's written down in my diary. Every detail correct.

I'm wearing my fantasy shoes. They're black and high-heeled and they have thin straps that clasp around my ankles, and he does what my fantasy man always does: he unbuckles the straps, places my feet so that my ankles are against the outsides of the spindly chair legs, and then he rebuckles the straps around the chair legs. Now my feet are cuffed as well as my hands. Now I'm helpless.

'What are you doing?' I breathe.

'Making sure you don't go anywhere.'

'Why?'

'Because I'm going to fuck you, later.'

'What do you want from me?' There's anguish in my throat; it makes my voice tremble. 'Why are you doing this to me?'

'Because I know you want it as much as I do.'

'That's not true. I don't know you. Let me go. Oh, please . . .' I twist in my chair as he goes out of sight behind my back. 'What are you doing?'

He pushes my face forwards again. He slides something black and silky over my eyes. I duck and fidget, leaning forwards and sideways, trying to escape the blindfold but he grabs me by the throat and slams me back in the chair. 'Please don't,' I whisper, as I'm blinded. He ties it tight around the back of my head. 'Please.'

'If you can't shut up I'll have to gag you as well.'

'Oh please. Please God. Please don't do that. Please, I can't stand –'

'Shut up!'

'Let me go.' I'm struggling, pulling at my ankle cuffs and trying to stretch the bindings around my wrists. For the first time, I am genuinely panicking. 'Please, don't do this to me. I don't think I can stand this. Let me go now. Untie me.' I listen for a moment. 'Are you there? Are you listening?'

I hear the front door click softly.

There's absolute silence apart from my breathing. The floor creaks slightly as my body slumps in my chair. I wait, straining for a clue that he's still here, but he isn't. He's gone.

I knew it would be frightening inside my mind. This is terror. The room is stiflingly warm but I'm sweating ice. Blind and dizzy, I'm trying to overcome the panic but it's impossible, tied to this chair. My restraints seem to tighten each time I pull against them. My neck muscles are hard with stress. I can smell fear; my fear. Adrenaline is being pumped through my veins and the message is flashing in my brain: get out! But I can't. And, above and beyond all of this, controlling my whole body and lurking behind every thought, my pussy is throbbing and wet. I push my hips forwards until my knickers are pulled tight over my crotch, and I feel the hardness of my clit rubbing inside the satin.

He comes back in, slamming the door behind him, and I jump, every muscle gripping. He ignores me and moves around the room, disorientating me as I try to work out where he is and what he's doing. 'Will you let me go now?' I ask.

201

He laughs. 'Shut up. You know you want this.'

'I don't. I don't. Oh. What are you doing?'

'Getting myself a drink.'

I listen to the sound of a glass filling. I hear clicking and whirring, then the sofa being sat on.

'What are you doing now?'

'I'm going to watch a video. If you'll shut up.'

I swallow hard. 'You're going to leave me like this while you watch a film?'

'No.' He gets up. He moves towards me. I feel him standing over me, and hear the whiz of material being pulled over material. 'I'm going to leave you like this,' he says, depraved delight in his low voice.

Something's stuffed into my mouth. Part of my fantasy, but it's still a shock to feel my mouth full. I guess that it's his tie. It smells slightly of him. I heave, trying to spit it out before the panic chokes me but he just pushes it further in.

'I wish you could see yourself now,' he says. 'You look so fucking sexy, all tied up like that, with your skirt hitched up and your blouse open and your underwear showing.' I hear him gulping his drink. A cold fingertip trails down my face. I fight against my ties, jerking my head away from his touch. 'There's no need to act,' he says. 'I know you're enjoying this too, you slut. Aren't you? Your nipples are erect.' His touch slides over the accentuated curves of my cleavage. 'I can smell your pussy. Are you wet?' A finger on my knickers. 'Oh, you are. You're loving this. You disgust me.'

I squirm, trying to move my hips out his reach. A muffled protest fights its way through the gag in my mouth.

'Oh. Don't you want me?' He grabs my chin. I flick my head away. 'Angry with me? Fine. I'll leave you till you can behave.' The sofa groans again as he sits down. The sound of a video starting: a fanfare, a couple of gravelly voice-overed trailers.

It's a porn film. I sit there, heaving with anger and the shame of it, unable to do anything. My thighs are wide open and so is my blouse. I'm in darkness, but he can see whatever he wants to see. Worse, he can do whatever he wants to do, and he chooses to leave me here in agony while he watches a dirty movie.

The ignominy. The shame. The hunger in my bowels.

The saxophonist who plays in all porn films is playing his tuneless theme again. I don't have to be able to see to know that women with huge, inflated football tits and men with moustaches are acting out some pathetic excuse for a story. The music changes: now they're fucking. A man is grunting and two women are moaning and screaming in a completely unnecessary way. I'm screaming inside. I'm being tortured.

He doesn't care. This is all part of his enjoyment, making me suffer like this. He grunts quietly and I hear the film being wound forward. This time there are two women, possibly three. More high-pitched squealing and it's wound forward again to two men and a woman.

I hear his flies unzipping. The sound is like the tearing of my soul – I'm desperate for him. The artificial pleasure coming out of the telly is an insult to the pain I'm in: not just physical pain, the stiffness of limbs that can't move and a jaw that's held open, but the mental agony of having to wait, trapped like this, until he decides.

The sound of him masturbating. My moan must be louder than I realise because he's standing up now. I can feel him in front of me.

203

'What's the matter?' he asks. 'Feeling left out?' His lips brush my ear. 'Want some?'

A faint, wordless plea from me. The gag is pulled out and before my jaw can recover, his cock fills my mouth. The smell of him fills my nostrils. I can taste his mustiness on my tongue.

For a moment it's heaven to have his cock sliding in and out of my warm, wet mouth. At last. But I should have known that, in this fantasy, shame follows right behind pleasure, stepping on its heels. He begins to pump too quickly between my lips. Holding my head still so he can fuck my mouth as hard as he wants to, he pushes in too far and touches the back of my throat. I gag but he doesn't stop. His grip is firm, his fingers pulling at my hair. I try to pull away but he won't let me. Anger at my own helplessness takes over and I do the only thing I can to stop him. I pull my lips back and let my teeth graze his cock.

He jolts and jerks himself away. 'You fucking bitch,' he mutters. Rage makes his fingers quick. Pushing me forward in my seat, he unbuckles the belt around my wrists. The leather chafes me as it's whipped away. 'Fucking bitch.' He pushes me so hard I fall off the chair. Despite my numbness my reflexes still work and I break my fall with my hands. I cry out as his belt cracks over my arse. Trying to crawl away from him, I forget that my ankles are still tied to the chair. Anchored by his weight, the chair won't budge and I'm stranded, lying blindly on the floor, sobbing quietly like a crash survivor who's just realised there's no escape after all.

'There's no escape,' he says quietly. 'I told you that before.'

I know. I know. I want this. But it's like the best orgasms – they're almost painful. Sometimes when

I'm masturbating, the feeling in my clit is so close to agony I have to stop, and at those times it's almost a relief not to come.

'Please,' I beg him, 'don't do this to me. Just let me go. I have to get home now.'

He snorts derisively. 'Look at you. You're a fucking state, lying on the floor like an animal.'

I am an animal. I've become the creature that lived under the floor: slavering with lust, dribbling with dark desire. Blind and always hungry, always quivering. Except that creature was powerful; I'm weak.

'Look at you.' Behind me, he slips off the chair and kneels astride my prone body. He pulls me up on to my knees. I mumble softly at the sensation of his body pressing into mine. He's so big, so firm behind me; everything hard – chest, prick, thighs. I'm soft. I'm falling.

He reaches around and squeezes my breasts. 'Look at you,' he says again, as my head drops back on to his shoulder. I try to look at myself; after all I've watched myself do this so many times. I see the picture quite clearly, looking down at us from inside my head. Compared to him I seem so small, so desperate, a prisoner behind my blindfold with my feet and knees held apart and my clothes half off. A prisoner in his hands.

His nails scratch me as he pulls aside the cups just about holding my breasts. My breasts feel big, heavy, and the tips are more sensitive than ever. He rolls my stiff nipples between his fingers and thumbs. He pinches them hard. My spine arches slightly as the pain makes its way down my vertebrae and into my pelvis. I rub my arse against his prick.

'You slut. Look at you,' and he moves around in front of me so that he can look at me. He kneels up facing me. I reach out a hand and finding his shoulder I hold on.

He's touching me. My stranger – he's touching me. I've willingly let myself fall into this, and now he's free to touch me wherever he wants. His fingers are on my blindfold, on my cheeks, in my mouth. I suck on his skin but he's moving on. Over my neck and shoulders. He tugs at my blouse and pulls it down hard until it hangs behind me, half on, half off. Fingertips swirl over my tits and down, over my belly. Around my waist. He unfastens my skirt and pushes it down over my thighs to the floor. He unclips my suspenders from my stocking tops. He shuffles closer to me and to one side of me. I can feel his breath on my face. He's staring at me, waiting for a reaction to what he does next. What he does is put one hand around the back of my neck and the other flat against my stomach. Then, slowly, he pushes his palm down into my knickers.

'Still don't want me, slut? Still want to run home?'

Sensation takes over. My nipples feel like sharp points jutting out. My pussy feels like a heavy, swollen fruit about to burst and spill its ripe, perfumed flesh all over his searching fingers.

'Fuck,' he sighs. The word caresses my face. He's found my nakedness and he's rubbing his fingers up and down over it, again and again, like he can't quite believe that it's smooth there, where there should be hair. 'Oh fuck. You slut.' With one hand, he pulls down my knickers, easing them over my stockinged thighs until they're stretched painfully across the gap. His hand clasps over my bare mound. 'Oh fuck. You pretend you don't want me, but you did this for me, didn't you? Slut.' The word's like a sting. His middle fingertip prises between my lips and easily slides into me. 'Oh Jesus.' He's found how wet I am.

His lips touch mine. I try to kiss him; I long to feel his tongue on mine, giving me some passion. But he grips my neck tighter, keeping me still. 'You're enjoying this,' he says, accusing me.

My breath sucks in as his finger slides out; then I exhale in a whimper as he roughly slides in again. My pussy's tight with tension. I'm clutching on to his finger, desperate to hold it inside me.

'You're loving every minute, aren't you? You don't know me, and yet you're willing to let me do this. You're willing to show me everything.'

His fingers are cruel around my neck, stopping me from squirming as his touch, lubricated by my lust, slips out and on to my clit. The tender, engorged lump of flesh and nerve endings and intolerable pleasure burns as he rubs me. I twitch like a creature that's dying, but I've never been more alive.

I'm deprived of my sight and my freedom, but my senses are overloaded. His tongue's on my neck, then sweeping across my lips; his mouth's in my hair, on my cheek, at my nipple, sucking hard; his fingers are inside me, on me, rubbing heat into my clit. I taste myself on his fingers as he puts them in my mouth. I smell him, sharp and male, and me, soft and heady.

I want more. He wants more. He undresses me, breathing heavily and pressing his palms into my skin as he reveals me. He has to untie my ankles to get my stockings and knickers and skirt off, but after that he puts my shoes back on again. I sit and kneel and stand, being pushed about like a small child being undressed by a rough and impatient older brother. Then I'm naked apart from my heels and my blindfold. I wait while he circles me, the sound of his breathing the only thing I have to cling to. I raise my hand to try and touch him.

He snatches it down. He wraps something soft but

strong around my wrist – one of my stockings – then does the same with the other end around the other wrist. The same with my ankles and my other stocking.

'You don't know me,' he reminds me, stroking my hair so gently it's menacing. 'And yet you just stand there, while I tie you up.'

I'm not gagged any more but still I can't speak. There's silence as he circles me again.

'You let me tie you up. You put yourself in my hands.' The back of his hand brushes my cheek. 'I can do things to you, you know, and you won't be able to stop me.'

I know. The fear tastes sour on my tongue and fizzes in my gut.

'I can hurt you if I want.' He slaps the cheek he was caressing. My face is thrown to one side and my breath is thrown across the room. 'Or I can be gentle.' Tenderly, he lifts my chin and kisses my smarting cheek. 'I can give you pleasure or pain. I can make you cry.' His lips touch my shoulder. 'I can make you scream.' The softness of his voice is terrorising me. 'I'd like to hear you scream.'

He leaves me there and pours himself another drink. I hear him swallowing it. I wait for him, cold with horror and hot with the humiliation of being stranded in the middle of a stranger's living room, trussed up like a bird. I bow my head, as if I can hide in my humiliation, but there's no escape from it. His eyes are all over me. I can feel them on my skin.

'What are you going to do to me?' I ask.

'What would you like me to do?'

I raise my head as his voice comes nearer. 'I want you to untie me. Let me go.'

'You don't mean that.'

'Yes I do.'

'No you don't.'

'Please.'

'You don't want me to let you go. Isn't this what you want?' His brandy-coated lips pull at a nipple. 'How about this?' His tongue licks down over my stomach. 'Is this what you want?'

His mouth is on my pussy. He licks upward in broad, lavish strokes all over my naked skin. He licks down, worming his tongue between my lips. Oh God. God. I open my thighs slightly to let him in.

'See. You can't stop yourself. This is what you want.'

It's true. His tongue slips inside me and I part my legs further, until my ankle restraint is taut.

He pauses in his licking. I gasp in frustration. 'Look at you.' His voice crawls up my body and spreads its claws into my neck. 'Tied up, wet, letting a complete stranger lick your cunt. You shouldn't be wanting this.'

I know. That's why I want it.

'You shouldn't be letting me do this.' He holds on to my thighs. His tongue flickers over my clit until I'm almost ready to collapse. This time when he stops, a sob takes hold of me like a spasm.

'You should be fighting me, not wanting me.'

I know. A tear escapes from beneath my blindfold.

'What's the matter? Ashamed of yourself? So you should be.' He French kisses my pussy, opening his lips wide and thrashing his tongue inside me.

'Stop it,' I gasp, as he stops again. The air feels so cold on my cunt when he pulls away.

'Want me to stop?'

'Yes.' No.

'I've stopped. If you want more you'll have to find me.'

My eyebrows twitch with confusion. I lift my

tethered hands, expecting to find his face still in front of me, but he's gone.

'Come on. Come and get me.'

'Leave me alone.'

'Come and find me or I'll use my belt on you again.'

I stand still, shaking with uncertainty.

The whip of his belt across my arse stuns me. 'Come and find me,' he commands. Stumbling, shuffling, stretching my bindings, I try to find him in the darkness. But I can see nothing; hear nothing but his near silent footsteps on the carpet; sense nothing but panic rising again. My single sob turns into a stream of tears as I trip around the room I once knew so well. Now it's a stranger's room, and things have moved. The stranger moves around me too, evading my pleading hands. Like a child, humiliation wells up into a tantrum and I stand in the middle of the room, my hands in fists, my lungs shuddering with fury.

From nowhere, fingers grip my ankles and pull me. I fall, bashing my knees down on to the floor. Those dismembered hands grab my hips and pull me further down until I'm sitting on my heels. I'm sitting on his face, although it takes a long moment for the tantrum to subside before I realise that pleasure is mine again. It's all over me now, and I can't stop myself from grinding down further on to his lips and tongue. I could suffocate him with my need but I don't care. I have to have this. I'm blinded and tied up but I can be free with his tongue unfurled in my pussy.

He starts to suck on my clit. My inner thighs tremble as I raise myself up an inch, shocked by the force of the climax already building. He sucks hard. He nips with vicious teeth and my body jerks; he rolls me with his tongue and I'm falling and melting. I'm coming. Oh Jesus.

I'm on my hands and knees. Behind me I feel his trousers brushing against the backs of my thighs. His zip is ripped open again and his cock slides into me. Oh fuck. I'm full. My clit's still screaming and my cunt is streaming with juice and he's pounding into me. His fingers dig into my sides as if he's trying to burst the skin and reach inside for my innards.

I don't know this man, and yet here I am being fucked by him. I have no reason to trust him, but I've stepped into the chains he held out for me. I don't know his name, and he doesn't know mine, and he's fucking me like a dog.

He comes as quickly as I did. Deep inside me. He shakes as he groans and empties his vicious lust into my gulping lips. I swallow him up.

His come dribbles down the insides of my thighs as he withdraws. Before I can make sense of anything I'm pulled by my wrist, up on to my feet again. He drags me along behind him. I feel carpet change into floorboards that creak as he flings me down. I tense myself for a fall on to hard floor but the bed comes up to save me. His body's over mine, his weight making the mattress dip. My hands are lifted back over my head. My wrists are released and retied to the headboard, my arms apart.

'What are you doing?' My voice is heavy with exhaustion. 'My hands are hurting. Please let me go now. You've fucked me. You got what you wanted. Now let me go.'

'No.' He moves down to the end of the bed. I fight but can't stop him as he unties my ankles and reties them to the end of the bed, with my legs wide apart. Spread-eagled. Vulnerable.

I groan in exasperation, although he knows as well as I do that I don't mean it. 'I want to go home,' I lie.

'No you don't.'

'I do.'

'You want me.'

'I don't. I don't want a man who treats me like this – like, like I'm an object.'

His hand slides over my body. Like a cat, I can't help reacting. A ripple of ecstasy flows down my spine. 'You're lying,' he says, fingering my swollen lips. 'You may not want to admit it to yourself, but your body doesn't lie. I'm going to leave you alone now for a while.'

'Don't, please.'

'You're confused, poor slut. Your mind's saying one thing, your body another. You need time to think.'

I try not to. My thoughts, if I let them out now, will be dangerous. But after a while the silence makes me lonely and it's better to have dangerous thoughts to keep me company than to shiver in the emptiness of the room.

It was a risk coming here. But the risk has turned on itself now. Now that I've tasted my fantasy, there are more questions than ever coiling in my brain. I thought I'd find the answers inside my desire, and I have found some, but they've mutated into question marks.

Would I want him in real life – if I had met him outside this room, would I have felt the need for him I now feel growing inside me?

What would my boyfriend say and think and feel if he could see me now? How would I explain this to him? Would I even try to, or would I shut him out, wanting to keep this as mine?

Why do I feel more liberated with my hands and

feet bound? Why does being blind and gagged and helpless make my orgasm explode more fiercely than it ever has before?

When this is over, and he unties me, will I be satisfied? Or will I crave more? Is it possible that what seemed so impenetrably dark before will become gradually lighter, and that I'll long to be plunged into a new, thicker, deeper level of darkness? Once my dream has been delivered, screaming and fighting, into the light, will I have to conceive another monster to take its place?

Does this have to end?

Beside me, the bed moves slightly. He had never left the room – dazed, I hadn't realised he was still here. He's been lying here all the time, watching me.

'I'm going to fuck you again now,' he warns. 'I'm going to fuck you so hard.'

'No.'

'The more you say no, the harder I'll fuck you.'

'No. No.' His weight looms over me. I pull on my ties.

'The more you struggle, the tighter those ties will become.'

'No. Please don't do this.'

'You say no, but you mean yes.'

'No.'

'I want to hear you scream.'

'No.' My voice is faint. 'No . . . oh.'

He's hovering over me. The head of his prick nudges between my tender lips.

He plunges in. 'No.' He reaches the neck of my womb in one violent thrust. 'No.' I can feel his bollocks banging between my buttocks. My hips are lifting off the bed, reaching up for more of him. 'No.'

'Admit you want this.'

'No.'

'Don't then.' He bangs hard into me. 'I'm going to fuck you anyway.'

He fucks me so ferociously I slide back and forward on the bed and my blindfold slides off. I blink in the light, and find him looking down at me.

My stranger. That look on his face – just how I painted it. Admiration and rage and vicious, angry lust. Proprietorial teeth baring as he forces his way into me. Sadness in his eyes because he knows this can never happen again, like this.

He still has his suit on. No tie, collar open, jacket crumpled, trousers shoved down around his knees. Supporting the weight of his lust on his hands, he's jerking between my open thighs the way my stranger always does.

He comes, his hips twitching as he goes into spasm inside me, and then, like my stranger always does, he pulls out, spurting his come over my naked flesh. He doesn't stop thrusting. He thrusts harder than ever with his cock rubbing over my clit. With his hard flesh he rubs remorselessly until the orgasm he started in the walls of my pussy spreads beneath his sliding cock. I jerk and pull, wanting it to stop, and he rubs harder. It's painful. I'm raw. I shout out, begging him to stop. He rubs harder, faster. Fucks my clit. I'm burning. I'm shaking uncontrollably. Harder. Hotter. I squeeze my eyes shut. More. He rubs away my consciousness. My brain floods with pleasure the colour of blood. Not pleasure; pain. I'm helpless. I fight it. I scream.

It's over.

He doesn't ruin it by speaking; by asking for my name or my number. He knows this will never happen again. He just loosens my ties and leaves the room.

He stands by the wall, sipping a drink and watching as I gather my clothes from the living room floor. He's thinking the same thing I'm thinking – what now? Why couldn't we have cut off the future and just stayed there for ever, suspended in that first moment when he slammed me against the door, and the anticipation was gnawing in our bowels? Now it's gone. Will anything ever be as good; as fierce; as real? Will we ever feel so alive again, or will we spend the rest of our lives drained of colour and ambition, wanting only to exist in that moment in our minds – trudging through the insipid, dull, blurred present with blank eyes and wordless mouths, searching for those lost hours and wishing they had never happened? We'll be like the undead.

I go to the door. I'm going to walk out without turning back, but he stops me.

'Wait.'

I wait as he walks towards me.

'This is yours.' He offers me my diary.

I shake my head. 'You keep it. It belongs to you too, now.'

The lights are off when I creep in. Reluctantly I run a bath, wishing I could keep the smell of the stranger on me for ever. But I have to wash him off, and as I do, I suddenly feel very tired.

I slump into bed. 'Mmmm. Hello, you dirty stop-out,' John slurs, flinging his arm over me. 'Did you have a good time?'

'It was all right. Nothing special.' My heart jumps at the monstrosity of my lie.

'You're late. What time is it?'

'Three. Go back to sleep.'

'Mmmm. Did I tell you I'm getting a new company car?'

'Great.'

'I ordered the hall carpet today.'

'Good.'

His breathing slows and deepens once again.

I feel relieved and drained and, most of all alone. My diary's gone, along with my stranger and my fantasy. They're memories now. All I have left is reality.

My mind should be empty, but I'm afraid to close my eyes. Afraid of what I might find in the darkness now; now that I need a new fantasy.

Afraid of where I'll have to go to find one.

Relight My Fire

Kristin sat up in bed and looked at the man she had married, twenty years ago. Twenty years ago, Martin had had thick, wavy hair and a flat stomach and hardly any hair on his chest. He'd had a cute, tight bum and a tan from skiing and sailing and tennis, and not a wrinkle on his twenty-five-year-old face. A lot had changed since then.

Some things never changed, like the way Kristin was always horny in the mornings. 'Come back to bed,' she urged, flapping open the duvet in an attempt to distract Martin from getting dressed.

She didn't look as good as she had twenty years ago either, but she still deserved more of a reaction than the 'Have you seen my stripey red tie?' that she got. 'It's on the chair,' she said, pointing with her foot, in the hope that the sight of a leg waving around in the air would do the trick. 'Come back to bed for a minute,' she said.

'Mmm? I haven't got a minute, darling. I've got a sales meeting at eight. Want to get there early and check my figures are up to date.'

'Why don't you come and check my figure?' She ran a hand over the short, silky nightie she'd put on hopefully last night. It hadn't been noticed.

'I haven't got time for that, darling.'

'You never have time any more.'

'Oh don't start, Kristin. You know how busy I am. There's a lot of pressure on me at the moment. I can't afford to slip up. I have to concentrate on my work just now.'

She pulled the duvet back over herself and glared at him. 'I'm under a lot of pressure too, you know.' But I still manage to feel horny for my husband. 'Perhaps you just don't fancy me any more.'

'Don't be ridiculous,' he said, but he didn't meet her eyes. He shuffled on his jacket, picked up his briefcase and just about remembered to turn at the bedroom door. 'Sorry darling. I've got to run. I'll see you this evening. I won't be late, I promise.'

'I won't be here,' she said, but he didn't hear her. He was already running down the stairs.

What started as a slow procession out of the conference suite threatened to turn into a stampede. Everyone was on overload, after seven hours crammed together in that airless, soulless room, listening to humourless lectures on sales projections, forecasts, revenue schedules and the latest selling techniques. Only the occasional slide show, and a distinctly unimpressive array of soggy vol-au-vents at lunch, had broken the monotony. Now, there was only one thing on everyone's minds, and the various reps and sales managers trooped off, like a battalion of zombies, in search of alcohol. Anything to dull the boredom of the day.

There was a selection of bars to choose from. The conference centre had a bar for every taste and mood

– or so the poorly written brochure proudly informed you. Kristin headed for the Jazz Bar, for no other reason than that it was the furthest one away from the conference hall, a long walk down beige corridors and across a walkway with views over the car park, into the next building. She hoped she wouldn't see anyone else from the company there. The last thing she wanted, after a day like this, was to talk shop.

She slumped on a bar stool, slouching over the bar. She was too tired to sit up any more. She'd sat up all day, trying to look alert and interested as the MDs had scanned the audience for possible promotion material. She'd had enough of being alert. She was going to drink herself into a semi-stupor, go upstairs to her airless, soulless bedroom, and run herself a deep bath. She might even get the tacky soft-core porn film on the in-house movie channel – to hell with the expense, and the fact that it'd show up on her bill.

To her relief, the bartender arrived immediately. 'Gin and tonic' was barked in stereo. Kristin, and the bartender, looked to her left.

She'd noticed him earlier on in the day. He'd caught her eye at the buffet and set off across the room towards her, but she'd turned away and pretended to be deeply involved in a conversation. Another thing Kristin loathed about these quarterly sales conferences was the flirting. Something about being stuck in Birmingham for two days and a night turned grown men and women into adolescents, dribbling over each other's flabby bodies and dying to rip each other's cheap suits off. But, oddly, her disappointment at being cornered was tinged with just the faintest excitement. He was attractive. Just the sort of man she'd go for, if she wasn't happily married. Tall, dark-brown hair, cynical eyes and a faintly wicked smile, like there was a very amusing thought dancing just out of view, behind his eyes. A dirty smile on a well-dressed man was so sexy.

'Snap,' he said. He turned to the barman. 'Two gin and tonics, please.' Back to her. 'I'm George.'

George was American. He had a deep, intelligent voice. Kristin had no choice but to accept the offer of his hand. 'Kristin,' she said.

'I saw you, earlier. At lunch. You were talking to, er, what's his name? David. From head office. You looked bored out of your mind.'

She laughed with relief: he obviously wasn't one of 'them'. 'I was.'

'I was going to come over and rescue you, but I got waylaid.'

'What's to say you wouldn't have bored me?'

'I might have done.' He shrugged. 'That's a risk I was just going to have to take.'

She smiled. She looked at him. He was attractive. There was something about him.

'Cheers,' he said, as their drinks arrived.

'Cheers.'

They clinked glasses and sat in silence for a moment while the alcohol numbed the pain.

'Are you enjoying this thrilling jamboree, then?'

Kristin answered with a sigh and a roll of her eyes. 'I hate these things. I just don't see the point of them. The first day everyone just sits there trying to keep awake. Tomorrow they'll all be so hungover, they won't even bother trying. There was an award for the loudest snore at the last conference.'

'So you think they're a waste of time?'

She shrugged. 'They're supposed to be good for morale. Team-building, I think they call it. The only good thing that comes out of these things is that everyone's bloody grateful to get back to work afterwards.'

He nodded. His wide mouth turned down at the corners. 'That's very interesting,' he said, staring into his drink. He thought for a moment. 'Can I quote you on that?'

'Why?' Oh shit, she thought. I've put my foot in it. 'You're not from head office, are you?'

'Not exactly.' He laughed at the worry on her face. 'I'm from A-Tech, the parent company in Chicago. We usually let you guys over here do your own thing, but these conferences cost the company more and more money every year. We've stopped them in the States and started one-to-one training programmes. Thought I'd come over and take a look for myself at what goes on here. We want to be sure it's a worthwhile investment. From what you've said, I think I've got my answer.'

She would have been embarrassed if it wasn't the truth. 'I'm sure some people get something out of them,' she said.

'There's no need to backtrack,' George chuckled. 'I wanted an honest answer. You certainly gave me one, Kristin.'

She sat up a little straighter. The sound of her name in his mouth was like an ice cube sliding down her spine. 'Would you like to get something to eat?' she asked, on impulse.

He seemed surprised, and pleased. 'Are you sure? I mean ... I imagine the last thing you want is to have dinner with someone from A-Tech, right?'

'That depends. Do you want to talk business?'

He shook his head.

Do you want to make a pass at me? she wondered. Because I wouldn't mind if you did.

* * *

They had to take their lives in their hands and cross the dual carriageway, but it was worth it. Five minutes down the road from the complex, a little pub offered a safe haven from shop talk – and, she suspected, from being spotted. She'd noticed George's wedding ring; and everyone knew that she was married. News travelled fast. Even the most innocent meeting could be turned into something dangerous by the company gossips, who had nothing better to do than imagine what was going on in other people's sex lives.

And this was innocent, she told herself, as they finished one bottle of wine and started on their second. She'd earnt a decent dinner and decent conversation – although she wondered whether Martin would have agreed. 'By the way darling, I'm having dinner with the Senior Vice President tonight. He's witty, loaded and rather sexy. He also listens to everything I say and has a very attractive, slightly dirty, smile.'

'Hmmm? Not now, darling,' Martin would say.

She caught herself looking at George's wedding ring again, as if she wanted to make sure it was still there. But it was, like a STOP sign.

Oh God. Why should that bother her? There was a STOP sign on her ring finger, as well, one that she was usually very glad of at these conferences.

But this was different. Maybe it was the combination of conference fatigue and booze on an empty stomach, or maybe it was the fact that George was American, and Americans are naturally more open, but she felt completely at ease with him. George was the first man Kristin had met, apart from Martin, of course, who she felt she could talk to about anything. And she did. George obviously felt the same. The conversation skated gracefully through subjects that were usually taboo between people who barely knew each other – from politics to religion to the state of their marriages.

'I adore my wife,' he said. 'I just wish I saw more of her. I feel like I hardly know her any more. We're like friends who lead separate lives, but happen to live in the same house.'

'I know what you mean. My husband works so hard, he barely has the energy to talk, let alone . . .'

She didn't need to finish it. George knew what she meant. If there was such a thing as a wavelength, they were both on the same one. Thoughts could be left unspoken: they were listening so intently to each other, they could hear the silences and read between the lines.

'This is weird,' she laughed softly.

'What is?'

'Life is weird. Don't you think it's amazing, how you can meet someone and you just know, immediately, that it's all right to talk about anything with them – even stuff you've never told anyone else before? I feel like we've known each other for ever. And then tomorrow we'll say goodbye, and you'll go back to the States, and we'll probably never see each other again.'

'Probably not. Maybe that's why it's so easy to talk.'

'Maybe.'

'You're right. This is surreal. I feel like – this probably sounds stupid – that we were meant to meet.'

She nodded.

'I feel like something could happen.'

What did he mean?

She didn't have to ask. The waiter came with

223

dessert and the conversation changed direction, but she knew it would return, later.

Something was going to happen.

The pub was closing before they knew it. George ordered them a brandy each. 'Well, this is the first time I've had a decent conversation with one of our sales managers,' he said, toasting her.

'Oh? Not casting aspersions on the calibre of your sales team, surely?'

'Not at all.' He smiled. 'You don't have to be cultured to sell electrical components. It's just nice to find someone in our company who is.' He winked at her. 'Usually when people find out who I am, they want to talk about work. It makes a change to meet someone who doesn't.'

'There's more to life than work,' she said.

'There certainly is.'

They looked at each other for a moment. It should have been uncomfortable in the silence, but it wasn't. It was a little too comfortable.

'Kristin.'

'Yes?'

He paused for a moment. 'I hope you don't mind me saying this, but I find you incredibly attractive.'

Ice cubes down the spine again. This felt too right. She tried to laugh it off. 'Are you making a pass at me, George?'

'Yes.' He wasn't laughing. 'I think I am.'

'Oh.' She didn't know where to look.

'Christ, I am sorry.' He reached across the table and touched her sleeve. 'I've never done this before. I'm sorry if I embarrassed you.'

'It's OK.' She glanced down at his hand on her arm. It looked strange, to see another man's hand so close to her. Strange and real, and so sharply focused,

224

like her life until now had been seen through steamed-up glass. 'I'm not embarrassed.'

'I want you to know – I don't make a habit of leching at women I've only just met. This is the first time I've ever ... oh Christ. I've ruined a lovely evening, haven't I?'

He was mortified. Kristin came to his rescue. 'It's all right. You haven't ruined anything. Your honesty's refreshing. And I'm flattered.'

'You are?' His hand slowly moved down her arm, until it was resting, barely touching, on her hand.

'You sound surprised. But you wouldn't have said it if you didn't think I wanted to hear it.'

'I thought you might be angry. Men always try to hit on women at these things.'

'It's Birmingham,' she agreed. 'There's something in the air here. Or perhaps they put it in the air conditioning, to try and liven things up a bit.'

His smile was unsure now.

'I find you attractive too,' she said quietly.

'You do?'

She nodded.

'Kristin . . .' His eyes narrowed ever so slightly. His smile began to return. 'Are you making a pass at me?'

She didn't know what she was doing. She'd never made a pass at a man before. All she knew was that she couldn't stop the words from coming out. 'I think . . . maybe I am.'

'Would you like to ... God, I can't believe I'm saying this.' He took a deep breath. 'Would you like to come back to my room?'

'Yes, I would.'

They hovered around the bed, not wanting to settle, like flies in an elaborate mating dance.

'I've never done this before. Invited a woman back to my room, I mean. Since . . . Well, since I met my wife. Not that I met her at a sales conference. I mean . . .' He took a deep breath. 'Start again.' He ran his fingers through his hair. 'I'm sorry. I'm nervous all of a sudden. I haven't felt like this for years.'

'Neither have I. And I've never done this before, either. I usually keep myself to myself at these things.'

'Me too.' He edged nearer to her. 'Kristin, I've got a confession to make.'

'You have?'

'I've been watching you all day. You were sitting in front of me in the lecture theatre. I couldn't take my eyes off you.'

She didn't know what to say. She hadn't been as turned on in years.

'I followed you into the bar, this evening. I couldn't bear to think of another man trying to chat you up.'

'Oh.'

'Does that scare you?'

Perhaps it should have done. It didn't. 'No,' she said.

'I felt like . . .' He moved closer. He reached for her hand. 'I just knew I had to speak to you. I knew that if I didn't, I'd regret it for the rest of my life.'

'Well, I'm glad that you did.'

'I don't know why, but I feel I could tell you anything.'

'Tell me something, then.'

'When the lights went out for the slide show, I closed my eyes and imagined . . .'

He didn't have to finish, but he did anyway.

'I imagined putting my hand up your skirt right there, in the lecture hall.'

'My heart's racing,' she said. 'Feel it.' She lifted his

226

hand to her breast. Staring into her eyes, he slipped his fingers under her jacket, over her blouse and on to her breast.

'Now you tell me something,' he said. 'Something no one else knows.'

Beneath his fingers, her heartbeat ran faster. 'OK,' she said quietly, afraid to break the tension with her voice. 'I'll tell you my fantasy.' She leant closer, until she could whisper in his ear. No one else was listening, but she'd never told this to anyone before. 'I want to do it somewhere where other people can see.'

They moved to the bed. In one fluid movement they sat, pushed off each other's jackets and unbuttoned each other's shirts. As Kristin told him more, her words strung together and wound around them, entwining them. George ran his hands all over her smooth satin bra, then slowly peeled back the cups to reveal her pointed nipples. He pinched them cruelly. She gasped and allowed herself to be pushed down on to her back.

Work, tired husbands, distant wives – distant lives – it had all gone. The world consisted of him and her; that room; that moment. The image of Martin flashed into her mind and she shut it out. He didn't belong here. This was for strangers who had nothing to hide. No baggage. Just lust.

Then the phone's dull ring shattered the moment, and it crumbled around them. 'Ignore it,' Kristin begged, but it was too late. The outside world had reared its head.

George sat up, rubbing his hair. 'Hello? Oh, Hello. Out of breath? No, I just ran out the shower.'

It was his wife. His guilty glance at Kristin told her. She sat up herself, arranging her breasts back in her bra and fastening her crumpled blouse. He reached out a hand to stop her, but they both knew it was over. She listened to his half of the stilted conversation, and realised it sounded just like her and Martin; just like happily married couples all over the world, who'd forgotten how exciting it had once been. And yet, just like her and Martin, George and his wife still loved each other. The strain of guilt was obvious in his voice.

Kristin looked at him for the first time, as if the lights had just come on. She noticed he had a little flab hanging over the waistband of his trousers, and grey roots growing through in his hair.

She smiled to herself. Reality had a way of throwing cold buckets of water on passion; leaving it damp and bedraggled on the grey nylon carpet. She should have known this was too exciting to really be happening in her life. Fate must have confused her with someone else for a moment. Things like this just didn't happen to people like her.

'I love you too,' he said, and he meant it. He put down the phone and turned to Kristin. 'I'm sorry,' he said. 'I guess that spoilt the mood a little.'

'Don't be sorry. I suppose it just wasn't meant to be. Perhaps it's for the best.'

'I'll try and console myself with that.' Self-conscious, he buttoned his shirt. 'I do love my wife, you know.'

'I know. I love my husband. This just seemed . . .'

'Still. It could have been worse. We could have never met.'

Would that have been worse? She didn't want to debate it now. She felt awkward, like she'd just noticed someone watching her. 'I should get back to my room. My husband's probably been trying to call me. He'll be worried.'

'It's late,' he said, looking at his watch. 'I hadn't realised how late.'

They hung at the door for a moment. Regret made her feel hungry, and her stomach rumbled. He smiled, and she almost ran and flung herself on the bed again. 'Will I see you tomorrow?'

He shook his head sadly. 'I'm leaving for the States in the morning.'

So this was it – their only chance. Gone.

'I'll write to you,' he promised.

'Yeah.' She smiled to herself as he kissed her on the cheek. Sure you will.

She sat staring at the figures on her computer screen. Her eyes were glazed. She had work to do, and a deadline to meet, but she wasn't going to meet it. The urgency had gone out of her life since Birmingham. She just couldn't be bothered any more.

She sat back and swivelled round in her chair so she could look out of the window. She used to think it was nice having the office overlooking the high street, and to be able to watch people without them ever looking up and noticing her. But ever since Birmingham, she found it irritating. It was like everyone was having fun, laughing, walking with a purpose, going somewhere. Except her. She just sat in her office, day after day. And night after night, she and John sat in and whiled away their lives, silently watching the telly, occasionally tutting when something was particularly shocking.

Where had it all gone? The excitement, the anticipation – even the contentment. There seemed to be nothing left but never-ending, grey nothingness.

It was worse now. Someone had dangled a morsel in front of her and she'd run after it, her mouth watering. She'd smelt it. She'd almost had it on her tongue. And then it had gone.

She closed her eyes and thought of him. But it wasn't him – it was someone; anyone; no one. It didn't matter who it was. George, Martin – the ancient security guard would have done. She just wanted to feel the thrill of being wanted. Her need to be needed – to feel desperation in his fingers – made her want to cry.

Kristin heard her secretary's pathetic knock but didn't turn around. There was a shy cough. Reluctant to drag herself back to the tedium she called reality, she slowly opened her eyes.

'Sorry to interrupt.'

Kristin waited, aware that Anne was being sarcastic and that it would be whispered round the office: 'She doesn't do any work at all. She just sits in her office with her eyes shut. I don't know what she's up to.'

'This just arrived for you, Kristin.'

She took the envelope. It was marked PRIVATE AND CONFIDENTIAL. Strange that Anne hadn't opened it.

'Are you all right, Kristin?'

She looked up at Anne. She was attractive, in a vacant, overly made-up sort of way. 'Be sure before you settle down,' Kristin advised. 'People say life is short. It's not. It's long.'

Confused, her secretary backed out, leaving her alone again.

Kristin sighed heavily and studied the envelope. She debated whether to open it or not. It was probably something very boring. But then she noticed that it had come from the States, and that it was addressed by hand, and the feeling of being alive ripped through her like the sound of the tearing paper.

K,

I wonder if you've been thinking about me as much as I've been thinking about you.

I can't stop. I usually work on the flight back to Chicago, but this time I couldn't. I couldn't sleep, either. I've barely slept since I got back. I just can't get you out of my head. And night-time is the best time to think of you, because I can do it in peace, while my family's asleep.

My wife met me at the airport and I almost broke down and confessed. To what? I only touched your breast. Nothing happened. But it's what I wanted to happen that makes me feel so guilty. That, and the fact that if my wife hadn't rung, I'd have done it without a thought for her. I know I would never have told her. It would have been our secret. A one-off. One of those chance meetings that makes life, and work, and all the shit we have to go through, worthwhile.

And now I'm back here, with no excuse to take me back to England again in the foreseeable future. We're probably going to put a stop to those sales conferences. You were right – they're a waste of time. So I won't see you again. You were right about that, too.

I'm an adult. I know that if we had fucked that night, it may have been a disappointment. We might have been embarrassed afterwards, and got dressed and gone our separate ways, kicking ourselves, full of regrets and feeling grubby and let down. I don't think we would have been. I know that you're the first woman who's ever had this effect on me. I love my wife, and always will. I wasn't looking to replace her. I wasn't looking for anything. And there you were.

Life drags on. A moment that could have defined my whole existence has been and gone – and we'll never get it back. Perhaps I'm being over-dramatic. Perhaps this is horny, meno-pausal, middle-aged man talking – but I don't think so. I just knew, when I looked at you, that you would have been the fuck of my life.

In the cold light of day, you might find this letter disgusting, but I know, that night, that you were as carried away by the certainty of it all as I was. It felt right, didn't it? It felt like we should be fucking until we couldn't physically do it any more.

I don't want to let this go. If you'll let me, I want to write to you. There's no need for you to write back. No need to even read my crap if you don't want to. Just let me believe that you are. I want to think of you reading these letters at work, and having to put your hand under your skirt. Take them home and hide them, and feel the fear of discovery every time your husband walks obliviously by your secret hiding place. That's the same fear I feel, whenever my wife looks at me, like I've got you stamped on my face.

You told me your fantasy, Kristin. I never got to tell you mine. Actually, I never had fantasies until I met you. I had dreams and vague ideas, like every man. I got most of them from porno films, like catching my wife with another woman – that one always got me hard. Fucking my uptight, middle-aged secretary was another one. But my fantasy of you is different. It's detailed. It's exact. And because you're not my wife, I can tell it to you without any fear of seeing revulsion in your eyes. It can be so hard,

232

telling the person you love that you want things that maybe she doesn't. She could be offended or disgusted, and she may never look at you in the same way again afterwards. But you – I know you just enough to want to tell you, and not enough to care what you think. Think what you want of me. My lust for you is real. It's about the only real thing in my life at the moment. I'm sitting at my desk now, with my office door shut. Just outside, my secretary is working and people walk by her desk, asking whether I can be disturbed. She tells them no, like I asked her to. I've work I should be doing, but I don't give a shit about it. Writing to you makes me feel alive.

We're at the sales conference. I see you, sitting two rows in front of me and slightly to the right. At first I look at you because you're the only attractive woman nearby. Because the lecture is so tedious, I'm audience-scouring. My attention was wandering, until it fixed on you.

I like the colour of your hair, and the way you wear it. I like your jacket. You don't look as boring as the rest of them. Your face is slightly in profile to me. I look at you, trying to concentrate and failing, and I smile. If only you were sitting next to me. I'd give you something to take away the boredom.

During the coffee break, I watch you. You feel someone looking but you don't find my face amongst the crowd. I'm poised, anticipating your every move so that when you sit down again, I get the seat behind you and just to the left. Another lecture. I stare at the back of your head and will you to turn around.

Just as the lights are dimmed, you shuffle in

233

your seat, using your fidgeting as a poor excuse to glance over your shoulder and see why you're feeling such heat on the back of your neck. You seem shocked to find me smiling. I pass you a note. You take it and turn around just as the slide show starts.

Your head bows. You struggle in the lack of light, to read what I've scrawled. I get a hard-on.

I watch the back of your head. I sense you blushing, as you wonder how to react. Is this exciting or disgusting, you're asking yourself.

You daren't move for fear of giving me the wrong signal. You sit, frozen, until the slide show ends and we're herded out for lunch. I stare at you across the room but you turn away.

But then we shuffle back into the hall, and you sit on the end of a row. I watch as someone asks whether the seat next to you is taken. You tell them it is. When I sit in it, you say nothing.

The lights go out again. There's a presentation about sales techniques which neither of us is listening to. I've got my hand up your skirt, between your legs. You're wet all over my hand. You come just as the lights are turned back on, and as you cry out, a hundred faces turn to look at you.

You don't even care. You sit, pressed right back in your seat, your legs open and your cunt swallowing my fingers. You actually want them to see how alive you are.

Letters crossed the pond almost daily. It was funny to think of the FedEx man handling all that paper lust; stamping it; giving it a bar code; assigning it a number. Kristin almost began to fancy him. There

234

was something attractive about the way he shuffled into the office in his polyester suit, carrying something wicked in his grubby hand.

Life had a purpose again. Her hand ached from writing; her head ached from lying awake at nights, planning what was going in the next letter. Everything went in. Their fantasies turned the air blue over the Atlantic.

It was a guilt-free affair. No physical contact. They touched themselves when the lights were out, or under the desk or in the toilets while they were at work. They pushed each other further into their minds than they'd ever had to go before. They were completely honest with each other.

Kristin kept the letters deep in a drawer that she knew Martin never went into. Every time her husband walked by, she felt a twinge of arousal tinged with guilt. There was nothing to feel guilty about, she knew – they weren't doing anything, and never would. But on the other hand, she'd told George things that Martin didn't know. She didn't actually want Martin to know those things – and that made her feel guilty. Why did it feel right to tell it to a stranger, and not to her husband?

In a way, it was so sad. She was more aroused by George's letters than by anything her husband could have done.

She knew something was wrong when she saw Martin's car pull into the company car park. Apart from the fact that he was here at all – he never came to visit her at work; he was always too busy – she could tell he was in a rage by the way he was driving. And then she spotted her bundle of envelopes in his hand, as he blazed across the car park towards the office.

Without a word, he stormed into her office. The letters splayed like a spilt deck of cards across her desk. Outside, Kristin sensed her secretary hovering, just lapping up the gossip. Without taking her eyes off her husband, Kristin got up and closed her office door.

'I was looking for something,' he said. 'And look what I found.'

His voice had never sounded like that before. Kristin's legs went shaky. She sat back down.

'You've been different ever since you got back from that sales conference.'

'Nothing happened,' she began.

'But you wanted it to. You went to his room.'

She couldn't deny that. 'But nothing happened.'

He was breathing quickly and heavily, filling the office air with the heat of his jealous fury. 'Is he good-looking?'

'Martin, don't do this.'

'Is he? Better-looking than me? Richer? Got a better job?'

'Martin –'

The phone rang. Involuntarily she reached for it, but he grabbed her hand.

'You're hurting me,' she said, surprised.

'Tell me about him,' he demanded. 'What's so special about him that you can tell him things you couldn't tell me?'

'It's not . . . It's just that . . .'

'Did you think I wouldn't understand your sordid fantasies? Think I'm too straight and boring to be allowed inside your filthy mind?'

'I . . . Martin, please . . .'

The rage in his eyes gave way, just for a second, and in that second she realised his anger was fuelling something else. She'd never seen her husband like this before. He wanted her, and there was a hard edge to his wanting.

He moved towards the window, pulling her out from behind the desk. 'Did you think I'd find it disgusting, that you want to do those things – that you want to be watched?'

He slammed her up against the wall of glass overlooking the street below. The window shook almost as much as she did.

'I do find it disgusting.' He pressed himself up behind her. Through her clothes and his, she could feel his cock pressing into her arse. 'You're disgusting,' he snarled into the back of her head.

She could almost feel Anne's eyes burning into her as Martin pulled up her skirt. Her lower back arched – a natural reaction as he squeezed his hand down inside her tights and into her warm, damp knickers.

His other hand prised its way between the glass and her squashed breast, and pulled at her blouse until it opened.

'I've never wanted you so much,' he groaned.

Outside the door, Anne squealed. Down below, for the first time ever, someone looked up from the street.

Kristin smiled.

My Life in Purple

'*H*ave I ruined your purple shirt?'
I raise my heavy head from where it hangs over the edge of the bed. I see my purple shirt, wrinkled on the floor where it was thrown. It's damp with sweat, and stained and streaked with sex; the overflow of our love. It looks beautiful.

My mind drifts to meet my body on that post-orgasmic, post-traumatic plane where lucid thoughts are coloured with sex and love. I think of the adventures I've had in that purple shirt. I think of the misery I've lived through, the desperate longing that kept my body shivering with cold for so many years. I think of how that shirt brought me to where I am now, and warmth flows between my legs and radiates over my skin, making me feel alive again.

My purple shirt has been around the world with me. Clothed in its strange colour, I've tasted seduction and submission. I've been in danger and control. I've hitch-hiked across continents, experimenting with drugs and men, sleeping rough, uncomfortable with myself. I vomited down the front of this shirt. I

238

contemplated suicide. I dabbled in lust and love, and through my darkest days, alone and dirty, discovered my darkest secrets – those I was trying to hide from myself. In this shirt, I've been to masturbatory purgatory; and, worse, to the hell that is marriage to the wrong person. And then, last night, this.

Right from the start, things happened when I wore this purple shirt. It isn't particularly expensive or revealing, and I'm not particularly beautiful. There's just something about this shirt: the way it makes me feel, the way I feel about it, the memories it stirs.

It's made of cotton. Good quality, soft cotton. It has a subtle pattern of tiny, occasional squares woven into the material. It has a wide, long, pointed collar and tiny mother-of-pearl buttons, which fall all the way down the front from my breastbone; a clean, pure contrast to the colour of the fabric. It's cut straight across at the hem, with deep slits at each side. The back is slightly longer than the front, brushing halfway over my arse. The sleeves flare out over my wrists to give an Eastern feel. Neither tight nor baggy, it's slightly fitted, curving inwards over my waist. It hangs beautifully – smooth over my shoulders, clinging at my breasts. But it's the colour that people notice; a strange, bluish mauve. Jack once told me it was the colour of a lonely soul. It was the colour of my soul.

I still remember the day I bought it, almost thirty years ago. Thirty years ago! Back then, I couldn't imagine being thirty, let alone being fifty. Life had seemed so long and sweetly slow. If only I'd known how swiftly the years would waste away. But I didn't. I had finished university, and was working in a women's clothes shop on Kensington High Street. It was my last day, which I was relieved about. I had finally found a job working in fashion design, which was what I really wanted to do. Excitement was eating me up (the blind hopefulness of youth!) and I decided to blow some of my paltry final wage packet on the purple shirt I had admired for a month.

The other girls watched as I tried it on, murmuring appreciatively. 'That really suits you, Zoe,' the manageress concurred, her mean hands unable to resist a feel of the cool cotton where it draped over my shoulder blades. She stood behind me as I looked in the mirror and I saw her smile. 'Would you keep it on for the rest of the day? It'll be good for sales.' It was the first time she had ever been nice to me.

As if to compensate, she asked me to clean the window display. It was a shitty job, tiptoeing amongst the headless mannequins, dusting, smoothing and shining with the sticky and obnoxious-smelling wax polish that was insisted upon by head office. Housework was tedious enough at home. But it was my last day, and I decided to be fastidious.

I was standing behind one of the dummies, adjusting its jacket, when I noticed him, on the opposite side of the street, staring at me. Me? Or was he just staring into space? Or at the jacket?

Me. He never took his eyes away, even while he crossed the road. I pretended to be busy, using the mannequin as a shield, and felt him watching, inches away from me on the outside of the glass. I blushed at his attention.

He stepped inside and touched my back, as if he knew me. I turned and we stared shamelessly at each other for a silent moment until he smiled wickedly. 'Are you a window dresser?'

'Yes,' I lied.

He looked at my breasts, which, since I was standing in the window, were on his eye level, while he

240

extricated a card from his jacket pocket. 'I've got three shops in Knightsbridge,' he said. 'I want you to do my windows. What time do you finish here?'

'Seven.'

'I'll come back at seven. We'll go for a drink and discuss it.'

I shrugged. My lack of resistance shocked and excited me. So did this man's blatant lust. 'OK.'

We didn't talk about window dressing in the pub. We didn't talk much at all. He stared at my purple shirt and I stared at him. His name was Asif, which seemed ironic, since he was extraordinarily beautiful: Asian, with shoulder-length, wavy black hair. Tall and slim, velvet eyes, long fingers. Sex in his smile.

He raised his eyes to mine, opened his mouth and leant over the sticky table. He touched one corner of my collar and said, 'I want to fuck you, now.' He stood up to go, and I followed him.

We went to the tiny park behind the church. He pulled me roughly by the wrist, searching for something. His skin looked darker in the moonless night. 'Can't see,' he muttered, panicking. 'I need to –'

He made a sudden decision and dragged me across the grass, into the corner of a flower bed. My spine screamed as he skewed me against the lamp-post. 'I need to see you,' he whispered urgently. 'I want to watch you come.'

He grabbed my jaw with one hand and pressed his dark lips to mine. I opened my mouth to him.

His mouth, his tongue. His hand on my breast. His breath, warm where I captured it in my throat. I felt hot with satisfaction at the urgency in his limbs, his body pushing into mine. I hadn't had sex for six months, since my boyfriend had gone to work in America. I hadn't really bothered about it until now.

241

I'd been happy with my fantasies and my fingers. Now I was reminded of what I'd been missing. It was so good to feel a man's strength again.

He unbuttoned my purple shirt and delved for my breasts, squeezing them together, fingers sliding greedily over the white satin of my bra. He fiddled with the hook at my cleavage then brushed the soft material aside, looking from one breast to another for a moment, as if he was staring into the eyes of the woman he loved. Then his lips dived to my wide, aching nipples, sucking and biting, his head moving beneath my hand with slow, arching movements of his long neck, like a wild cat tearing at its prey. My fingers moved through his soft hair and I felt his muscles straining, sinews and tendons flexing, blood coursing. My pussy clutched involuntarily and suddenly I shivered, despite the night's humidity. I wanted his cock. I found myself hoping it was as long as his fingers.

His mouth left my nipples and his eyes found mine again. His forehead glittered with sweat beneath the dull orange light above us. He looked down at me and hissed, 'I'm going to fuck you now.' He pinched my nipples until he heard my breathing falter. 'Tell me you want it.' He bent his wild neck and bit my lips. 'Say it.'

'Fuck me,' I agreed.

His fingers snatched at my waist and my trousers fell to my ankles. I kicked them off while he took off my knickers, his palms smooth over my thighs. He pushed me down on to the soil, knelt astride my hips, unzipped and unfurled his long penis. He reared above me. I spread my legs. His skin looked purple in the mix of night and light. He balanced his lean body forwards on his hands and poised himself.

'Say it.'

I reached down, opened myself with one hand and pulled him into position with the other. 'Fuck me.'

My back arced in spasm with the force of his first thrust. He seared into me, my body roaring with relief, animal noises straining forward from the back of my throat. He slid easily in and out. I was a soaking wet wanton, spread wide for him on the dry earth. The church clock began to chime softly in time with his remorseless rhythm and for a moment of astounding, shattering clarity I understood my smallness on this earth, and at once it was both devastating and exciting. I saw the stars, counted every one; felt the soil, dry between my fingers; realised its power and smelt its strength. I was infinitesimal and omnipotent. I was alive, and yet with every push of this man into my soft flesh, the earth billowed higher around me, and I sank into nothingness, willing and unafraid.

I felt drugged, out of my mind, on a different plane. I blinked and the moment was gone and I understood only him: he was ripping me open, my legs fastened around his neck. I was almost screaming in desperation. He shuddered inside me but realised I hadn't come and continued to thrust, long and slow now. He began to rub my clit between finger and thumb, watching with fascination as my head began to twitch and roll. He plunged and tweaked until my cries became violent and my body gave in beneath him. He withdrew. His come dribbled between my damp thighs as he leant right over me and his face hovered above mine.

'You slut,' he concluded, gleefully.

'Yes,' I sighed, wondering what had come over me. I'd never slept with a stranger before. I'd never acted like this before.

'Who's Jack?' he asked.

My brow twitched with confusion. 'Jack?'

'You whispered his name when you were coming.'

Jack was a pathetic, loathsome character. I hated him. He called himself an artist. Piss-artist, more like it. He was an arrogant, lazy, selfish sod. He was married to my best friend, Rachel, and he sponged off her shamelessly. While she went out to work, he stayed at home and toiled over his 'art', which seemed to involve a lot of nicotine, alcohol, watching television and little else. I had often told Rachel I didn't know what she saw in him.

I'd despised him, with a passion that was almost sexual, since the moment we'd met in the student union bar. 'Great tits,' were the first words he ever said to me, the minute Rachel left us alone to buy another round. Stunned, I could only blush helplessly as he leered at me. He got so much pleasure from my discomfort that he got an erection – and he told me so. By the time I caught my breath, Rachel had returned from the bar. I found an expression that contained as much condescension as possible, muttered an excuse and left them alone. As I watched him with my friend, my heart quickened with rage. How dare he? I was so disturbed by his arrogance that I had to go outside for some air.

The day I bought my purple shirt, after I'd been fucked by Asif, I went round to Rachel and Jack's house. I wanted to talk to Rachel, to share the news that after six months of unwilling celibacy, I had finally got some. And, although I daren't admit it to myself, I wanted to see the face that had filled my mind as I'd got laid in the park. I wanted to know why, at the pure, clear moment of orgasm, my thoughts had been stained with him.

Rachel wasn't home. Uncomfortable, I waited with

Jack. I felt him staring, laughing at me, as he always did. Eventually he moved his chair directly opposite mine, and smirked as I unflinchingly met his eyes. 'You've got grass stains on your trousers and a very smug look on your face,' he said. 'You've just had a shag, haven't you?'

I huffed and turned my face to the window, trying to look cool as white-hot sparks prickled my skin.

'That's a nice shirt,' he added. 'Your tits look particularly lovely in that shirt.' He paused to light a cigarette. 'I bet you've got fantastic tits.'

I looked him up and down. He was tall and too skinny. He had dark-brown, lank hair which was cut in an affected way to flop over his face. His angular chin was constantly covered in greasy stubble, a dark rash across his translucent pallor. He looked, as he always looked, as if he had been up for a week, existing only on a diet of Rothman's, lager and caffeine, which wasn't surprising since his diet did consist of Rothman's, lager and caffeine. He held his cigarette as if it was a fashion statement. He draped his ranginess with confident ease across the chair. His whole existence was contrived. I detested him.

And yet, for some insane, inconceivable reason, I had the urge to unbutton my purple shirt and show him my lovely breasts; to let him lick them slowly. I wanted to unzip his jeans, straddle his hips and devour his arrogant machismo inside the softness of my cunt.

Instead I said, 'I have wonderful tits, Jack, but sadly for you, you will never get to see them,' which was a pathetic retort, way beneath my capabilities. He did that to me. He made me nervous.

'Calm down,' he mocked. 'Keep your knickers on.'

He was laughing at me. Anger at myself for wanting him boiled over. 'Why can't we have a normal conversation without involving my tits? I've known you three years now, Jack, but you've never once relaxed with me. What's wrong with you? Is this it? Are you really this pathetically shallow?'

He was wounded. He stared into his palm for a long minute. When he raised his head, his expression had changed. The hardness had gone and his brown eyes were as rich and smooth and promising as a freshly poured pint of Guinness. I could see he was about to explain, but at that moment Rachel walked in. 'Zoe finally found someone desperate enough to shag her,' he said viciously, slouching out of the room.

By the time I was twenty-four, three and a half years later, I'd forgotten about Jack. Life was perfect: I was working in Paris, I was in love with my job, and I was married to my rich and charming boss. Then, in the course of one mad moment, everything changed and I was made homeless, jobless and single again. My husband caught me shagging his son on the conference table. I was wearing my purple shirt at the time.

I went back to London. Rachel and Jack put me up – and put up with me. I had slumped into the numb comfort of depression, curling it around me like a blanket between myself and the pointless world outside. I had fucked up, big time. I had no job, nowhere to live, and savings which were running out fast. I lost all interest in life.

Rachel was the only one who persevered during that time; the only one I would allow to persevere. I had known her since primary school. She almost understood my state of mind. She tried her best to encourage me to pick myself up and start again. But I had no energy, no fight, no desire to start again. I preferred sitting round the house with my depression and her husband.

My relationship with Jack became strange and intense. Rachel was out at work all day. Jack, who was by now a fairly successful artist, stayed at home to paint. I would watch him, sometimes in silence; sometimes we'd talk. About everything. Alone with me, his defences gradually came down and the colourful emotions he used to paint with began to shade our conversations. Then, Rachel would arrive home and he'd revert to his sneering, obnoxious self. I knew, as well as he did, that this was just an act to hide our growing closeness – from himself as well as from Rachel.

Then Rachel invited some of our old uni friends over for Sunday lunch. She thought it would cheer me up to see them. God knows why it should cheer me up to hear how successful and happy everyone else was, compared to me. Everyone else had marriages and mortgages and careers and babies on the way, a whole host of things to tie them down. I had nothing. The only thing tying me down, and stopping me from floating away into the ether, was the weight of my depression.

There were nine of us altogether. As usual when he was in company, Jack showed off.

'Your tits look great in that shirt,' he said. 'Get 'em out for the lads.'

'Fuck off,' I snarled, but a cold thrill tore its way through my numb depression. I'd worn my purple shirt for him, hoping he would remember how he'd admired me in it once before. My rationalisation of this thought, my need for him to crave me, was infuriating. I wished I could push it back into my subconscious where it belonged. He was married, to my best friend. We had never got along. He was good-looking – if you liked the junkie-at-death's-door look, which I didn't.

Why then, while we were having lunch in the garden, did I put my sunglasses on so that I could watch him? Why, when I was bending over the fridge door and I felt him leering down the gaping front of my purple shirt, did I let him look – and then escape to the bathroom and bend myself to the mirror, to share the view he'd had? Why, when the others went for a walk, leaving me alone, did I pray it was him when I heard a key in the door?

'Forgot my wallet,' he explained breathlessly. Then, realising he had invaded a heavy silence, he asked, 'Are you all right?'

It was too hot and I'd come indoors. He found me leaning out of his lounge window, vacantly watching the empty street, listening to the chaos in my mind. 'I'm fine,' I said, but I was crying. Crying, not because I'd messed up my life, but because I wanted Jack, and I knew I couldn't have him.

I heard him move closer behind me. I hoped he was looking at my legs – I had a short skirt on. I reminded my lungs that they should be expanding and contracting.

'What's wrong, Zoe? Why are you crying?'

I didn't answer. My tongue was numb.

'Zoe.' He stood by my side. His fingers brushed into the small of my back. The cotton clung to the sweat on my spine. 'Zoe.'

I turned my face slowly. His eyes had changed. The usual sneer had disappeared. 'What?'

'I didn't come back for my wallet.'

'Oh.'

There was a long, comfortable silence; so comfortable, I could happily have moved in and spent the rest of my life in it. Then, slowly, his gaze drifted downwards. 'That shirt,' he said. 'I always fancied you in that shirt.' He looked up and his eyes were morbid. 'I always fancied you desperately, from the first time we met.'

'I know,' I whispered. 'So did I.'

We kissed, at last.

Slow, everything slow. Grabbing my shoulders, he eased me away from the window and against the wall. His fingers slipped over my wrists and he raised my hands above my head. He crossed my wrists as if they were tied and I held them there while his fingertips trailed down my arms, down to the swell of my breasts, and we both sighed quietly. I watched as he unbuttoned me and pushed my shirt from my shoulders. He blinked slowly.

'Oh God, Zoe.'

I looked down, seeing what he was seeing. My bra was very low-cut. The edges of my nipples were visible. I'd worn that bra for him, knowing he wouldn't see it but hoping he'd be able to tell, by the look in my eyes, that I'd dressed with his eyes, his mouth, his fingers in mind.

He traced the crescents of soft brown skin with his thumbs, palms cupped, fitting me perfectly. 'I always knew you had beautiful breasts.'

He took off my bra and pulled me towards the sofa, then sat, his long legs apart, me standing semi-naked in the gap. He reached for my breasts; he made gentle swirling patterns at first, intensifying into soft squeezing and kneading. My nipples stiffened. He kissed my stomach so tenderly a tear raced down my cheek and dropped on to his face.

He looked up. 'Have I done something wrong?'

How could I explain? Ever since I'd known him, I'd denied my attraction for Jack. The release was overwhelming. He had reached into the core of my depression and pulled me awake; I was alive again, intensely so, grateful. I had been defeated, and it was a relief.

'No,' I assured him, touching his face. 'I just can't believe it. You, and me.'

He hesitated, his fingers unsure now. I slipped my knickers off and guided his hand beneath my skirt. 'Touch me. Please.'

He discovered me with a delicacy that made me gasp. Then he slipped deep inside: one finger, two, thumb looping round my clitoris, pressing, loving. Trembling, I came. His fingers in my mouth, I tasted myself, and the tears flowed.

'Make love to me,' I whispered.

His clothes gone. A pale, thin body revealed, surprisingly sensual in its androgyny. A long, hard cock rising from his dark crotch. He pulled me on to him, and my skirt rucked over our hips. The narrowness of his chest, his boyish fragility, brought a lump to my throat. I squeezed him within the walls of my pussy; my breasts bounced in his face; he poked out his tongue. Our joining was hidden under my skirt, as if it was sacred – and it was. This felt right, and real. The first real moment of my life.

'I love you,' he whispered, his white, sickly frame tangled around mine, his long white fingers on my waist. He bit my neck as we came together, groaning so loudly we didn't hear the others coming back.

Rachel was two months pregnant at that time. Jack did the decent thing and stayed with her. I did the decent thing and disappeared, leaving them to sort out their marriage.

Depression merged into obsession. I never saw Jack again; saw him everywhere. Europe, Asia, America – I left England and hitched across the world, trying to escape the fixation that was stalking me. I craved another moment with him, an instant of freedom from myself. I sought relief in the arms of men who possessed an angle, a shade of Jack, a sense of him; in the chemical comfort of drugs; in the solitary gloom of masturbation.

I had never been very good at it, but found that if I wore my purple shirt and short skirt, if I played out every second of every scene between myself and Jack, I could build enough false tension to make myself come as I was poised above his imaginary cock. But it wouldn't work if I touched myself. Just the sensation of my own fingers on my clit was enough to destroy the carefully preserved images in my mind and send them shattering to the floor. It had to be something else; something that wasn't my fingers, my skin, and therefore could, with faith and determination and tightly closed eyes, be mistaken for him. Almost anything would do. I'd rub my swollen, desperate clit with vibrators, vegetables, even the handle of my toothbrush. The whole tragic episode always took a full hour, and always ended with tears which were nothing to do with my orgasm.

I didn't have to be alone. There were men who told me they loved me, and even a couple who meant it. But I didn't want them.

I drifted aimlessly for the next few years until, driven to search for sense or conclusion, I moved back to England. I heard that Rachel and Jack were living in the States. I closed down the part of my brain that belonged to love, sealing it off for good. I got a job, lived alone, lost myself in London. I blinkered myself. Carried on.

* * *

I'm fifty now. In the years between then and now I married again, had children and divorced again. I watched my children become teenagers, felt their adolescent condescension turn into hatred and rejection of the way I lived, then saw them leave home and in the distance, grow to respect and love me. But they have their own families now. I bask in their unconditional love once a year, at Christmas, if I'm lucky. The rest of the time I live in numb isolation. I'm resigned to it now. It's my existence. Or it was, until last night.

Last night, suffering badly from the insomnia that plagues me, I put on my purple shirt (which still fits me) and tried to masturbate. Despite the best efforts of my humming, buzzing, swirling, all-singing, all-dancing vibrator, I couldn't make myself come, so I got up and went for a walk instead, hoping the rhythm would soothe my restless soul. I walked for miles from my flat in Battersea, over the bridge and all the way to Earl's Court. I found a tiny, slimy cafe, narrow and fluorescent-lit, the type that's open at three in the morning, and sat in the window watching the outrageous gays parading outside. A hand on my shoulder jerked me awake.

'I've been looking everywhere for you,' he said.

It was him.

As he told me about his life – about how Rachel had left him soon after their second son was born, about how he'd tried in vain to find me, about how he'd been on his way home from the opening of his latest exhibition when he'd glanced out of the taxi and seen an unmistakable flash of the purple that had coloured his every waking thought since the last time we'd seen each other – I stared at him. Waves of silver had overtaken his brown hair, his skin was weather-beaten and his frame had filled out with age. But he hadn't changed.

I peered into his face and saw a bleakness I recognised, a darkness which echoed inside me; the hollow expression that spoke of so much wasted time. We'd lived in the same city, only a few miles apart, for the last twenty years.

He touched my mouth, took me to his house, and made love to me till sunlight streaked across the grey.

I will never forget last night, the night he saved me. We kept the lights on and our eyes open.

Standing on the rug in the living room, we looked into each other. He undressed me slowly and reverently touched every part of my body. He touched my breasts delicately, gratefully, as if they contained the secrets of his life, as if they were still smooth and pert and lovely. We lay down and he rested his head between my legs and breathed me in. He kissed me there as if he was kissing my mouth.

Later, we fucked violently, as the realisation that it was finally over made us delirious.

This morning, while he was still asleep, I went out to get some croissants for breakfast. I wore one of his T-shirts; an old, faded beauty, like him. It was clean but felt of him, smelt of him. I thought of him for every second of that interminable walk to the bakery and back. I laughed out loud. I sang to myself. People stared at me.

I let myself silently into his house with the key he had proudly offered the night before. He was playing Mozart's *Requiem*, loud, but above the music I could hear him, or perhaps it was just a sense of him, and I crept towards the open door of his bedroom.

A lesser man would have stopped, or at least

flinched, paused, laughed. Not him. On the bed, his torso was draped with my purple shirt. Buttons fastened, he caressed his chest – my breast – through the cotton, with one hand. With his other hand, he clasped one sleeve to his prick, and I watched as he masturbated – as I masturbated him. He saw me in the doorway, saw me reach into my knickers, and he came all over my purple shirt.

'It's the only thing I had of yours,' he said. 'I woke up and you weren't there. You were gone so long.'

I joined him on the bed. He removed my clothes and his face plunged to my cunt. I lay back, my knees spread so wide I felt the pull of the tendons in my inner thighs. I pushed myself to him; showed him how much I needed his tongue, lips, teeth. He sucked my insides out, lapped me up, swallowed me whole. He carried on so long I came more than once.

He flipped me over and poked his tongue into my anus. I winced as I wondered how it tasted in there, but he didn't seem to care. He reached between my legs and made me tilt my hips backwards until he could reach my clitoris. I cried out in protest at the intolerable pleasure.

He hooked his fingers under my pelvis and raised me on to all fours, sideways across the bed. He stood behind me and plunged slowly in, and it was so deep I cried out again. My body was stabbed with the reality of him inside me, hooking my innards around his cock and wrenching my guts out each time he withdrew. He held on to my hips for leverage and rocked into me. He touched my anus, eased a finger inside my grasping hole. I begged for him to stop or at least slow down – the feeling was too much, too intense – then we came. He grunted and collapsed on top of me, crushing me beneath his sweating weight. He pulled out with a long slurp and we lay still, listening to the music, alone in our thoughts, together in our loneliness, no longer alone.

'Have I ruined your purple shirt?'

I raise my heavy head from where it hangs over the edge of the bed. I see my purple shirt, wrinkled on the floor where it was thrown. It's damp with sweat and streaked and stained with sex. It looks beautiful.

I roll over and face you. Your eyes don't stray to my breasts or pussy, but stay with mine; courageous, vulnerable. I feel my innards, my vital organs, liquefying at your honest stare. Now that we've found each other again, can I be honest with you? Can I uncoil my charred, fettered insides, pick apart the knots of the last of the last thirty years?

I love you, Jack.

I am in love with you. I always was. For years I didn't realise it; for years I tried vehemently to deny it; for years I tried desperately to forget it.

Now you know. You feel the way I clutch at you when you're inside me. Eyes. Sharp fingers. The muscles of my cunt. I want you deeper. I want you imprinted inside me. Fuck me hard, Jack, until I cry, scream, until blood oozes from my pores instead of sweat, until the bed is flooded with us and we thrash, crying and struggling above the sticky waves; until we drown. I want to feel my arteries clogging with you. I want to feel myself suffocating with you. I want to feel full with you. I've felt empty without you, all this time.

I want to watch you paint, and feel your paint-stained fingers sliding over my age-worn skin. I want to wake up and watch you sleeping. I want to roll over in the middle of the night and feel the warmth of your breath, your body, your love, beside me in

255

the bed. On those nights when insomnia will strike, and I'll lie awake and silently cry, acid tears carving bitter paths across my wrinkled face at the thought of all those years wasted, I want you to wake up and know what's wrong without asking me, and to hold me until the feeling of your heart beating next to mine makes it all right again. I want to go to dinner parties with you and to look at you during the intelligent conversation, and to catch you staring at me with love and pride and longing in your dark eyes. I even want to see you looking at other women, younger women whose bodies are fresh and firm and whose eyes hold the bright eagerness of youth; because then, to feel you turn and look at me, and to know that I'm the one you love, will make my life complete.

I want to be with you every moment from now, until we die. If you die before me, I'll spend the rest of my days crying and smiling, thinking of you and overflowing with gratitude that you were put on this earth for me. And if I die before you, I'll approach infinite nothingness with the rage and frustration and blackness pushed away like grey clouds sent packing by a fresh sea wind. And I'll be cushioned on my way to death by the pure, calm white thought that my life was not a waste, because I knew you, and I knew love. That thought will be the silk in my coffin; the breeze that carries my ashes over the lush lawns of the campus where we first met.

But enough of death. Now, we have a life to live together. Together, we can pretend that the wasted years never happened. Only our wrinkled skin, and the sadness in our eyes, will tell the truth.

BLACK LACE NEW BOOKS

Published in April

HAUNTED
Laura Thornton
£5.99

A modern-day Gothic story set in both England and New York. Sasha Hayward is an American woman whose erotic obsession with a long-dead pair of lovers leads her on a steamy and evocative search. Seeking out descendants of the enigmatic pair, Sasha consummates her obsession in a series of sexy encounters related to this haunting mystery.

ISBN 0 352 33341 3

STAND AND DELIVER
Helena Ravenscroft
£5.99

1745, and England is plagued by the lawless. Lydia Hawkesworth feels torn between her love for Drummond, a sea-faring adventurer turned highwayman, and her all-consuming passion for his decadent younger brother Valerian. With the arrival of the icy Madame de Chaillot, Valerian's plans to usurp his brother's position and steal his inheritance turn down a sinister and darkly erotic path – one which Lydia is drawn to follow.

ISBN 0 352 33340 5

Published in May

INSOMNIA
Zoe le Verdier
£5.99

A wide range of sexual experience is explored in this collection of short stories by one of the best-liked authors in the series. Zoe le Verdier's work is an ideal reflection of the fresh, upbeat stories now being published under the Black Lace imprint. Many popular female fantasies are covered, from sex with a stranger and talking dirty, to secret fetishes, lost virginity and love. There's something for everyone.

ISBN: 0 352 33345 6

VILLAGE OF SECRETS
Mercedes Kelly
£5.99

Every small town has something to hide, and this rural Cornish village is no exception. Its twee exterior hides some shocking scandals and nothing is quite what it seems. Laura, a London journalist, becomes embroiled with the locals – one of whom might be her long-lost brother – when she inherits property in the village. Against a backdrop of curious goings-on, she learns to indulge her taste for kinky sex and rubber fetishism.

IBSN: 0 352 33344 8

Special announcement!
THE BLACK LACE BOOK OF WOMEN'S SEXUAL FANTASIES
Edited and Compiled by Kerri Sharp
£5.99

At last, Black Lace brings you the definitive *Book of Women's Sexual Fantasies*. This special collection has taken over one and a half years of in-depth research to put together, and has been compiled through correspondence with women from all over the English-speaking world. The result is an astounding anthology of detailed sexual fantasies, including shocking and at times bizarre revelations.

ISBN 0 352 33346 4

To be published in June

PACKING HEAT
Karina Moore
£5.99

When Californian Nadine has her allowance stopped by her rich uncle, she becomes desperate to maintain her expensive lifestyle. She joins forces with her lover, Mark, and together they steal a vast sum of money from a flashy businessman. But the sexual stakes rise when Nadine and Mark try to put the blame on someone they shouldn't. Their getaway doesn't go entirely to plan, and they're pursued across the desert and into the casinos of Las Vegas. Full of sexual intrigue, this action-packed erotic novel is reminiscent of a *film noir*.

ISBN 0 352 33356 1

TAKING LIBERTIES
Susie Raymond
£5.99

When attractive thirty-something Beth Bradley takes a job as PA to the arrogant Simon Henderson, she is well aware of his reputation as a philanderer. She is determined to turn the tables on his fortune through erotic manipulation. But she keeps getting side-tracked by her libido, and craving sex with the dominant man she wants to teach a lesson.

ISBN 0 352 33357 X

If you would like a complete list of plot summaries of Black Lace titles, or would like to receive information on other publications available, please send a stamped addressed envelope to:

Black Lace, Thames Wharf Studios,
Rainville Road, London W6 9HT

BLACK LACE BOOKLIST

All books are priced £4.99 unless another price is given.

Black Lace books with a contemporary setting

ODALISQUE	Fleur Reynolds ISBN 0 352 32887 8	☐
WICKED WORK	Pamela Kyle ISBN 0 352 32958 0	☐
UNFINISHED BUSINESS	Sarah Hope-Walker ISBN 0 352 32983 1	☐
HEALING PASSION	Sylvie Ouellette ISBN 0 352 32998 X	☐
PALAZZO	Jan Smith ISBN 0 352 33156 9	☐
THE GALLERY	Fredrica Alleyn ISBN 0 352 33148 8	☐
AVENGING ANGELS	Roxanne Carr ISBN 0 352 33147 X	☐
COUNTRY MATTERS	Tesni Morgan ISBN 0 352 33174 7	☐
GINGER ROOT	Robyn Russell ISBN 0 352 33152 6	☐
DANGEROUS CONSEQUENCES	Pamela Rochford ISBN 0 352 33185 2	☐
THE NAME OF AN ANGEL £6.99	Laura Thornton ISBN 0 352 33205 0	☐
SILENT SEDUCTION	Tanya Bishop ISBN 0 352 33193 3	☐
BONDED	Fleur Reynolds ISBN 0 352 33192 5	☐
THE STRANGER	Portia Da Costa ISBN 0 352 33211 5	☐
CONTEST OF WILLS £5.99	Louisa Francis ISBN 0 352 33223 9	☐
BY ANY MEANS £5.99	Cheryl Mildenhall ISBN 0 352 33221 2	☐
MÉNAGE £5.99	Emma Holly ISBN 0 352 33231 X	☐

A FEAST FOR THE SENSES £5.99	Martine Marquand ISBN 0 352 33310 3	☐

Black Lace anthologies

PAST PASSIONS £6.99	ISBN 0 352 33159 3	☐
PANDORA'S BOX 2 £4.99	ISBN 0 352 33151 8	☐
PANDORA'S BOX 3 £5.99	ISBN 0 352 33274 3	☐
SUGAR AND SPICE £7.99	ISBN 0 352 33227 1	☐
SUGAR AND SPICE 2 £6.99	ISBN 0 352 33309 X	☐

Black Lace non-fiction

WOMEN, SEX AND ASTROLOGY £5.99	Sarah Bartlett ISBN 0 352 33262 X	☐